STOP
HERE

STOP HERE

a novel

Beverly Gologorsky

SEVEN STORIES PRESS
New York

A Seven Stories Press First Edition

An earlier version of Chapter 3 "Imaginary Friends" was published in
Hamilton Stone Review, February, 2010.

Seven Stories Press
140 Watts Street
New York, NY 10013
www.sevenstories.com

College professors and middle and high school teachers may
order free examination copies of Seven Stories Press titles. To order,
visit www.sevenstories.com/textbook or send a fax on school letterhead
to (212) 226-1411.

Book design by Elizabeth DeLong

Library of Congress Cataloging-in-Publication Data

Gologorsky, Beverly.
Gologorsky, Beverly.
  Stop here : a novel / Beverly Gologorsky. -- A Seven Stories Press First
edition.
    pages cm
  ISBN 978-1-60980-504-3
  I. Title.
  PS3557.O447S76 2013
  813'.54--dc23

                                    2013008793

Printed in the United States

9 8 7 6 5 4 3 2 1

As always, for
Charlie Wiggins,
Georgina, Dónal,
And especially Maya

In Memory of
Frieda Trestman
Dave Gologorsky
Billy Capozzi

The Best of It

> However carved up
> or pared down we get,
> we keep on making
> the best of it as though
> it doesn't matter that
> our acre's down to
> a square foot. As
> though our garden
> could be one bean
> and we'd rejoice if
> it flourishes, as
> though one bean
> could nourish us.

—Kay Ryan

Contents

1

Usable Truths

There's no way to ignore the warmongering on Fox News, though Ava is trying. The screen takes up half the wall. Hours ago, it seems, she searched for the remote to lower the volume, but no luck. She went so far as to ask Murray to turn it off, but instead he began jabbering about our brave boys, keeping the country safe, on and on like he knew something no one else did. That sent her mind reeling back to the evening her son pulled her onto the couch to watch the invasion of Iraq. Shock and Awe, he said, repeating what he'd heard the newscasters call it. Then, too, she wanted to close her eyes. She told him the sights were frightening, nothing to celebrate, but it didn't dampen Bobby's childish excitement. That scared her, too.

No one seems bothered by the TV. The party is in this room where the food table and bar are set up, where wraparound windows allow only blueberry darkness, where vaulted ceilings create echoes as people talk and gesture and take up space. If she could find a corner to be alone—to hide, actually—it would help, but no luck there either. She avoids parties, fears the expectations, the false gaiety, and worse, strangers' idle curiosity.

Maybe another glass of wine, but her head feels spacey, her fingers tingle, and when she tries to breathe deep her body tenses. It's been a while since anxiety dogged her, though it happened a lot after her husband was killed. Damn TV. It's boring through her senses.

Wending her way to the bedroom, she switches on a lamp. A ghostly amber light slides across a bed larger than hers by far; piles of bulky winter coats cover the pale satiny spread. It will take forever to find her jacket.

She hurries out, finds her friends at the makeshift bar. "I need to leave. Right now. Could you get my jacket with yours?" From the way they look at her she hasn't disguised the desperation.

"Absolutely," Rosalyn says. "Wait in the foyer."

"We've been here long enough," Mila agrees.

"Murray, I'm leaving. Early shift tomorrow," her voice ridiculously high. Before he can say a word, she heads for the vestibule, but not fast enough. The eerie feeling of nothingness begins to sink her. She takes hold of the doorknob, something solid.

⁕⁕⁕

Picking her way over gravel, she glances back at the enormity of the house with its walls full of windows. Overwhelming. Murray insisted on a never-ending tour, room by room, pointing out each piece of furniture as if she didn't know what a couch or a chair looked like. The décor was beautiful, it's true, but cold; maybe if more people lived there. . . . But just Murray and Sylvie . . . How will they care for it? She beeps open the car doors. Home, she wants to be home.

Rosalyn slides into the passenger seat. Mila, in a puffy jacket as iridescent as pigeon feathers, climbs in back. The doors slam, the sound magnified by the ocean. She flicks on the high beams. Sand dunes loom up like headless figures. She turns the key and the ignition makes a dreadful sound. Praying to gods she doesn't believe in, she counts to five, inserts the key again and turns it. Nothing. Her foot on the gas, she tries again and again and again.

"Ava, stop, don't flood it. I'll call Triple A." Rosalyn pulls a slim phone from her velvet purse. They listen to her give directions for a tow truck. "At least half an hour, probably longer."

"I'll pay for it," Ava promises, wondering which part of her budget to raid. She sees the neat pile of envelopes on her dresser labeled *food, gas, telephone, utilities*; there's one for emergencies. Also one marked *fun*, in which she feels compelled by a force she doesn't understand to add a dollar or two, depending on tips. It's grown thick.

"Don't worry, I'm a member," Rosalyn counters generously.

"I can't wait back at Murray's." There's alarm in her voice.

"God forbid," Rosalyn's large eyes examine her as if for the first time. "Let's walk to the shore line, kill some time."

"Are you drunk? It's freezing out there," Mila says.

"What if I am? I'm going to be forty."

"What does that have to do with anything?" Mila mumbles.

"I know Murray's watching us." Ava peers into the darkness. He'll insist they come inside.

"Who cares? The stars are beautiful and ours. Come on, we'll hear the truck when it gets here." Rosalyn is out the door, her shapely body hidden in a red wool coat that reaches her ankles.

Ava hesitates; the car feels safe.

"Rosalyn's right, let's kill some time," Mila is out the door as well.

Does she want to sit here alone? Reluctantly stepping into a vastness she can sense but not see, a faint shiver rides through her. She breathes in the salty air. It's a cold night of stars.

"Little ol' Murray, can you believe it?" Mila's shoes crunch the gravelly sand. "The house dwarfs him. Ava, did you see the height of those ceilings?"

"Who could miss it," her tone too harsh. These are her friends.

Tell them she's anxious. Yet how to describe nothingness? She tried once, didn't she, to a military doctor who looked as young as her husband had been. What could he understand? In the end he said bad things happen to everyone as if she didn't know that. It wearies her to correct and explain what feels beyond language. At home she'll be alone. Bobby's sleeping at Dina's. She'll undress, wrap herself in the old robe, maybe flip through a magazine or sit looking out the window. The anxiety will lift, her mood will change. It always has.

Slowly, they follow the dimming cone of headlight toward the wind-driven sound of breaking waves.

"Rosalyn, you do know how to needle Murray. Your warnings about keeping up such a big house . . ." Mila begins, her tone more joyful than critical.

"He expects Sylvie to be his maid, his cook, god knows what else. In Murray's eyes, that's what a wife's for. Anyway, he kind of enjoys my defiance. I certainly do," Rosalyn muses.

Ava steps gingerly over pockets of sand, careful not to trip. It must be nearly midnight. If the tow truck arrives here in thirty minutes it'll be an hour getting home, another half-hour to drop off her friends. She's due at the diner by five. She doesn't mind leaving home before dawn, the houses still dark, no cars or people, the world silent, and she there to witness the morning.

"Nick and Bruce are stuck working the diner all night," Rosalyn says, reading her thoughts as she often does. "Bruce isn't going to be that helpful. There's another man whose wife I wouldn't want to be."

"Shelly's a strong woman. They'll get through this," Mila counters.

Ava's reminded of Shelly's early morning calls to the diner. The flat, powerful voice tinged with irritation as if the person listening were at fault and not Bruce's lateness.

"I'm sure Nick's happy not to go to Murray's housewarming. I could've done without it," Rosalyn admits.

"Then why go?" Mila whips a hat from her pocket, tugging it low over her thick, reddish hair. Only her small, determined face peeks out, which doesn't look much older than her daughter's.

"Because we three rarely get a chance to play . . ."

"I wouldn't call it a fun party," Ava mumbles, watching Rosalyn trek easily over the sand in heeled boots.

"Ava, what's going on with you?" Mila's coal-dark eyes try to read her.

"The joyous occasion lasted too long, that monster TV running the same awful war video over and over. And the things people come out with would drive anyone crazy." The words come quickly but suddenly have little meaning.

"The TV was a bit much, but after a while I didn't notice." Rosalyn can do that, shrug off what she considers unimportant, something she wishes she could do.

"Except for a few of Sylvie's friends, we were the only ones Murray knew to invite. How depressing is that?" Mila sounds gleeful.

"He's a lousy host, lousy boss, and he'll be a lousy husband, too," Rosalyn declares as if she'd never said as much before.

"Are you maligning the man whose money helped buy your condo?" Mila teases.

"Not on Murray's salary."

"Then whose?" Mila asks.

Rosalyn hesitates. "Oh . . . previous, more lucrative jobs. Besides, I'm quite frugal." She's not, but neither of them says so.

"Murray has so much," Mila says.

"Is there something you need?" Rosalyn wants to know.

"Cash. Not stocks, bonds, or plastic. Twenties and fifties, this thick." Mila holds her fingers inches apart.

"Money for what?" Rosalyn asks.

"Know how much a pair of Darla's boots cost?"

"What do you want for yourself?" Rosalyn persists.

"A lot of things."

"For example?"

"Is this a quiz?"

"Sort of."

"If I had lots of money, I wouldn't waste it on a big house. I'd stop working."

"And do what?" Ava asks, faintly alarmed.

"Oh, this and that," Mila's voice drifts off the way it does when questions become too specific.

Ava too frets about money; but such worries are personal. Shapely clouds move across the sky, obscuring the stars, darkening the space around them even more. It reminds her of another night at the beach. She and her husband-to-be wrapped in each other's arms, the cold wind howling; how they laughed. Nothing could touch them, not wind, cold, or anything out there. It was years ago, when she assumed pleasure was her due.

"Ava?" Rosalyn tugs her arm. "I'm talking to you."

"What?" her voice low. The wind whistles past her frozen ears, the thrashing water close too close.

"I said unlike Mila, I don't mind being a waitress. Do you?"

"I'm grateful for the work." It's the closest to the truth she can trust just now. Being busy, moving resolutely, hurrying to get a task done suits her, may even bring her somewhere better faster.

"Sylvie left *her* job, and why not? Murray isn't as stingy with her as he is with us," Mila says.

"Did you see how Murray sidled up to listen whenever I talked to Sylvie? It's sort of sweet he's afraid of my influence," Rosalyn seems pleased.

She, too, chatted briefly with Sylvie, who revealed tidbits about her decision to leave the theater, her decision to get an ordinary job, to let go of the familiar . . . to try new things . . . have new experiences . . . Words that made her edgy, as if Sylvie was a pioneer whose risks paid off.

At the water's edge, the horizon sucked into the black sky, she wonders . . . If she wades in, experiences the danger of sinking, faces the fear, would the sensation vanish? But what if she can't find the shore again?

Rosalyn teases the water with the tip of her patent leather boot.

"Murray was watching Sylvie everywhere she went tonight," Mila says definitively.

"I'd rather be alone than with a man who didn't trust me," Rosalyn's tone serious.

So often her friends' words provide sustenance, proof of what it means to go on. Tonight, their chatter is useless, something her cop father wouldn't abide. To him conversation had to be useful. He believed usable truths could be shared. Anyway, usable would give her a method, a handle, something to grab on to.

"None of what you say is usable," she says in a soft voice, surprising herself.

"What is it, Ava? You're somewhere else tonight. It's not like you," Mila says impatiently.

Mila's right, it isn't like her, she's generally as grounded as a flat road. She gets things done and rarely complains. "Let's go back to the car," her voice close to a whisper.

They trudge back, sandy wind in their faces. Walking ahead, her friends' voices lost in the crash of waves, she focuses on tomorrow's tasks. First thing, she'll call a taxi to drive her to work. If it takes more than a day to fix her car she'll have to rent one, won't she? Pick up the rental after her morning shift, then stop at the hardware store for lightbulbs, an extension cord, soap pads, new broom, the list on the fridge etched in her head. She'll have to visit the supermarket as well. Bobby wants those precooked pot-pie things for his school lunches, no doubt expensive, no doubt unhealthy. Ordinary thoughts any mother would have. It's where she needs to be now.

She slides into the car, Rosalyn beside her. Mila settles noisily in back. Doors slam. The dunes look pitifully like what they are, piles of sand. Glancing at the time, she calculates the tow truck should be there any minute. They'll scrunch in beside the driver. Rosalyn will keep up a stream of chatter. Mila will ask a thousand questions, answering none. She'll sit there quietly.

"Call Triple A again, it's been more than thirty minutes," Mila says.

Rosalyn obediently pulls out her cell phone. They listen. Clicking off, she tells them, "Busy night. The truck won't be here for another half hour."

She's making her friends wait in the car when they could . . . but she can't go back in there. "I appreciate your staying with—"

"We're not doing it for you. We're not that pure," Rosalyn says.

"Isn't that the truth? What now?" Mila asks. "Want to share fantasies?" A game they once played after a few drinks.

"You first."

"I buy a lottery ticket every day and fantasize what'd I'd do with all that money."

"Hmmm, well . . . heavens . . . mine is weirder. I fantasize the discovery of a pill to preserve my body . . ." Rosalyn's tone subdued. "You're quiet, Ava. Does that mean you won't reveal your fantasy or that you refuse to have one?"

"Not sure." Her plaintive tone saddens her. Her fantasies, if that's what they are, seem stuck in the past, which makes no sense, nothing can change there, but everything's known.

Rosalyn pats her arm comfortingly, then stares out the window.

Mila sighs loudly.

It's her fault, souring her friends' mood. "Is there something else we can talk about?" she asks softly.

"How about a Bobby or Darla story we haven't heard before?" Mila offers with little enthusiasm.

"No offense, but that's duller than looking through a stranger's photo album." Rosalyn flicks open her cell phone to search her messages.

"Then you come up with an idea. Or we'll sit here listening to our breathing," Mila scolds.

"Fine." Rosalyn shuts the phone, drums her fingers on the dashboard. "Let's tell a story. One of us starts, another continues, and on it goes."

"Like a once-upon-a-time thing?" Mila asks.

"No, no. Not a fairy tale. It has to be real, important, dramatic, revealing, something that'll hold our attention," Rosalyn tells her.

What in her story would be revealing, important? A shameful event from her teen years? Everyone has one, but which is hers? Something dramatic? Stealing a lipstick? Lying to her mother? Who cares? What would hold their attention? Maybe something about her dead husband; or that she hasn't had sex in years; or that she can't feel much. Or how her . . . Searching the night sky wishing her story were scripted there because whatever's ahead can only be imagined, yet wishing, too, she could scroll down dates and events and discover what led to here.

2

Reunion

Between five and six a.m. the weirdos arrive for coffee or handouts or just a booth for a nap. It's too early for real people, but somewhere out there, beyond the still-dark parking lot, Ava can hear the first few cars in what will become the morning rush. Nick is in the kitchen checking inventory. Bruce will show up late; Mila won't get there till ten; Rosalyn is probably still asleep. And Murray . . . well, he'll arrive at eight sharp to check on everyone.

The first pale light skips over the missing floor tiles illuminating the ashy black linoleum beneath. Soon the sun will burnish the white Cape Cod houses that dot the nearby shallow hills. Even on cloudy days, a narrow strip of pink appears in the sky for a few seconds. It's the play of light that tells her the hour, not the bold round clock on the wall.

For the only time all day, the marbled Formica counter is free of dirty dishes. On the back ledge there is an array of pies and cakes that arrive when she does. Taped on the wall over a tray of water pitchers and glasses is the list of blue-plate specials. Murray insists on varying them daily and it drives Nick crazy. How many different ways can you serve a piece of meat? The gold-edged mirror reflects empty red vinyl booths and small black tables. The last sugar container is filled and, bored, she's propped on a stool leafing idly through an old *Newsday* when the door chimes its ridiculous tune, and he walks in.

"Morning." Clean blue eyes seem to seek her out.

"Coffee?"

"I'm starving." He straddles the stool next to hers.

"What can I get you?" she asks as she stands up and moves behind the counter. She's already pouring coffee and laying out silverware as she hands him a menu, which she normally does without thinking. This time she feels different, questioning herself.

He points to number three, *Lumberjack Special*. Ham, eggs, hash browns, rye toast, and pancakes.

She gives herself a second cup of coffee.

"My name is Mark."

She waits for a second. Clearly he isn't from around here. "Ava. You passing through?" She registers the blue denim shirt tight across square shoulders, and guesses he's entering his fifties. A thin man carrying weight. Her husband was barrel-chested.

"I'm the new owner of Cross Country Trucks, Long Island and Denver. You must've seen the green and white billboard on Sunrise Highway. I'll be working both places now. I'm renting an apartment in Wantagh."

It's where she lives. Her small house is one of many look-alikes, the highway close enough to hear the traffic, but she hasn't seen the billboard. She piles two orders of toast and serves his eggs, then waits at the open ledge between the kitchen and the restaurant for Nick to deliver the pancakes. For a moment Nick's dark eyes fasten on her. It seems he has something to say, but he doesn't, so she makes busywork at the other end of the counter till she hears the plate slide toward her.

"Is this the end of your night shift?" Mark asks.

"I work four hours dawn and four noon. It gets me time to sleep."

"That your son?" He points at Bobby's photo, stuck into the side of the mirror. She never wants to be far from him. She nods, unsurprised since Bobby looks just like her.

"How old is he?"

"Soon to be eleven." For a moment she too gazes at Bobby's thin, sharp-featured face, his blond hair a bit long and shaggy, a sociable child who is curious about foreign places.

"His father must be proud of him?"

"He was killed in an army helicopter crash. He never met Bobby." The words leave her mouth before she can check them.

He puts down the fork. "How awful for you."

She looks at him, a customer, not even a regular. There's no way he can understand the unceasing pain that was her husband's death, which finally faded to an indifference she's vowed never to disturb.

"I was lucky," Mark says. "Too young for Vietnam, too old for Iraq."

Luck is for people with money, she doesn't say.

"I imagine you never get over that kind of loss," he offers softly.

"You go on," she says, more to herself. When Bobby was a baby and threw his toys on the floor, she'd retrieve them—again and again—to teach him that what leaves comes back. Except she doesn't believe it herself. Or in the power of love to last either.

"Breakfast is fuel," he declares as if suddenly embarrassed, and mops up what's left of the eggs.

She was never good at small talk. She begins filling napkin holders and hears the swiveling stool, senses him watching her.

"You're good at that."

"I can eat fast too, but what does that get me?"

She stuffs the last container with too many napkins, thinks about wiping the counter even though it doesn't have a speck on it.

"No insult meant, truly." He catches her eye with his surefire blue gems.

"None taken. Is this your first time in New York?" she's surprised to hear herself ask.

"Lord, no. I lived in Manhattan for seven years a decade ago. Still miss it."

"Why?"

He takes a sip of his coffee. "People, I'd say. I like people, all kinds. It's what you have there. Turn a corner, hear one language, next corner, another. It's exciting."

"It's refreshing to hear the city described lovingly for a change."

"You ever been to Colorado?" He leans toward her with his elbows planted on the counter. She notes the grime-free nails, odd for someone working trucks. Then again, he's the owner.

"No." When was the last time she left Long Island?

"Imagine a hammock in a field of wildflowers, spectacular cloud formations. Think you'd like that?" He smiles, two dimples.

"Sounds like a resort."

"I suppose . . . You ever travel?" His expression is inquisitive as if he's discovered something in her that sets her apart.

"I don't see travel in my near future."

"It's close by plane, my house in the cup of the mountains. You'd fit right in." He smiles once more. Men flirt with her all the time, though she can't imagine why. Her narrow face with its too-thin nose is intense, unsmiling. Some try to coax a smile, which makes her self-conscious, tighter, as if giving in would be a loss. Dina tells her to rouge her pale cheeks. Maybe she will, someday. Once in a rare while she has a drink with a regular, usually Mila or Rosalyn with her. A mother can't allow strange men into her bedroom.

She gathers up his dishes, sweeps the counter clean, and notices Nick watching her before he glances at the clock. Because of Mark she's missed the sunrise and quickens her pace for the early rush. Mostly it's men with faces weathered from outdoor work in the new construction sites near Jones Beach. They arrive famished in SUVs and vans, dropping half-lit cigarettes on the diner steps, which Murray picks up each morning. Women come on later after leaving their kids at school or day care. She lifts a two-pound bag of coffee off a nearby shelf; fills three urns with water. Then she twists her hair into a ponytail, fastens it with a barrette, and sticks two pencils in her pocket. Mark's eyes are on her all the while.

"I'll be using the diner's hospitality for my meals, unless you know a better place." Only it isn't a question.

⋆-⋆-⋆

Two weeks of diner breakfasts, two weeks of conversations, and she lets him visit Bobby and her at home for the first time on a Sunday morning. Most people talk about how a boy needs a father, but who discusses how a man needs a son? She's seen men play nice with kids to get to their mothers, but his interest isn't feigned. Bobby is the missing ingredient in his life, and Bobby knows it immediately.

On a few of her days off he drives them to places they've never been: a strip of beach at the end of Long Island with edge-of-the-world rock formations; a park where the scent of cherry blossoms is thick enough to bottle; a seafood restaurant where he teaches Bobby how to crack open a lobster's shell with a knife blow to the belly. After two months he asks to stay over. To her surprise, she doesn't demur, except to say she hasn't slept with a man in years, which probably makes her a virgin again. He chuckles, even though she hadn't meant it as a joke.

That first time he makes love hesitantly. As he does, the memory of her husband enters the bed along with the long-forgotten certainty of her husband's arms, his repeated promise to please her like no one else could, which he had. It was eons since she'd heard his voice and it felt like a warning.

Mornings she has to be up by four and she makes Mark leave with her. Although Dina comes by each day to wake Bobby and help him prepare for school, she isn't ready to have her meet Mark.

By May, they're at her place most of the time, where he spends hours teaching Bobby the mysteries of the outdoors: the difference between a boat and a ship, how to read trail markers, what flies lure trout. He describes the privilege of meeting ravens, hearing birdsong, discerning wind direction, a life invisible to city boys.

In bed together it's easier, although she blames herself and her dead husband for never fully relaxing. Time, she needs more, she tells herself, except he's preparing to leave in a few weeks. The Denver piece of his business needs tending to, and he won't return until September.

❖-❖-❖

On a June night as sticky as August, the three of them are in her living room playing Scrabble.

"That's it. My game," she declares.

"Mom always wins."

"We'll have to work harder to change that." Mark winks at her.

"Very hard, indeed," she says.

"Bobby, would you like a summer in Colorado?" Mark asks.

For a moment her son is as stunned as she is, then he grabs her hand. "Mom, please, can I, please? I'd really love it. Mom?"

"We'll camp in the mountains. There are some old caves to explore. I have a canoe, a sailboat, too. We'll hike; we'll trout fish . . ." Whatever Mark sees in her face checks his eagerness. He folds her hand in his. "I should have asked you first. It kind of came on me. If you don't agree . . ."

"Mom? Listen. It's hot in the city. I'll hardly have anyone to hang out with. It's such a good idea. And you have to work."

True, and Murray's about to change her schedule yet again, straight shift, ten to dawn, beginning in July. She's already taken over a chunk of the ordering. Now he's showing her the books, bills, lists of salespeople. He isn't a good teacher; she has to concentrate. She'll have to sleep some during the day. What will Bobby do? Languish in this old living room watching TV, the couch too shabby for words, the walls in need of painting? Is that the kind of summer she wants for him?

"Will he have his own room?" That's not what she needs to know, but it's a start.

"Yes. And don't worry about expenses. Believe me, the fare's no big deal."

Bobby's pulling on one hand, Mark pressing the other, and King Solomon comes to mind.

"He's not used to country life." Okay, that's closer, but to what?

"He'll go to the warehouse with me now and then, but we'll have plenty of time for everything else." He releases her hand but his eyes remain steady on her.

"Let me think," she says, but thinking is impossible. Bobby's fingers are cuffing her wrist like she's his prisoner. It's clear what he wants. And yet . . .

"Mom? Listen. If I don't like it I'll come home. But Mom . . . listen? I'm going to love it. Sailing? Where can we go sailing here?"

Her son's excitement is infectious. She glances at Mark. He's been reliable, consistent, even devoted, she'd say. He has a good effect on Bobby. On her, too. The last months have been positive for the three of them. Isn't that enough to hold on to for seven weeks?

⁕⁕⁕

Bobby's face is still glowing in her head when she arrives at the diner. He was so eager to get on the plane, his hug and kiss so quick. It was all she could do not to grab him before he disappeared past security.

Dina is having an early lunch at the counter, as usual. "You let him take Bobby for the summer. A stranger? I don't care if you slept with him. I don't care how much they like each other." Mila, who never keeps a thought to herself, promptly starts talking about those priests: You know, the kindest men on the planet. Who would have guessed! Her friends' words fire her imagination. Rosalyn slips an arm around her. "Listen, trust yourself. You know the guy, don't you?"

"Of course," she shoots back. "Mark isn't a stranger. I know where he lives, where he was born, his upbringing, where he went to school, his past jobs, what he wants for this new business."

"So?" Rosalyn says, "What more do you want? Unless . . . something in you isn't sitting right."

"That's not the point. The man hasn't passed the test of time," Dina says.

"It'd be different if you went with him, but that's expensive," Mila offers.

"Hey," Murray calls from the kitchen. "What is this?"

⟡·⟡·⟡

The lunchtime crowd is heavy, demanding. She won't miss it when she starts her new hours. She moves fast from table to counter to kitchen, all the time listening for the ring of her cell phone in her pocket. He's only been gone a few hours, but her nerves are shot and her friends' warnings are corrosive. She tries to put their words aside, but it's no use. She apologizes twice for giving the wrong check to a customer. She hurries the hours. Bobby will call as soon as they land. When the phone rings she runs out to the parking lot even though Murray is watching. Bobby's voice sounds so near. He's at the Denver airport; elated, he says they're leaving early the next morning for a few days of camping. The two of them alone in the mountains. That spooks her too.

Two days later, she finds herself at the Port Authority bus terminal, ticket in hand, a small travel bag over her shoulder, her adrenaline pumping. Dina, Mila, and finally Rosalyn, too, agreed that she had to do this or never sleep again. She weaves her way past food kiosks, panhandlers, and vendors to the Cruiser Line gate. Murray's displeasure follows her. She told him she'd only be gone several days; it was family business. "Who would you know west of Long Island?" Yeah, she said, that far.

❖-❖-❖

The bus plows through the night. Occasional headlights streak the darkness. The wide aisle is now littered with paper bags, candy wrappers; an empty soda can rolls desolately past her feet. No one sits beside her and she's grateful. A talker would have shattered whatever is holding her together.

She keeps glancing at his photograph, her son's face caught in the light of a waning sun. Is he wishing she'd come or is he too busy, too happy to remember her at all? For several weeks after her husband was killed, she took Bobby into bed with her, kept her arms around his tiny sleeping body. Protecting him made her feel safe.

The driver's voice interrupts her thoughts. "In a few minutes we'll be arriving at the bus terminal. You have fifteen minutes to stretch your legs, get a cup of coffee," which his tired voice sounds in need of.

The bus pulls up in front of a small depot with a dirty plate glass front. She stares out the window. She can just make out a ticket counter inside and the uncertain flicker of fluorescent lights. Two soldiers bring their coffee outdoors and watch the bus as if it might take off without them. She wonders if they're bound for Afghanistan. The last time she saw her husband he was in uniform. They'd spent that week in San Francisco huffing and puffing up the hills, eating and drinking and making love like there was no tomorrow.

Two magazines are stuffed in the mesh pocket of the seat ahead. There is no way can she digest other people's stories now. She remembers Mila saying that diners are a better source of gossip than beauty salons because salons don't include men's input. Rosalyn disagreed, saying men talk half as much as women, and even then you can't believe a quarter of it.

She checks her purse for the tenth time, one hundred dollars and a credit card. She also has her checkbook and a roll of quarters in case her cell phone doesn't work.

Back on the road, the bus picks up speed. But for one or two reading lights, it's dark again. Outside, though, there are glimmers of light in the sky. Across the aisle the two soldiers are asleep, something tender in the way their heads nearly touch. Almost two days, now just another few hours and she'll be there, and she still doesn't know if what she's doing is right.

Loneliness, she'll say, not used to Bobby being gone. Mark will understand her decision to take him back with her. By next summer her trust will be complete.

⋄⋄⋄

For a while the taxi drives along the same highway as the bus, then turns sharply to begin a gradual climb on rutted dirt roads. Lemony sunlight opens the morning and the beauty of it all silences her. She'll arrive there at breakfast time and wonders what Bobby's face will do when he sees her.

The cab drops her off at the foot of a long driveway leading to a white stucco ranch house. Blue wildflowers march uphill like toy soldiers. She walks slowly between trees in summer glory. A dog barks. Maybe she'll say hello and go home. If she feels Bobby's safe, why rob him of this?

Through a picture window she sees a woman. No sign of Bobby or Mark. What if he gave her the wrong address?

She knocks. The woman is in her early fifties, sturdy build, blond hair pulled back from a broad-boned face. Jeans, T-shirt, sandals, her arms deeply tanned. Two rings circle her fingers, one pearl, the other a band of gold.

"Hi, I'm looking for the Dobson house."

"This is it," the woman says huskily, like a smoker.

"I'm Bobby's mother."

Just for a second, the woman's expression freezes. "Oh my goodness, hello. I'm Lydia, Mark's wife." She opens the door wider and yells out, "Mark! Bobby!" Her eyes settle into a gaze, a calculation. "Come in," she finally says in a near whisper. They stand in absolute silence. Not a bird sings, not a dog barks. She feels eerily calm. She already knows the problem here isn't her son's. It's been hard enough for her, why should she make anything easy for any of them?

Suddenly Lydia begins speaking far too quickly.

"What a great son. I know you've heard that before, but he's so smart, so easy to talk to, such a pleasure. He and Mark just came back from camping. The three of us plan to go sailing later. Will you join us?" Her words are friendly, but her gray eyes are hesitant. And why shouldn't they be? No doubt Mark told her Bobby is some needy kid whose poor, overworked mother couldn't give him anything. Certainly not that she's the woman he bedded down with all these months.

Lydia pours her a cup of coffee at the table. She can't remember the last time anyone did that for her.

Feet drum across wooden floors. Entering the kitchen, they both stop.

"Well . . . hello . . ." Mark says. He licks his lips and manages a smile. "You're a long way from home."

"Mom, did something happen?" He's alarmed as if caught somewhere he shouldn't be.

"No, honey. I had some days off and decided to see some of the country. I was near enough to save Mark a trip and pick you up."

Mark leans against the counter, ankles crossed, arranging himself in a pose—no doubt familiar to his wife—she's never seen.

"But I've only been here a few days." His words are half-apologetic, half-accusing.

"Yes, I know. We never did decide how long the vacation would last, did we?" And she touches his cheek.

Sensible words but her brain flashes another headline: duped, betrayed, his sweet talk, endearments, promises, all lies. Never mentioned a wife, did he? Her skin stings. Man needs a son to play with and takes hers. This weird kidnap, isn't that what it is? Her roiling mind searches for a way to upend this ludicrous reunion. She's a cop's daughter, taught to take action. She won't allow Mark to violate two women. Only Bobby's puzzled gaze causes her to hesitate.

"But Mom, we have so many plans. Me and Mark, I mean . . ."

"Won't you reconsider," Lydia asks with little enthusiasm. She must be wondering who this younger woman is.

"No, but thank you. Bobby, pack your stuff. We'll talk more on the bus." Or not, she thinks, because he's so upset by now that his lips are quivering, his eyes narrowing against the tears. She can't allow his disappointment to reach her. If he stayed the summer, he wouldn't be mistreated. But it would be like stealing, wouldn't it? Stealing her trust and then her son. Stealing what only money can't buy. Why should Mark get the pleasure of her son?

"Mom, listen, I have an idea," Bobby's jerking her arm as if to shake some sense into her. With his pale skin and wheat-colored hair, he could disappear into any cornfield.

"I'm listening," she says gently.

"How about if I stay for July? Then you and me can have August together. How about that?"

She can feel it and she's strangely touched. He's trying to negotiate her happiness as well as his own. She stands there in a circle of calmness that nothing in this situation justifies or explains. She knows her job as well as she would if she were working the diner. She has to reassure Bobby that none of this is his fault. And Mark hasn't said a word, doesn't dare to influence the moment one way or the other. If they go on much longer, Mark's reticence will hurt Bobby even more than her insistence.

"I have some plans for us, a surprise, but you need to pack up now." And what would that be, she wonders, but it doesn't matter. Surprises are the easy part. She'll send him to sports camp and worry about how to pay later. He's about to try one last time, but she adds with all the emphasis a mother can bring to bear, "Bobby, go do it, please."

After he's clumped out of the room, she sips her coffee. The fury of a bird's flapping wings speeds past the window.

Mark stands there, a poster of the good husband. Why shouldn't his wife know the truth?

Lydia wipes the table and places the milk carton in the fridge. Nothing left out. Dishes, cups, tumblers in glass-fronted cabinets. A rack with every kind of condiment. A microwave, a Krup's coffeemaker, a Magic Chef stove, all shiny new and ready to come to life at the press of a button. The micro-pearl lights above the white sink sparkle. A room with a view approved by *Good Housekeeping*. It's nothing like the bare-bones kitchen where Bobby eats his breakfast without her or the diner where she dishes up the eggs and hash each morning; where not so long ago she dished them up to Mark and took him into her home where except for the small window above the cracked sink, there was no view. Now Bobby has a comparison. And just like that she realizes it isn't to Lydia she owes the truth.

She'll make it simple. Mark lied to her to spend time with him. Mark lied to his wife to spend time with her, which makes him untrustworthy. Mark was good to him, which convinced her that he was a good man, but anybody who'd lie so easily is without a conscience and a man she should never have left him with. Bobby won't like hearing it, but he'll get it.

"Thank you for your hospitality," she says to Lydia. "Would you mind calling a taxi? I'll wait outside for Bobby." Without a glance at Mark, she gathers up her purse and traveling bag and heads for the door.

Facing the alley of trees that leads to the road, she remembers a story about a slave child whose mother beat her methodically for five nights; on the sixth morning the mother escaped. When the master took a cane to the child to learn where her mother had gone, the child hardly felt the blows. That's her. Her disappointment must be profound, yes, but it doesn't hurt like when her husband died. And isn't that a relief?

Orange suede plateaus surround her. A bittersweet scent pierces the thin, crisp air. She's never seen the depth of an open sky before. It does make her wonder where she might be next summer.

3

Imaginary Friends

Just the way he likes it. Packed booths, a cacophony of voices, clanking dishes, the sizzling grill, the breakfast smells. Any time of day, Murray knows what's cooking in the kitchen. Ava moving smoothly from counter to tables, wonderful. He's changed her hours several times; he likes her there for the morning rush. He hangs up the wet coat, takes off his boots. Everything has a trade-off, though; he learned that from his father. Even marrying Sylvie?

He remembers it like it was yesterday. She appeared at the diner asking for directions back to the city and then lingered at the counter with coffee and a muffin for a good hour. He was intrigued by how she explained things, so energetically. Her light brown hair shot through with golden strands swept around her face whenever she moved. He remembers being amazed that she wasn't married—and then wondering how come.

He glances outside; snowflakes fall rapidly. Still, he worries: a man of fifty-two has his habits, and marrying late has its inconveniences. It's not like he never dated. He enjoys women; they're good listeners, natural nurses for whatever ails you, and a man needs caring. Until Sylvie, though, the women he met . . . well . . . too soon the cream dissolved.

He deposits several rolls of quarters in the register. He counts the bills, jots down the amount and the time. Okay, he's not thrilled with her theatrical past—the looseness of actors. Her appearance, though, that's something else. Those wild green eyes. The woman needs no makeup. She adds to his presence. Five seven, the last time he checked, with shamefully small hands and feet, although it'd take a boulder to fell him.

Of course it's not quite a year; they're still in the honeymoon phase. Beginnings are like that, filled with talk and a little mystery, but everything becomes routine, and how she'll behave when it does, he's not sure.

He notices the regulars are here despite the storm. A good sign.

Never a generous man—who did he have to spend it on?—he's now the owner of a home in East Hampton, a mansion by anyone's standards. With Ava taking over some of his chores, he's easing up on evening hours.

Black watermarks pool near the diner's entrance. If anyone slips it's a legal problem. He hands the mop to Ray, who is young enough to be his son. It is too late for children of his own—and he does regret that—though he's devoted to his Dobermans.

Ava has the pies out on the counter the way he likes it. He sorts and arranges the bread in several bins, then heads for the kitchen. The dishes are stacked properly; sponges lined up on the lip of the sink, the surfaces clean. A good cook and kitchen person is the heart and soul of a restaurant. Nick is the best, much cleaner than Bruce. Where is Bruce anyway?

"How's it going?" he asks Nick.

"Fine."

Nick talks to him the least. Rosalyn says he probably believes bosses are the enemy. Well, this is America; he can believe what he wants as long as he keeps it to himself. He hands Nick the empty paper bread sack, watches him discard it. He could've done it himself but the order of things is important, and Nick's in charge of the kitchen.

❖·❖·❖

"Sumptuous" is the word Sylvie comes up with because labeling a thing is as important to her as a handle on a teacup. Still, what's she doing in a house with cathedral ceilings? A velour couch—gray like an impending storm—stretches ridiculously long across one living room wall, green club chairs protect each side of a teak coffee table; the lamps have silk shades. It's all too fresh, too precious. New paintings waiting to be hung, prints she could never have afforded. Was it wrong to leave her job when there's nothing more for her to do but walk the spacious floors and marvel at the strangeness of the architecture?

One windowed wall faces the beach, but she can only watch the wheeling gulls for so long. She eyes the dogs near her feet. Wherever she goes, they tail her. It's oppressive. She dislikes their names as well as their menacing snouts.

She told Murray she isn't fond of animals. They're like children, he responded, give them love and food and they'll offer unqualified devotion. Is that true of her marriage too?

She may not be totally honest with her husband but she is with herself. A woman of forty-one, still single, no savings, moving through life at a decent but unremarkable pace, meets a man who wants to give her everything. How could she not? She flashes on a passing remark from Shelly outside the diner. It was one of those late autumn afternoons when the last rage of sun drenches houses in a golden light. With eyes closed she lifted her face to the warmth. Take what you can when you can where you can, Shelly said, the words odd but Shelly's tone neither mean nor sarcastic, just certain.

The dogs follow her to the kitchen, a room crammed with devices she has no use for. The trash disposal makes a loud sucking sound that upsets her and the dishwasher fills so quickly she's sure it will flood. Where she grew up, clothing was washed in the bathtub, and the scruffy field next door was where she spent her time with imaginary friends, who unlike her dreamy, alcoholic mother, attended to her every wish.

Taking a bowl from the cabinet she begins kneading ground beef. Some of it spatters on the floor. The dogs lap it up, then one licks her hand. That's a first. She tosses each a meat patty, watches the food disappear, feels their heavy warm bodies sidle past her the way cats would. Raw meat, she thinks, the key to their miserable hearts.

Suddenly she's not in the mood to cook and shoves the bowl in the fridge. She grabs her jacket and, wrapped in a scarf, slips on boots and fur mittens, ready to brave the weather. The dogs wait at the door. Murray warned her not to leave them home alone. She has a vision of them wading into the ocean and being carried away.

Together they trek the wet beach, snow-blown wind in her face, gulls screaming into the roaring of the waves. In the snow-veiled distance she can just make out a figure. Curiosity or plain boredom keeps her moving toward what turns out to be a man dressed in a long coat and woolen hat. A backpack is slung over one shoulder.

"Hi!" she calls into the wind. And the dogs begin barking. Damn! She shouts at them to stop but they don't listen. Undaunted, the man lets the dogs sniff his fingers and offers them crackers from his pocket, which quiets them. A youthful handsomeness is apparent in his craggy, ancient face. He's tall and lanky, white hair streaming from under his hat.

"Can't hold a conversation here!" he shouts. "I have a lean-to up the beach!" Without another word, he leads her to a tarp barely held aloft by shivering poles and battened down with bricks. An unzipped sleeping bag covers the sand; an easel is set up nearby. Coals smolder in a fire pit.

"My winter lair. Have a seat." And to her amazement she does. He tucks the edges of the sleeping bag around her. It's ridiculously cozy. After tossing the dogs more crackers, he seats himself in front of her as if to block the wind with his delicate body.

"Liam, here, I live on Jessup Road." Outside the howling wind is but a breath. His voice is soft, courtly, so unlike Murray's rough-edged tones.

"I'm Sylvie. We're new here and I haven't gotten my bearings yet."

"Yes," he muses, "bearings, very important . . . I must admit it took me years."

"So you've been here a while?"

"Since I retired from business and . . . well, so many other things . . ." Something confessional lurks here and she finds herself unexpectedly embarrassed. She points to his backpack.

"Can I see?"

He hands her a bunch of paintings as easily as if they were sandwiches at a picnic. Winter beach scenes. White, gray, silver without a drop of color, yet they shimmer. Could these be the landscape she finds so forbidding, cold and untouchable? She catches him staring at her.

"Too bleak for you?" he asks.

"No. The opposite. Is that how you really see what you see out there?"

"There's no metaphor for the ocean, only how I feel when I try to capture it."

"In this one the waves are ferocious. They're filled with warning . . ."

"Because my fingers were stiff and my knees hurting, the waves spoke to me of what's impending."

"Was that depressing?" Is she probing?

39

"At my age death is a comrade, a way of leaving, an exit."

"I don't believe everyone your age feels like that." Nothing about him seems tired or worn, though he must be near eighty.

"Maybe not. But there isn't much I'll miss. I love the beach, but I'm alone now. Do you have children?"

"No."

"I had a son killed in 1970, in that dirty war."

The sea, the sky, his death, his son's. He says it all in the same matter-of-fact way.

"How awful," she finally says.

"It was worse than that."

"I'm so sorry."

"You're born, you die. Everything in between is mostly illusion, but there are still sins. The avoidable deaths of young people is one." He gathers up the canvasses and slides them into the worn backpack. "It's no mystery how the dinosaurs disappeared. War kills the young and it's the beginning of extinction."

"You sound pretty certain." She's thinking of Murray, who believes war is a way to keep what you have.

"I did go on, didn't I?"

"Oh no, not at all. Not in the least."

❖·❖·❖

For the third time Murray punches in the number, his eyes on the snow mounting outside the diner in the empty parking lot. She's supposed to drive in but it's not a good idea. He'll take the train home. Buy some flowers from the guy on the platform. He enjoys bringing her presents; it's a new sensation. So is knowing she'll be waiting for him. Sharing space is easier than he thought. Each night her chatter and that creamy body. It couldn't be finer. He adjusts the thermostat. The windows are steaming up, the snowy world vanishing. He does what he can but the weather is beyond him. He dials the number again.

"Hi?" She sounds breathless.

He imagines her anxious to get to the phone.

"The wind is something else."

Is the woman crazy? Yesterday, too, she was out walking. "Where'd you go?"

"Just along the water. I can't always tell where I am until I look back and see our house."

"The dogs must be frozen." The coffee urn, he notices, is low, the floor beneath the corner stool gummy.

"Do you think so?"

"Yeah, you'd be surprised how delicate they are." He wiggles a few fingers at Rosalyn, who's stamping her boots on the rubber mat. Her dark, piercing eyes beneath heavy brows take in the scene.

"Okay, I'll keep an eye on them."

"So pick me up at the station at eight, it's too dangerous to drive in." He hangs up and draws water for the urn. Who goes for walks in the middle of winter? It's not like anything out there changes.

"Work half-day," he says to Rosalyn, without looking at her. "It's going to be slow." Paying hourly help to sit around irritates him.

"Murray, I drove here in a storm. Unless you close shop, I'm doing full-day." Rosalyn enjoys combat more than a marine.

"Well, don't blame me if you're bored." He wonders if she'll mop the gummy floor without being asked.

"So how's Sylvie?"

"You should see how beautifully she rearranged the living room, a real show."

"Nice of her to pick you up every night. I wouldn't."

He laughs. "Me or anyone?"

"Any man who could drive himself, to be exact."

"Can you take care of that spot on the floor?"

The train station looks quaint beneath a mist of falling snow. He spots the dogs in the backseat and then kisses Sylvie's cheek, cold and smooth. The promise of a warm house and dinner excites him. "How's it going," he asks, taking over the wheel, not really wanting an answer. It's been a long trip.

"Murray, you never told me why you weren't in the army."

She surprises him constantly. "What brought that up?" Cars are pulling out of the station at a slow, careful pace. He waits his turn impatiently.

"Reading about Iraq, Afghanistan . . ."

"Yeah, I wanted to go . . . badly, but they found a TB spot on my lung."

"TB?"

"I caught the bug somewhere but it never infected me. Happens, I'm told." Actually it was flat feet that did him in.

"How strange. TB may have saved your life."

"It was frustrating. My father thought I was some kind of misfit." He waits for a word of sympathy.

"You must've been relieved. I mean, who wants to go to—"

"Sylvie, war's a man's sport like hunting, no more no less." He maneuvers the car onto the road. The snowplow ahead forces him to reduce his speed to a crawl. Hell.

"So it has nothing to do with patriotism."

What's she nattering on about? Something challenging in her tone annoys him. "It has everything to do with it, everything to do with this great country of ours. And what's all this about anyway? Why are you so interested in stuff that happened a million years ago?"

"Listening to the news . . ."

"Well, read a book."

Just as he expected, the house is warm and cozy.

"Sylvie," he calls from the bedroom, "let's eat where we can watch the storm." She doesn't respond. "Sylvie," he calls even louder.

"Please don't shout." She appears in the doorway, startling him.

"Let's eat—"

"I heard, okay, we'll do that." She turns to leave.

"Wait." He grabs her arm, nuzzles her ear, sniffs vanilla or maybe something else, he can't tell. He wishes the flower guy had been at the station. "You smell delicious."

"Must be the cooking oil."

Watching her walk out, he pats the bed and both dogs jump on; after wrestling with them awhile, he says, "Okay, boys, down. Now!" They obey, which makes him stupidly happy.

He changes into his sweats, ready for the evening.

She's uncorking the wine, her silvery kimono shimmering in the lamplight. He inhales the luxurious surroundings, nothing like the faded furniture and cracked plaster of his old apartment.

Two dishes of pasta with vegetables steam on the low coffee table. He was hoping for fish or meat, real food.

"Great, baby," he fills their glasses. The wine is so tasty; she knows what to buy. He refuses to ponder how many intimate dinners she had before this one. He leans back, his fingers caressing the velour.

"So how was your day?" she asks.

"Rosalyn pisses me off by the minute, a dyke if ever I saw one."

"Please don't use that word."

"Don't be so sensitive, Sylvie. People are people. I know that. I run a damn restaurant, don't I? All kinds." It's not the first time she's called him on his language. Reminds him of his stiff-assed second grade teacher warning him to talk right or no one would respect him. He's halfway through his first glass and refills it. Sylvie's hardly touched hers. "So you went into town today?"

"I signed a petition against the war, first one ever. There were hundreds of names on it."

"Jesus," he mumbles, "bad move."

"Murray, I've a right to express my beliefs."

"Men are dying over there for your rights."

"That's ridiculous. I want them home alive."

"Sylvie, you don't understand."

"Of course I do."

She's hell-bent on ruining the evening. "Let's not argue, please baby?" For her, he's willing to forget the whole deal. "What else did you do today?"

"Walked, cleaned, read, talked on the phone with Jenny, who's gotten a part in an out-of-town play."

"Oh yeah, where's that?" Jenny is one friend he wishes she'd forget. He'd have to stand on his head to get a smile from her and even then . . .

"Kentucky. Real pretty place. We should visit."

"Oh, you've been?"

"A play in Louisville eons ago."

"No kidding? That's impressive."

"Murray, I've told you about that episode. How the agent saw me in a little commercial and invited me to audition . . ."

". . . And you got the part, yeah I remember." But actually he doesn't like remembering. God knows the people she slept with . . . "On my day off we should hang those paintings. Three in the living room, two in the bedroom, one in the vestibule. You pick."

"Okay, Tuesday?"

"Not sure. I'm still teaching Ava to do some of the ordering. The woman's lonely, I can tell. She ought to marry again. Marriage is good, right?" He can hear himself slurring a bit, but so what, they're home. Before long they'll be in bed and her sweet body will be his.

❖ ❖ ❖

As they've done for the past week, she and the dogs go straight to the lean-to. Armed with baggies of raw meat, she keeps the dogs content. Liam pours two cups of sweetened coffee from a thermos. The afternoon's chill demands heat of a sort. With Liam beside her, she watches the ocean swallow the snowflakes.

"If anyone had told me I'd enjoy sitting outdoors in this weather, I'd have said they were loony . . . I mean it wouldn't be something I could do with Murray. He likes his comforts. He's very ritualized. The thing is, when I imagined a husband it was someone more . . . audacious."

"My wife always knew disaster awaited her outdoors. She was terrified of slipping on ice, she wouldn't consider getting on a plane, kept her distance from tall buildings. After our son was killed, though, her fears vanished, which scared me silly. You never know what'll provoke change in a marriage."

Is that what she's waiting for? "It's not that Murray isn't loving. He is, and he's giving to me, but he doesn't spread goodness easily. The people who work for him . . ." Why does that bother her?

His voice drops falling on a dark memory. "My son's death refocused my work life."

"I'm sure it did," she murmurs, staring at the horizon. Her father's death upended everything.

"What is it?" He touches her arm.

What indeed, she wonders. Was she happier in her studio apartment, coming and going with no one to care where or when?

❖ ❖ ❖

As she plows home through the wet sand, the dogs loping ahead, Liam's concern warms her. She wonders how he sees her. Daughter, neighbor, intelligent woman? In the theater she would analyze each role: Who is she before she walks onstage? Who now? What's to become of her? The dogs begin barking, then dash into the curtain of white and disappear. Murray must be there, though it's early. An urge to run back down the beach sweeps over her. The front door swings open. "Hi baby! When it started snowing again I decided to leave work. Mila was a little too happy to see me go."

"Want something to eat?"

"Yeah," he says, but he's already unwinding her scarf, removing her coat, embracing her waist, and she knows just what he wants.

Oh lord, not now, she prays. But refusing is as beyond her as an excuse that would convince.

He undresses quickly, perhaps sensing resistance. He's spread-eagle on the bed, his cock stiff; his arms reach for her.

"Haven't I said a hundred times I don't want the dogs in the bedroom with us?"

"Rummy, Cheney, out, now," he orders.

She slams the door. Wishing to sustain the anger but having no reason to, she slips off her sweater, her sweatpants.

"Hey baby," he whispers, "come here, speak to me. But it isn't words he wants; she knows that. She slides in beside him, his leg capturing her thigh, his head pinning her chest. Her fingers bite into his shoulders; the need to push him away is so strong. But she can't bear the thought that he'll be furious, that he'll sulk all night, or worse, demand to know how come, what's wrong, where she's been. And what would she say then?

"Something the matter," his tone soft, far away.

"No," she offers in her breathy just-walked-onstage voice, wondering who is she now? And now, as she draws him closer. And now as she strokes his back. And now as she closes her eyes on a memory: seventeen, in rehearsal, the director pulling her into an empty room, and his first kisses and her thought that rebuffing him will come at a price and—as any good actress would—that last thought: what's a little kiss or two.

⋖·⋗·⋖

When she and the dogs arrive at the lean-to, he isn't there. She tucks the sleeping bag around her to wait. If Murray discovered her sitting shoulder-to-shoulder with Liam he'd be a lot more than unhappy.

The purple-tinged sky promises more snow. The forces of the universe are sending a message: inclement weather as punishment. An idea Liam would appreciate. Usually he arrives before her; morning light is what he's after. Could he have been and gone? He did say, see you tomorrow. She searches the beach for his figure but windblown sand impedes her view; seagulls glide overhead, the endless waves.

⋖·⋗·⋖

She drops the dogs at home and begins the trek over the opalescent sand toward the dunes where an exit leads to his road. The tiny A-shaped house squats on a postage-stamp lawn obliterated by snow. The blinds are drawn on the few small windows. She might regret this; it's none of her business. They've only known each other two weeks; he must have other friends who look in on him, but she's already knocking on the door with an insane urgency and shouting his name into the swirling wind. Trudging through the snow, she finds no back entrance, no porch, just two small windows, also with shades. Apprehension fills her. She flashes on her father hanging from the barn rafter. The chair beneath kicked halfway across the floor, sunlight in a cracked mirror flooding the space.

Even if she phoned the police, what would she say? Liam didn't show up at the beach on a blustery day? Liam's not at home? She pounds on the door once more and nearly stumbles forward when he opens it; shoeless, his open shirt revealing a mat of white hair.

She can't tell if he's sad or glad to see her. "Are you okay?"

"I didn't sleep well. Not at all actually." He ushers her into a small living room: bare walls, couch, rocking chair, easel, TV.

"Does something hurt?" she asks because his face is pale, his eyes bloodshot. Strands of hair fall untidily across his wide forehead.

"At my age, things hurt."

"What's wrong, then?"

"I can't explain." And he sighs.

"Of course you can." Jesus, she sounds manic. She takes a breath. "I expected to see your paintings everywhere."

"They're in the closet. Choose a few if you want."

"I will, thank you." And wonders what exactly she'll tell Murray.

"There's coffee in the thermos on the counter."

It's a closet of a kitchen; hardly enough room to turn around. She's about to offer Liam a cup, but he's leaning against the wall as if standing were too difficult. Without a coat he looks thin, fragile. "Liam, why don't you take a nap now?"

"Will you stay?"

"Yes." It comes out before she can think and when she does, she knows this is where she wants to be. She wonders is he afraid to be alone the way she is? When he's alone does he wonder: Who am I? The way she wonders about herself as if she had just wandered on stage, a seventh character in search of an author? But she knows he has no such thoughts. He doesn't seem frightened, only weak.

She follows him to the bedroom and sits down on a folding chair while he stretches out that matchstick frame on the full-size bed. "I am exhausted," he admits. For a few minutes, he stares at the ceiling while she gazes at a photograph of a boy in uniform that sits on the small chest of drawers, the only photo in the room. He's the one to break the silence. "Would you lie next to me?" he asks, his gentle tone almost apologetic.

He's fully dressed; so is she and who's to know? She slips in beside him, inhales the scent of lavender soap. She almost holds her breath, listening for his to even out. She'll leave once he's asleep. He takes her hand, his fingertips icy. His breathing has a raspy edge now. Should she call 911? If she'd been home with her father that morning, what then?

"I'm being visited by the end," he whispers as if reading her thoughts.

"It's your imagination."

"No, death sends a message before he arrives."

"What message?"

"A calming one," he says with quiet assurance. "All weariness to be erased along with pain, regret, ambition, and a thousand other burdens."

Is that what her father felt? She slides her arm around his waist, his words strangely comforting.

❖·❖·❖

The train crowded with commuters is so raucous he can barely think. He's tried calling her all afternoon. He wondered if she was walking in this weather. He left a message: Pick him up at six. What if she's not at the station?

The man next to him reading a newspaper closes his eyes. He closes his but it's no use. She did seem distant this morning. He probed, but her responses were vague. If she ever left him . . . God, her soft warm body removed from his life? Can a person die of a broken heart? If this is love it's getting difficult. Is he panicking? Worry isn't new to him. But Sylvie gone, that would be something else.

The man, awake now, has resumed reading the paper.

"Some weather," he says because he'd rather talk than think.

"It's going to get worse."

He looks at his watch, another ten minutes. What's the matter with him? Of course she'll be at the station. He peers out the dirt-streaked window; it's snowing heavily.

❖❖❖

It must be nearly six, the darkness ashy; a flashlight would help. Gusts of cold wind burn her face. A veil of snow obscures her view; the unplowed road is hard to navigate. But she's not bothered, her body energized, a reprieve offered. Her arm around Liam went numb but she didn't remove it until he woke. It was as if she were hanging on to him instead of holding him.

She picks her way carefully along the shoulder of the road. Snow-laden trees and bushes hide vacant summerhouses. If she shouts no one will hear but the aloneness rejuvenates. A neighbor, an elderly gentleman she met on the beach, was ill and she helped him, the paintings a thank-you for her ministrations. None of it a lie.

Glancing at the darkened house, she sees her car beneath a cape of snow. Wet flakes hit her face. She's reluctant to call it a day. The dogs bark, and she fishes in her bag for the keys.

Switching on the living room light, she freezes. Chewed couch, torn chairs, gnawed tables, toppled lamps, ripped shades, clawed paintings, scratched walls, splintered floor, ruined, all of it ruined. "Bad, bad dogs," she cries. They look at her dolefully.

Murray will have a fit; he'll curse her and the universe, maybe worse. Better pack a few things; be gone before he arrives. Lord knows what he'll do to the dogs; still, she can't take them with her. What motel will let her in with them in tow? "Bad dogs," she mutters, and peers out the window. It'll be treacherous driving, no visibility at all.

Ignoring the phone's pulsing message button, she hurries to the kitchen, pristine, untouched, appliances gleaming. She quickly fills the dogs' bowls with food and water. They sidle past her; she doesn't want their affection; they could be dead tomorrow.

Lights sweep the window. Christ! A headline flashes: Man in temper kills dogs, wife.

She takes a last look at the animals, meets him at the door. He throws his arms around her. He's mumbling something she can't make out.

Her words, though, are precise. "I left the dogs home alone."

He strides into the living room. He runs his hand along the damaged couch, studies the ravaged coffee table, stares at the paintings, traces the scarred wall with his fingers. "Rummy, Cheney, you bastards . . ." his voice breaks.

"It's my fault," she offers.

"God," he says, "God . . ."

"Leave," she stage-whispers; the dogs sit.

"Miserable, stupid curs," he grabs the back of a chair.

"Murray—" she begins.

"Everything's wrecked, everything."

"Murray?"

"How could you?"

Is he talking to her? "Murray . . . Look at me."

He turns; eyes wide, astonished, wet, skin blue-white and taut, mouth slack. She's never seen him this way, it's scary, a whipped man resigned to the next lash. He's no youngster, a seizure, stroke, anything is possible. Prying his hands from the chair, she walks him to the bedroom, lies down beside him.

"Murray," she whispers, "they're things. They can be replaced . . . we can reupholster the couches . . . and the chairs. The paintings, okay, they're destroyed . . . Are you listening? . . ." She looks into his nearly unblinking eyes. "It's okay, it doesn't matter, it's not important . . ." But he's not responding.

"Say something, please, you're frightening me."

"I never lived this well . . ."

"I know." But does she? She was expecting anger, not collapse.

"You can't imagine what this house, the furniture, means to me," his voice a whimper.

Her eyes slide to the mahogany dresser, the floor-to-ceiling mirror, wicker rocker, all of it inanimate. How can he be so emotional; no one's died.

Suddenly he grabs her arm. "We'll make it beautiful. We did it once, we can do it again." The volume loud, he could be screaming.

She sees herself in one of the large suburban shops, salesmen circling her every move, furniture arranged by room, pillows galore, tables set for eight, peering at materials until her head aches.

"Money's not a problem. We can spend," his voice revelatory, gleeful, which should reassure her, except her energy's gone, a pricked balloon, the air seeping away. She takes a deep breath, but it doesn't help.

"I'll get rid of the dogs. Everything has a trade-off."

"A trainer can teach them to behave." Does she care?

"Are you sure?" his tone childlike, high-pitched.

"Yes."

"It'll all be the same as before, I promise." He's breathing heavily.

Once she watched an actor playing King Lear suffer a heart attack during his last scene. The audience applauded.

"You believe me, don't you?" His voice shaky, he takes her hand. "Are you okay with me?"

She looks past him at the darkness and visualizes the moon's tangerine light above the storm.

"Yes," she replies because the truth now would do him in.

4

The Way Things Work

Shelly stares out the kitchen window, cell phone in hand, as a few cars pass by. Across the road her elderly neighbor wearing a sweater over a robe is watering the lawn as she does every morning. Maybe it's penance, or a pact with the devil in exchange for something. If the devil approached her offering relief, what would she agree to in return? she wonders. She glances at her cell phone. God knows she doesn't want to make this call. Bruce . . . he's killing her. It's the fourth time this week she had to call to say he'd be late. If Murray happens to arrive earlier, if he picks up before Ava, if . . . it won't happen. Sylvie told her he goes to sleep and wakes at the same time every day, no exceptions. Sylvie sounded disappointed, but isn't it a good thing? He functions at a high level, doesn't he? Runs the damn diner like he was born to do it, doesn't make business mistakes that she's heard about and can be counted on to get to work on time. None of which she said to Sylvie. Once more she glances at the phone. It's no use, either she calls or . . . The diner is on speed dial and she listens to it ring. When no one picks up, she exhales and leaves a voice message.

Her cold coffee on the table, she eyes the muffin. Can't eat that. God! Even her oldest, after he sees his father, asks what's happening. She could give him an earful but all she says is, Dad's getting on and it's not easy in a diner kitchen. Bruce was never tidy, but now it's impossible. Leaves things wherever, but, okay, she's used to men doing that. She has three sons for god's sake. But at least he used to shower every day. It's making her crazy. They've shared a bed for twenty-seven years, ever since she was nineteen. She can't do it anymore.

Her eyes slide to the newly painted kitchen walls. Apricot. Lord, what possessed her? She hoped it would cheer her baby before he took off. He did say he'd remember the color, something bright in the desert. It's painful to think of Michael there. She can't watch TV, either, though since Michael left, Bruce is a news junkie. What she can't say to her sons or to Bruce is that fear for Michael's safety has her by the throat, though she confided as much to Ava and Mila during breakfast at the diner. Women with children, they understand the terror.

She glances at the clock. Three times she's told him to get up. He'll lose the damn job. Murray isn't the type you want to piss off too often. She strides out of the kitchen and smashes open the bedroom door. "Bruce, I swear, you don't get out of bed now I'm leaving for good." She hates shouting; it's so crude. Even when the boys were little, she didn't raise her voice. Now she's beginning to sound like her mother who screamed everything.

He rolls slowly toward the side. He's gained weight. He used to have a good build, he jogged and pumped. Now he does none of it. She waits till his feet touch the floor, then walks out.

Leaving Bruce has become a daily fantasy. Then she'd have only herself to care for. Her sons, too, of course, but with Michael away and her oldest married, already saddled with a baby, and the middle guy in Seattle doing whatever with computers, it's just Bruce, isn't it? What would she tell her sons? I can't live with your father anymore. He doesn't bathe, doesn't talk. They're not going to be sympathetic to that. Even if they are, they'll want him to get help;

you can't leave a man when he's down. It's immoral. Well, let them come live with him.

Bruce shuffles in, dressed in baggy jeans and a sweater.

"Want breakfast?"

He nods.

"Coffee and a muffin? Because you don't have time for a big one."

He nods, again.

"Why couldn't you get up?" She cuts up the muffin the way he likes. Sweeps the crumbs off the smooth surface of the counter, which she planed and stained herself.

"It's hard."

"Tell me something I haven't heard."

"Just is." She pours the coffee and he gulps it down, though she's sure it's too hot.

"Bruce, be careful, you'll burn your tongue." Habit. She shouldn't bother when the man asks nothing about her well-being.

"Jam?"

"On the table there. I was thinking before how Michael likes the color of the kitchen, I mean he said so in his last—"

"He's a baby. He shouldn't be fighting in this frigging war. He didn't even sign up . . . what's the National Guard doing there anyway," his face reddening.

"Jesus, Bruce, calm down. I agree with you, but what can we do? He's there."

"Do?" He looks at her like she's posed the sixty-four-thousand-dollar question.

"I know how you feel. But Bruce, there's nothing we . . ." She stops, no point repeating herself like an idiot.

"I'm too jittery to drive this morning," he says. "You take me."

"Why not. I have nowhere special to go."

"What about work?"

"I told you twice, they cut my days to three. After twelve years, it's a shame. People are saying they'll call me back. Who knows?" She's one of two assistants to the head bookkeeper. They check accounts, payment errors, and merchandise received. It's satisfying, the order of it, the repetition, the predictability. She watches the colorful bustle on the supermarket floor from the little glass cage of an office. If she slides open one of the panels, the cacophony rises up to remind her there's a world out there.

❖ ❖ ❖

As she drives through familiar streets, her eyes flit past houses with extensions not half as good-looking as the one Bruce's brother built onto their place. His brother is creative but can't stop drinking no matter how many programs he attends. Once, sitting at the kitchen table crowded with empty beer bottles, he said AA meetings leave him so desolate only a drink can help. Bruce laughed. It wasn't funny. Later, in bed, Bruce mumbled people choose the way they die. When did he make his choice, she wonders, glancing at him gazing ahead, his face empty of clues.

"Heard anything from your brother?" she asks.

He shakes his head.

"He must be on a bender," she offers.

"Why do you care?" He sounds bothered, as if she's taking something from him.

"I'm just talking, that's all."

"Things on the news now that no one's seeing."

"Bruce, millions of people watch TV."

"Watching and seeing are different."

"Well . . . that's true." Is this the beginning of a conversation? "It's hard for people to really . . ." but he's turned away to stare out the window with the same intense look that comes over him when he watches TV, as if there's something he has to catch before it disappears.

In the diner parking lot, she waits for him to begin his slow climb up the few steps, her eyes glued to the front door till it closes behind him. She could go in too, have a cup of coffee and chat with Mila, but it's the morning rush; Mila will be busy. The sun too bright by far, splashes the front windows. She flips down the visor, steps on the gas, and wonders where she's headed.

⬥⬥⬥

Could be too early to drop in, she thinks, pulling up in front of her son's garage. Well, she's here, isn't she? Ricky rented the small Cape Cod with a deal to buy in two years. He's working his heart out, but he can't control construction. It happens when it happens, he'd be the first to say. He's on a site now, thank god.

Ricky holds open the door for her. "What's up?" He sounds concerned. Firstborns are like that, always waiting for the shoe to drop.

"Hi son. Drove your dad to work and thought I'd pop in to kiss the baby. Hope it's okay."

"Joni still has the coffee hot."

Joni is sipping coffee at the table, her thin body hidden in a cotton robe. Shelly notices the mess in the sink, must be two days' worth of dishes. Should she offer to wash them? She doesn't want to. Besides, Joni might take offense.

"What time do you go in?"

"In a few minutes. We're on weird shifts now. It's a big piece of property near Jones Beach. How's Dad?"

"He felt too jittery to drive this morning."

"Poor guy's beaten down, is what I think."

And what about her? she'd like to ask, eyeing the baby swing next to the high chair, neither of which has been used yet. They were presents from the baby shower where she and Joni's mom

57

were the only people over thirty. Damn thing lasted for hours. Then the men arrived, including Joni's father, but no Bruce.

"Dad needs to get checked out. A doctor might give him something."

"I've suggested it a million times. He looks at me like I'm asking him to climb Mount Everest."

"Ricky, you talk to him," Joni says, which surprises her. Joni's a quiet girl who's loved her son since junior high. And why not? He's earnest, handsome, and energetic. He used to polka his mom around the living room, lift her right off the floor, and laugh. Or was that Bruce? There was a time when Bruce was the man. They were married, but they were lovers, four or five times a week, which is no easy feat with a bunch of kids in the house. Bruce always had his quirks, he's a vet, isn't he? When he first returned all those years ago, he'd open up after a few drinks and talk about the war. She never liked what she heard, but comforted herself that it was over and done with. Except maybe things don't go away, maybe they go into hiding like bears and come out when you're too old to fight them. Bruce will be leaving his fifties real soon.

"Want something to eat?" Joni asks, her tone less than inviting. She can't blame her; these kids don't have much. Besides, Joni's got her hands full with the house, the baby, her telephone canvas job.

She shakes her head. "Where's the baby?"

"Asleep in the carriage. He was up all night. I had to wheel him around. Don't wake him."

"No, I wouldn't think of it." She turns to Ricky, "Joni's right, talk to him. Maybe he'll listen to you."

"I'll take him out for a few beers."

"Like he needs the calories."

"What?"

"Never mind. Pick him up at the diner after his shift."

He nods. "Gotta go." He grabs his jacket. She's about to tell him it's pretty warm out there, but it's none of her business. It's Joni's business now. Joni kisses him hard on the mouth. The girl's still crazy about him, but just wait. Such negativity . . . it's not like her. Where's the bright-eyed, perky Shelly, a woman determined to get what she wanted? A woman who said yes to whatever it took to make it happen, and god help any who stood in her way. Bruce used to laugh at her combativeness, said it would put a grunt to shame.

She's careful not to slam the car door and wake the baby. No point hanging around without Ricky there. Maybe if she'd had a daughter . . . but her sons, they're men, they feel with their dad. Oh they love her, but sometimes she's on a planet by herself. Joni's sweet, but the only thing they have in common is Ricky. She doesn't want to hear Shelly's problems. Does she want to hear Joni's? She could find a therapist who'd listen, or maybe she could go to confession for free. Except you have to believe to receive solace. She could drive till the car runs out of gas and see where she ends up. Her fantasies of flight are beginning to scare her. But what scares her more are the thoughts piling up in her head like so much garbage she can't get rid of.

⟡ ⟡ ⟡

Searching the mall for a shady spot to park, she pulls in between a pickup truck and an SUV. With keys in hand, she slings the bag over her shoulder and hurries toward the bakery. As usual, the mall seems endless and unrewarding, but where else to go? A hotel in the city for a few days, not too expensive, with room service, a bar, a restaurant? A temporary escape. She'll take in a show, something deep, not a musical. Ricky will fire how-come questions at her she won't be able to answer. Her sister, too, will be calling to ask if she's okay. Well, she's not.

The well-dressed, stout woman who owns the bakery sits on a stool behind the cash register. The warm scent of fresh bread fills the shop. A gorgeous display of cakes and cookies offer themselves behind a domed glass. She spies a man near the large oven icing cakes on a flat table, his apron a palette of colors.

"Shelly?" From behind the counter, her sister throws her a questioning look.

"Take lunch early, please," she whispers. "I'll be at that café across from the shoe store." She's out the door before Patti can refuse.

Slipping the keys in her bag, she heads toward the café taking in people's expressions on the way. What does her face say? she wonders. The first few years of their marriage, Bruce would study her for long minutes, then try to guess her thoughts. She didn't like it, said it was intrusive; he was invading her head. Some of that would go a long way now.

The café isn't crowded. A waiter loiters near the counter looking bored. He follows her as she finds a table away from the window. Her watch reads eleven. It's too early for anything but coffee, which she orders black. Then she decides on a scone. They're going to be here awhile, is what she thinks. A huge mural covers one wall, a French countryside, she thinks. A trip to Europe by herself would be exciting. She'd go places if Bruce weren't around. But where would he be?

Patti hurries in as she always does, a kind of tic with her, rushing.

"Hi sweetie. What's up?"

"Order something," she says.

"I can't look at cake."

The waiter arrives, pad and pencil in hand. Her sister orders a cappuccino.

"Time of day tells me this isn't a how-are-you visit," Patti says.

She gazes at Patti's long wavy hair dyed the same honey-blond color since she was fifteen; her eye makeup hasn't changed either.

Her sister doesn't look different from ever before. "It's Bruce. I don't love him. I can't live with him." The words run out before she can test them, and they surprise her.

"After so many years it's not unusual. There are months I can't stand the sight of Peter. Then, I don't know, some little thing happens, the way the light hits his bald spot, the way he rubs his eyes, it brings it all back. You have to wait for those moments to rekindle." Patti talks fast.

"They're not here, they won't come back." Peter is jovial. He cooks. He loves the house. In their worst periods, he brings her flowers every Friday night.

"How can you be so sure?" Patti asks.

"It's been too long, more than a year. I'm reaching the edge."

"Then talk to him."

"It's no use."

"Why not?"

"He's shut down. Either he takes me to the bottom with him or I let him hit it alone. How can I get out of the marriage without being hated by my sons, you, Bruce, everyone else in our lives? You don't leave a drowning man, and Bruce is drowning."

Two teenage girls make a noisy entrance, laughing like they own the future. Why aren't they in school?

"Shelly, you're going through that time, not yet fifty but closer than further, when we start asking ourselves what is this life? I've been there. I turned fifty last year."

Patti's right, before long she'll be looking back at fifty, then how quick to sixty. There'll be limits that aren't here yet. "So stick it out and one day all will be fine? Is that what you're saying?" She can't help the sarcasm.

"It's the way things work," Patti asserts in that voice of hers that claims to know everything. "You can't hold on to dreams that promise another life, because there isn't any. Maybe for rich folks who travel the world, own mansions. Not us. Think of the struggle, how long it took to create the homes we wanted. You won't be able to do that again. Why give it up because Bruce is going through hard times? You'd be sorry."

"I didn't expect you to agree, but you're not getting it." She should've waited to catch Mila on break. Single mothers know a thing or two about struggle that women who live with men don't. What exactly she'd be hard pressed to explain.

"What's there to get, Shelly? A marriage falls into a pit. Who climbs out first? The woman does. Remember Dad's depressions, what did Ma do? She walked around them till he snapped back. He always did. It never occurred to her to leave."

"We don't know that. It isn't something she would've told us. Anyway, Ma didn't expect anything better." She's not her mom, won't be.

"Shelly, what part in this do you play? What should you be doing that you're not? Is it all Bruce? It might be. But do you know that for sure?" Patti's bright blue eyes, so like her own, remain steady on her. Then she glances at her watch and takes another quick sip of coffee. "I couldn't take lunch, it's too early. I'm on break. It's over. Sorry. I'll call you later." Her sister drops three singles and rushes out. The door slams, she and the teenagers the only customers there.

Is Patti right? Is she contributing to Bruce's behavior? She badgers him constantly. Wear the new boots, take off the hat, pick that up, don't drop it, too hot, too cold, not right, a thousand ways to control. He lets her, Bruce does. Actually, she does pretty much as she pleases, always has, with her sons, the house, her hours at work.

⸙⸙⸙

In the pharmacy next door, she buys a box of Epsom salts and a packet of bubble bath. Then she picks up a steak at the food mar-

62

ket. She'll hash brown potatoes the way he likes, though he doesn't need the starch. Wine, yes, that too, and a candle for the table. Maybe some unexpected shaft of light will illuminate his face and rekindle her.

She takes out her cell phone and leaves Ricky a message to pick up Bruce another night.

⸙⸙⸙

Shoving the pillows deep into cases so they're plump, she turns down the duvet, exposing the pretty blue hem of the sheet. She remembers how the bed gave itself up to them as if it too was a star performer, the naughty pleasures that followed her into the next day. Remembers too the years of Bruce's whispered words, always the same endearments because they belonged to her. It's what's left of their marriage. Memories.

She scrubs the bathtub till it's as white as one in a soap commercial. He used to like it pristine. Peering into the crystal clear mirror, the face that stares back hasn't begun to reveal the truth. Strong-boned like her mother's with skin that promises to age gently. A few laugh lines would be good. Her touched-up dark hair is graying at the temples. She doesn't care the way she used to. There was a time she'd dress up on a Saturday night, heels and all, even if they weren't going out. He always noticed, Bruce did. He called her his dark Irish beauty, his one and only. He was her mirror, her happiness reflected there. Now her makeup sits unused on a shelf near the sink. She unzips the pouch, takes out foundation, eyeliner, blue shadow, frosty pink lipstick, all the while thinking this is even crazier than some of her fantasies.

⸙⸙⸙

She places the unlit candle in the center of the table set now with matching plates, stemware, and cloth napkins. She won't broil the steak till he gets out of the bath, then a few glasses of wine. It's strange, the fussing without the excitement that used to rise in her as naturally as her energy. Still . . . if she doesn't try . . .

Hearing the front door, she hurries toward it in the high-slitted long purple dress he brought her from overseas. Her eyes made up, she's wearing earrings and perfume. "Bruce? Honey?" When was the last time she called him honey?

"Something happen?" His face drains of what little color it has.

"No. Everything's fine. Let's have us an evening." She touches his shoulder. "I bought salts and bubble bath for you. I'll fill the bath for you. You'll feel refreshed. Then we'll have some wine. What do you think?"

"Too tired. I'll watch TV in bed."

She sees herself walk past him out the door.

"I need to say a few things. Come in the kitchen. Just for a minute. I'll make you a steak. You can eat it now or later."

She pours wine for both of them. "Sit, Bruce. I can't talk with you standing there like someone's outside waiting for you."

He slips into the armchair and watches her warily. She sits across from him. His curly black hair peppered with gray flattened now from the ridiculous cap he wears, though it's no longer winter. All of her sons have his large, round eyes and long lashes. Always a strapping guy, the kind who could pick up a woman and carry her over the threshold without losing a breath, and he did. Not anymore, though. She wonders if recalling the good times or the better times or just the times when he wasn't the way he is now would be helpful.

He drains the glass in two long gulps, and she refills it. "Just today I had an image of you with your strong arms pushing the stuff that bothers you into a carton. After so many years, the carton splits apart. The stuff floats around looking for a new hideout but it can't find one. I think it's what's happening to you, to us, Bruce." Okay, it's not what she actually thought, but the bear-in-the-cave thing won't work for him.

He looks interested. He puts down the glass and seems to be figuring out something to say. She doesn't want to pressure him, so she goes to the stove and turns the potatoes, only the sound of spitting grease. She waits a beat, then returns to the table. "I was also remembering some of your war stories. They were horrible, particularly . . . and there must be many you never told me. Not that I want to hear them, god help me, but I was thinking . . . if you could vent to . . ." She's taking a chance here, trying to get him to open up when he doesn't want to. The last time she did that, after 9/11, he mumbled, why bother, said it was the beginning of the end anyway. "Bruce, what do you think about what I'm saying?"

"Why do you care?"

She tells herself let him go to bed. She can't. "Bruce, I care, and I'm waiting for an answer."

"Michael's carrying forty pounds, plodding through the mud, afraid of any noise in the trees. He's only nineteen. He doesn't want to die." He leans toward her, breathing hard, his face tense, eyes wide, the tendons swelling in his neck. A cold hand squeezes her gut. It's himself he sees slogging through the mud, being pursued, his old demons creeping up his back and what can she say to prove it.

"Our son is nineteen, yes, Bruce, but he's in the desert, not the jungle. It was you in the jungle."

He gazes at her but lord knows what he's remembering. "Yesterday, a helicopter was shot down. It was on the news. Everyone killed." Then, scraping back the chair, he walks out slowly.

Once Ricky brought home a stray dog that kept growling at them. Why keep a dog that might bite the children? She called the animal shelter and asked for someone to come get it. When the man arrived, the dog stopped growling. He knew it was over.

She turns off the oven and takes the pot of potatoes to the sink. She carries her wineglass to the bathroom. Starts the bathwater, shakes in a cup of salts, adds the bubble stuff, and waits for it to fill. Heat dampens her face, the aroma gardenias, she thinks. Someone brought home flowers for one of her birthdays. Was it her thirty-sixth? Bruce ordered a gigantic cake and Ricky insisted on putting all the candles on it. "Make a wish," they all shouted, even solemn Michael. What did she wish for? Was there something she wanted just for herself? A piece of clothing, a trip, a better job, she can't remember now.

What she does remember is what she feared even then, that Bruce wouldn't last through the marriage, that she'd be left alone with three young children. There were always clues she was good at ignoring. Things can turn on you when you refuse to pay attention.

She undresses, the purple dress a dark puddle on the floor. Then lowers herself in the bath, slowly stretches out. She reaches for the wineglass. No use letting good stuff go to waste. Faint voices reach her from the always-too-loud TV, sounds that will follow her into the den where she sleeps on the pullout couch. Where she gazes at the painting of three little girls in a field of daisies, cherubs with smiling faces lit by the sun.

The phone rings. No doubt it's Patti. Bruce won't pick up. She'll ask Patti for two days' work at the bakery, save enough for a vacation. When's the last time she left home? Bruce will have to fend for himself. He'll never get out of bed. He'll eat a bunch of crap, gain more weight. He'll develop heart problems. She'll return to find him in the ICU with just enough time left for her to say sweet nothings before his eyes close forever. The water tickles the back of her neck. Her body relaxes despite her thoughts as the bubbles quietly disappear.

5

In the Silence

Wiping his hands on the damp towel, Nick peers over the divider. Amazing the junk customers leave behind. Ava's clearing tables with the haste of someone stalking free time. She seems more energetic since that lying-faced guy vanished. Bursting past the kitchen door, she deposits a load of trays and turns to go.

"How's your son?" He can do better than that.

"Frisky. Girls are different. How's Glory?"

"She's looking for a job, not sure about college, moping, sharing little."

"Yeah . . . well . . . give her time."

"As much as she wants."

"Nice beard. I'm going to get the newspapers."

How about a drink? What's so hard about that?

His ear picks up the incessant drip of the sink tap. He'll fix it tomorrow. Charge Murray a plumber's fee. Yeah, right. Bruce shuffles in through the back door, an hour late. A man so worn he makes Nick feel chipper. Bruce wasn't always this way. He used to pay attention to whatever crossed his path, kept an eye on unsavory possibilities. He would think nothing of taking a heavy bin of dirty dishes out of anyone's hands. A helper. Now, well . . .

"What's happening?" he gathers his gear.

"Nothing." Bruce speaks even slower than he moves.

He ought to stay a minute and make conversation. They're buddies, sort of, or would be if they were on a desert island together. Instead he heads out the back door.

Except for Ava and Bruce, he has little to do with fellow employees. His run-in with Murray still tastes sour. He tried to enlighten him about the war. Murray insisted in that loud voice of his, the boys over there are saving New York from another attack. Why did he bother? No matter the facts, the man has an opinion about everything. Yesterday it was Nick's beard, but he's not about to conform to some cockamamy dress code to work in a kitchen.

⊰·⊰·⊰

Early morning driving. He loves it—no traffic, Glory still asleep. She'd better be. A girl of eighteen isn't always where you want her. He's headed toward Jones Beach, his usual stop before home. No one around but a few male shapes sprawled on the sand. From their garb, he'd guess they have little reason to wake up. The boardwalk is shuttered, light splattering the dark horizon like a cracked egg. He locates his bench facing the ocean. If it weren't for Glory, he'd stretch out here, count a few sheep. But she'd know he didn't come home.

He breathes in the sea air, conjures up his usual vision: China Beach, nurses frolicking in the water. Joyce, his big-boned mate who wasn't yet his wife. Inhaling those weed killers took her lungs as sure as any soldier's. At the end she moaned because anything louder would've put him in a box beside her. One tough lady who kept his mind focused, his body functioning, which was no easy feat. She had a mantra: life's a jigsaw puzzle.

⊰·⊰·⊰

When he peeks into Glory's room, the computer screen is silver bright stars into the stratosphere. Asleep, her curly red hair is bright against the white pillow, one freckled cheek hidden. He tiptoes out and leaves the door open, the signal he's home. In the four years since Joyce died he and Glory have worked out a routine of sorts broken by his occasional bad days. Which reminds him . . . he follows the worn runner to the bathroom where an array of pill bottles summon him. A handful each morning to ease blood pressure, scare away migraines, lower the decibel of voices. A tiny aspirin to keep him alive. It's a joke.

Glory comes up behind him. "Skip one and Mom will clobber you."

"I hate these damn things, get stuck in my throat, turn my piss orange. Jesus, even if I want to forget mortality, I can't."

"Some people are deaf, blind, and paralyzed, but they still manage to smile if it's sunny out."

"I smile."

"When?"

"You mean that?"

"Totally."

He gazes at her, trying to remember where it was Joyce offered him ten dollars to laugh.

"I need to brush my teeth, and other personal things. You going to be long in here?" she asks.

"I'm out of here to sleep. What about you?"

"What worthy tasks am I about to undertake for the day?"

"Yeah, something like that."

"How about job interview. Or a college visit?"

"Sounds good."

"Well, truthfully, that's not it. I've been meeting with people who started a local antiwar collective. I bumped into them online a few weeks ago. They're very interesting. We meet in one of their houses, not far from here. But after, I really do have a job interview at IHOP."

He groans.

"It's just temporary, till I figure something or everything or a little bit of everything out." She kisses his cheek, making a loud sucking sound the way she did as a kid.

❖-❖-❖

For reasons he can't locate, sleep eludes him. Is it the start of one of his bad days? He's tired but not edgy, his mind blank, not whispery. He imagines Ava beside him, her lovely hair unpinned, flowing. His affairs have been brief, itch-fulfilling but nothing to ruminate about, no one to bring home. Anyway with Glory here, it's not particularly lonely.

❖-❖-❖

He opens his eyes, the room is hot, his mouth dry. A dreamless sleep, thank god. Hoisting himself off the bed, he stares at his feet, but remembering depresses him. The old wall clock reads 6:20. Yesterday he conked out for two or three hours, today ten. His whole life lacks regulation. Glory's in the kitchen noisily preparing dinner. The girl can't cook but whatever she serves, he eats.

After a shower, he pads to the kitchen; the table set for two.

Glory seems nervous, excited even, as if she can barely contain news.

"What is it?" he asks.

She studies him for a second. "Let's eat first."

Tension grips his body. "I don't think so."

"The group I told you about, the one I spent the afternoon with, they're amazing. They're part of an organization that's global.

People from lots of different countries go together to become witnesses for peace in the Middle East. It's a way to stop the killing and the torture, to show the rest of the world all the evils that are going on so we can eventually stop them." She's nearly breathless, her eyes shining.

"Out of the question."

"Dad, I don't need your permission. I thought I'd have your approval. You believe in peace."

"I'm not sacrificing you for it."

"I'm not going to die. Honestly, dad..." She gestures impatiently.

"I can't process this now . . ." His hand flies up to swat it away. The colors of a migraine seem close.

Her light blue eyes take him in. Her translucent skin tight around that tiny nose, her rosebud mouth. She's barefoot in jeans and a T-shirt, her costume of the month. But there's nothing petite about her broad shoulders, her sturdy body, as solid and shapely as Joyce's ever was.

"Later, then," her tone upbeat. She's handling him.

After a one-two, hurry-up dinner of pass-the-salt talk, he drives to the beach. Sits in the parking lot, a blanket of darkness about to fall. Even if he demands Glory not go, she'll do what she thinks is right. It's how kids her age navigate the world, impulsively. It's his fault and Joyce's too. They brought her up to believe everything is possible. Glory standing in some no man's land between tanks? It's insane, suicidal. Shit.

A cluster of young drinkers saunter by, beer cans in hand; their voices compete with the buzz in his head. He pulls out his cell phone.

"Ava, it's Nick. I'm tending a headache. Can you cover till I get there?"

"Sure. You take it easy," her voice curious but restrained.

He could ask what she'd do in his shoes but hangs up instead.

Her input might increase his anxiety and he doesn't have any pills for that.

He inhales sharply, warns himself not to drive fast. Useless.

⸎⸎⸎

It's late, but Glory is staring at the computer like it has the last word. Something in him wants to smash the screen.

"Hi sweets. We should settle the deal now." Otherwise it's farewell to sleep and work and sanity.

"Okay." She presses a few buttons and the screen is back to saving stars. "Have a seat. You're looming."

He sits on the bed. She rolls her desk chair around to face him. Only one lamp is on and the dresser fan whirs annoyingly. It's been hot since the last snow melted. He offered her a small A/C but she said it would pollute the air.

"I'm not going to say witness for whatever is a bad thing. Except there's so much turmoil in that part of the world . . ."

"But Dad . . ."

"Wait."

She leans back, stretches out her long legs.

"Your values are no different than mine or your mother's. But neither of us would put ourselves in jeopardy."

"But Dad . . ."

"There are safer ways to protest. In the chaos of Gaza, the West Bank, or wherever the fuck . . . you'll be an ant, a tiny bump, an annoyance, and nothing more."

Her expression closes down. Her eyes lower, her mouth tightens. "Look, I'm going. I need you not to worry. It's three months. I'll e-mail as often as I can."

He begins pacing, wonders if he should threaten her, but how? "Glory, you just met these guys. I'm sure they're sincere, but Christ,

72

who the hell are they? I mean what makes them witnesses? And the money, where's it coming from?"

"Rich people, older people, people who agree with us but can't participate physically."

"Wonderful. They remain in their cream-colored houses while you sleep in the sand."

"Dad . . . please . . . stop pacing, you're not in an emergency room. I need to be involved with something bigger than me," she explains as if he were the child.

"I don't want you going." He's trying to keep the volume down.

"Dad, even if I chose this for pleasure, or out of curiosity . . ."

"I don't want you going." He'll never budge.

". . . It's my life, my time to do such things."

He stares at his daughter, at the band of freckles crossing her forehead, the clarity of her eyes, the strong jaw, the length of her fingers, and realizes he's memorizing her.

⋰-⋰-⋰

In the silence of her room the computer stands as a gateway to the rest of his life. Her messages were coming two a day, one every two days, once a three-day interval, but it's been six days. Jesus, God, Crap! How's he supposed to survive that? Rereading previous e-mails, which he never deletes, the information is lodged in his brain. She arrived; she's fine; it's too hot. She needs another couple of pairs of shorts; don't send them, no real address. She's bunking in a camp-like situation, electricity on and off. The beauty can feel like an insult: clay-colored dunes, sky so blue it hurts her eyes, stars so bright they light up the night. The misery, the poverty . . . the kids are killing her; hopeless, depressed by age eight. Her last e-mail bragged she could say words in Arabic, some in Hebrew. Tan, Dad, she wrote, I'm so tan, it's amazing.

He picks up the bottle, takes a long swig of bourbon. It'll be a month tomorrow. Two more to go. He's crashing in Glory's bed now. Without the sleep pills, dreams and crawly, creepy stuff wake him every hour or two. Even now his feet feel itchy. He peels off his socks and checks for fungus. Clean.

Then he remembers . . . begins rummaging through the desk drawer, slides a piece of paper out from under others; three names: Josh Towns, Emanuel Walker, Robert Messenger. He takes another long drink from the diminishing contents, finds himself on the faded couch in the living room punching in the first number. It rings until voicemail picks up. He leaves a message. He dials Walker's number.

"Hi." Sounds like a child.

"Is your Mom or Dad there?"

"Who should I say is calling?" Her little voice is prissy.

Who indeed? "A friend of . . ." —and here he takes a chance—"your brother's."

"I don't have a brother."

"Your father's Emanuel Walker?" The decibels rise.

"I can't say."

"Let me talk to your mom, now, please." Jesus! Damn, the bourbon's still in Glory's room.

"Hello." It's a voice so dull he wants to hang up.

He introduces himself. ". . . and I haven't had an e-mail in nearly a week, so I wondered . . ."

"My husband and I . . . we're not communicating much. If I hear anything . . . leave me your number."

He does, but she'll never call.

Staring at the third name, he decides he needs hope; he'll try it tomorrow.

Two groups of noisy young people take over several diner booths. It's the middle of the night and they're ready to eat everything including the inventory. He works the orders nonstop. A few strays come in as well, probably because there's nowhere else to go. The kitchen is steamy; he's sweating. He stares at a chit but the letters scramble, so he blinks a few times, tries again, but the words still blur. He cups some cold water in his hands and splashes his face, tamps it dry with a paper towel and tries deciphering it again. Better. Except there's a pull in his stomach even though he visited the bathroom minutes ago. "Ava," he stage-whispers over the divider.

She turns her perfectly shaped head to look at him and hurries into the kitchen.

"Have to go home . . . need to check the machine . . . I've been away for hours . . . haven't had an e-mail in days . . ." his voice trails off.

"That doesn't mean a thing, Nick. It's not New York. It can't be easy to find a computer."

"All the orders are done. I'll be back. Can you cover?" Before she can answer he heads out. Great, she thinks he's crazy. Maybe he is. So what? Crazy or sane isn't the issue. Something happens to Glory, he's fucked. In the parking lot, he thumbs down hard on the car keypad; damn door won't unlock. The car begins beeping loudly. Shit, shit. Take a breath. Try again. The noise is deranging. Someone help. Did he say that out loud, because Ava's running out the back?

He hands her the device. She makes the beeping stop, bless her beautiful soul. She's had her tragedy, losing a husband, but it was a long time ago. She can't still be mourning. "How about going for a decent dinner tonight before our shift? On me." See what happens when drink collides with crisis?

❖ ❖ ❖

Sunlight brightens the adjacent wall, illuminating the nearly empty bottle. Across the road is a house like his, except it's yellow with blue trim. Inside there is an intact family, a husband, wife, two children, very American. His house is white with green trim chosen by Glory before she was old enough to determine her life. Glory would not want him going to the State Department for help. Then again, the State Department wouldn't be sympathetic. Is he going to sit in front of the screen all day? Ava walks into his head. She's home getting some shut-eye. He wouldn't mind having an afternoon drink with her. But what would that mean for dinner tonight?

A distant ambulance siren penetrates the silence. Someone's life is about to change. It's what he thought as he lay in a makeshift hospital tent listening to the docs talk about amputating his infected foot.

He drags himself to the living room and tries Messenger's number.

"Hello," a woman's annoyed voice. Does she understand where her son has gone?

"I'm a friend of Robert's—"

"I clean. He's not back for months. You call later."

But he won't call later, and he can't sit in front of the computer another minute without losing it.

⁂

In the car in front of Ava's house, he tries to talk himself out of what he's about to do. Fails. He rings the bell with short staccato stabs.

She opens the door, a queen in a purple robe.

"I'm freaking out."

She leads him to the living room where the furniture looks almost as old as his, and he thinks to console her with this observation but finds himself unable to speak. She's pushing something that smells like whiskey under his nose. Should he drink or sniff it? He drinks.

"What happened?" She stands arms crossed, wavy hair falling past her delicate shoulders; her light eyes weary but concerned.

"I could go to the State Department except they'd probably arrest me. It's a lot of money to fly over, and I don't even know where she is exactly. It's stupid of me to barge in like this, but—"

"We're friends, right?" She sits beside him, her clean soapy scent instantly calming. "If something bad happened, you'd be contacted. You're next of kin." She sounds certain. Except his stories don't have happy endings.

"She was e-mailing, so what changed? The thing is, Glory's never on the same computer. If I'm at the machine, I reply instantly. I told her I have to hear from her."

"Children," she sighs. "Have you slept?"

"Couple hours. I should go home, but I'm too wrecked to drive." Is that true? Does she believe him? Her face reveals nothing.

"Do you want the couch for a while?" He wants to close his hand around her long, thin fingers.

"Sure," but to his surprise he follows his body to her bedroom. He takes in the yellow daisy wallpaper, the yellow lampshades, sunshine in the dark. A portrait of her husband is on the wall, the face gigantic. He recognizes the R&R quality, charcoaled too quickly in some godforsaken place; and wants to ask if it's how her husband really looked but decides not to.

The bed is queen-size, the pillows numerous, waiting. He slips out of his shoes, turns down the yellow-and-green-flowered cover. He stretches out. He's lost it.

When she slides in beside him, he remembers hearing about men so exhausted they begin dreaming before their eyes close. But once more he inhales the sweet scent of her.

"Who are you? Why do you care, or something along those lines?" he asks.

"Who says I care. You're suffering."

"It's a motherish thing?"

"You're older than me, I can't be your mother."

"So?"

"It's probably a mistake, but I need . . . I want to be adventurous, a little."

He palms the cool smoothness of her cheek. "You're wonderful, hauntingly . . ." But a weariness he doesn't want shoots lead through his body. "I can't believe this," he mumbles—not that she wouldn't notice his limp prick. He strokes her hair, the silky strands tangle between his fingers, then subsides like a ship in harbor.

❖-❖-❖

Opening his eyes at an unfamiliar ceiling, the shades drawn, he remembers. Is he mortified or contrite? She's not beside him. Should he call her name? Her husband stares at him without affection.

He walks into the living room. The TV is on, the volume low. She's dressed in a long black skirt, silky, with a white blouse open deep at the neck.

"Drink before dinner?" she asks.

"Dinner?"

"It's nearly six."

"You're kidding."

"No," she says so seriously he's embarrassed.

"Where's your son?"

"Helping Dina next door. I told him you collapsed, and why. He offered to look online and see what he could find out about Witnesses for Peace."

"You're extraordinary." He drops on the couch beside her. Slides an arm around her slim shoulders, dips his chin in her soft hair, done up in some fancy knot. His fingers wander inside her blouse, find her velvety breast . . . With the heat of her throat against his lips, he cradles her head, maneuvers her legs onto the couch; she curls her body to make room for his. He thinks to say a few lovely words, but her eyes are closed, her limbs wrapping his. He enters a land where only distraction and satisfaction exist.

❖·❖·❖

He watches her attempt to organize the mess he's made of her outfit. "I could offer to have it cleaned, but it'll only happen again."

"Why was that so exciting?" She sounds genuinely surprised.

"Unexpected love. It's the best kind."

"How would you know?" She searches his face.

"I wouldn't."

"Is dinner still happening?" she asks, but he can sense her withdrawing.

"Tonight and tomorrow, if you want?" He means it.

"Bobby's not always going to be conveniently busy."

"Let's take him with us tomorrow."

"No."

"He knows me from the diner, remember?"

"I'm going to change."

❖·❖·❖

His time with Ava yesterday gave him courage. His car glides into a space beneath a huge tree, which he wants to identify as oak, but he wouldn't know. Hidden by afternoon shadows, they can't see him. Then again these people don't gaze out windows; they have security do that. He stares at the estate. If the house were any

79

nearer the water it would float. The last time he saw this much property he was mustering out of the Marines. But the base was a flat, ugly, brown expanse, dotted with huts that passed for barracks. That anything this lush exists a mere twenty miles from the cheek-by-jowl places he sees daily is staggering.

He replays the voice message in his head. "Come by, we're home all day on Thursdays." What can he possibly say to the rich and famous? They probably own a piece of the Middle East. If someone opens the door, he'll be chased away. A bearded man dressed like a panhandler? He's not wearing his good shoes. Find a bar in town, two drinks to dissolve the edge, then return here.

Finding his cell phone, he calls Ava. Probably napping. Well he needs to talk to her. As the machine picks up he hears her real but tired voice.

"I'm parked outside a mansion. It's me, Nick."

"Yes?" Her plaintive voice, so girl-like, encourages him.

"Parents of one of Glory's friends invited me for tea."

"And?"

"I'm not dressed for it."

"I see . . . You mean your clothes are dirty?"

"Not exactly." He eyes the beige pants and blue shirt.

"Holes in your shoes?"

"Why does everyone focus on shoes?"

"You want to make a particular impression?" Is she being sarcastic?

"I'm Glory's dad."

"Could be they're idiots."

"Not with this estate."

"Nick, who cares? They have information. You'd walk through fire for Glory, so?"

"I didn't mean to wake you."

"Yeah well, it's becoming a habit."

"I wish you were with me."

"You'd better go in."

He clicks off. He does wish she were with him, though it makes no sense. What makes even less sense is the way she's invading his thoughts. These flings work a certain way. Sleep together a few times, then she discovers his faults. Many. She begins to make excuses. Too busy to meet . . . not good for employees to fraternize . . . If Murray catches us . . . Murray? Who cares about Murray? His mind is bending, that's what. Glory's killing him. In his state how can he think about Ava?

Yet her non-dismissive voice helps him out of the car. He lopes up a driveway to what he hopes is the front door, feels the first drops of rain. He discovers a brass knocker. Is that an ornament or real? No bell. He uses the knocker. A maid with brown satin skin, dressed in old movie-style black and white, opens the door. She can't like her costume. So soft-spoken he can barely catch the words. It's his name she wants and he tells her. Then he waits in a vestibule larger than his living room.

The maid ushers him into a den or library or maybe it's a living room. Mr. and Mrs. Towns stand together in front of a fireplace. She's tall, thin, wearing black slacks, a gray blouse. In her early fifties, he'd say. Her husband, too, is tall, thin, in his fifties. He decides Mr. Towns in khakis and polo shirt just returned from playing golf. They look like brother and sister.

When the maid leaves the room he feels alone.

"Please have a seat." Mr. Towns takes the wing chair facing the couch, his wife the chair next to his.

Nick sinks into a leather sofa so soft he may never be able to get up.

"We haven't heard from our son recently. No doubt they're all on some exciting outdoor mission, traveling who knows where." Mrs. Towns seems charmed by the idea.

Maybe he should enlighten her about the outdoors there. Trying to sound matter-of-fact, he says, "When last did you have an e-mail?"

"Josh phoned us ten days ago, right dear?" the husband asks but doesn't wait for an answer. "We spoke a very short time. We agreed, well, he's so involved he can't think about keeping us up to date. At any rate, his voice was gleeful." He reaches over to touch his wife's arm.

Gleeful? How does that word apply to the Middle East? Would Josh tell his father if one of his friends were kidnapped? Wounded? Killed?

The maid brings in a tray with tea and a square plate with flat white crackers that look as if they'd crumble at the touch. He wants bourbon.

"Mr. Towns is certain everything's fine. Josh is our youngest, more of a challenge than Chad or Douglas. Eighteen and already curious about complicated places."

Mr. Towns? Complicated places? What language is this? Mrs. Towns hands him an empty teacup. Christ, he doesn't want to deal with tea stuff.

"If we don't hear from our son in the next two weeks—" Mr. Towns pours himself tea.

Two weeks? He'll be certifiable.

"—Martin will take a look?"

"Martin?" He says, relieved to speak.

"Mr. Town's business associate is somewhere near Saudi Arabia, certainly closer than we are." She gives him a crisp smile. "Martin will investigate, discreetly, make sure all is as it should be. You know how children are? They become so invested in the moment they can't remember to contact us. We'll let you know either way."

Either way? They don't sound a bit worried. Why should they? Their problems are delegated, resolved by others. The green slime of envy fills his veins. Not the mansion or the money, though a little of the latter would get him on a plane. It's Mr. and Mrs. working in tandem, reassuring, affirming each other, refusing disaster.

Carefully, he replaces the unused cup on the tray. With muscles he didn't know he had, he hoists himself off the sofa. "Thanks so much. If I receive a message from Glory, I'll let you know." Do they care? So he adds, "And yes, I'd appreciate hearing anything you learn."

❖❖❖

"I've never met people like them, cool, not as in hip, as in distant. Not snobby . . . almost innocent. Of course Josh's okay. I could've pointed out the guns and tanks, but why do that?"

Ava looks at him tenderly the way she does when they're alone together, except they're seated at a deeply scarred wooden table in the rear of Sully's bar. Far from fancy, the pub has the right amount of noise at this early evening hour to set problems aside, albeit with a little help from booze. The beer is cheap, the wine not cold enough, but they've decided on bourbon and Coke.

"Tell me everything." Her long fingers splayed on the table, no wedding band, only a small reddish gem embedded in a silver ring. He wonders if it's her birthstone. He folds her hand in his.

"His wife calls him 'Mr. Towns.' Jesus, what does she call him in bed? They were a pair of . . . I don't know"—and he doesn't although the experience is still fresh in his mind—"birds squawking a language I couldn't grasp."

"Rich and secretive, I've read about people like them. She cries in bed without making a sound. He drinks too much and wouldn't hear anyway."

"Even if the Towns worry in private, they aren't fixed on disaster. Otherwise Josh would be on a plane home tonight, Martin no doubt the escort. Are they stupid, can't they see the misery there, or do they know something I don't?" He downs the last of the drink.

"Did they manage to reassure you at all?"

"They're in la-la land."

"And you?" Her eyes still on him. He's starting to like being watched, at least by her.

"Me? I'm an ex-marine; reality's my specialty." He wants to tell her how lovely she looks, that her red blouse is exciting, but she's focused on the details of his day. And how often does that happen?

"You get in your own way," she says a bit too soberly, as if she is about to reveal some gruesome truth about him.

"I'll get us refills."

At the bar, he catches the bartender's eye, holds up the empty glasses. Who else in this place is agonizing over a son or daughter? He studies a few faces that reveal nothing but lines. Is it that he can't bear being apart from Glory? He understands the order of things. It's time for her to leave him, but not gunned down or kidnapped by some lunatic. "It's a worthy deed, Dad, better than serving pancakes. There's something big at stake here." It's what she'd said, and not just once.

With a cold glass in each hand, he studies the very real woman waiting for him, has an urge to say thank you, but she won't know what he's talking about.

Setting down the drinks, he asks, "My place or yours, as the saying goes. We have two hours before our shift."

"Yours . . . but—"

Is this the first of the excuses? He waits.

"After, I want to spend time alone with Bobby at home, arrive at the diner in my car."

"I couldn't agree more."

Sheets of rain splash against the sides of the car, hard pellets of hail drum the roof, the windows fogging. It feels like he's inside a plastic bag. The meteorologist drones on about high meeting slow-moving front, and sounds baffled. He switches off the radio. Only a few miles from his house to the diner but the deepening puddles force the car to a crawl.

The imprint of Ava's slim, strong body still warms him. They made a decision together. If there's no e-mail from Glory in the next three days, he'll phone the State Department, find out the protocol for locating a missing person. Not a solution but it's something—waiting is driving him under. He's on the two-a-day antidepressant now, his mouth dry, nightmares, and worse, sometimes he can't get it up. Thank god that didn't happen this evening.

Is it mist circling a tree? An apparition? He can just make out a figure walking the edge of the road. He swipes the side window with his forearm, cracks it an inch. Peers out. Christ, what's he doing? "Hey," he calls, sliding the window all the way down, water splashing his face. "Bruce!" He stops the car. "Get in, for god's sake."

With a black woolen cap pulled low on his forehead, his round, dark eyes blazing, Bruce stares like he doesn't know him. Water drips off his nose, chin, everywhere. "Get in," he orders, leaning over to open the passenger door. Bruce delivers his bulk.

"Where are you going?"

"That way." Bruce points in the opposite direction.

He's wearing an army jacket, backpack in his lap now. "What, you running away?" He tries for the smile it's impossible to get from Bruce on a good day, and this isn't one of them, of that he's certain.

"Need to get to the National Guard office."

85

"It's not open this time of night."

"That's what I want."

"Bruce? What the fuck?" Silently, he ticks off possibilities: flashback, sleepwalk, hallucination. Does he want to know?

"National means in the US," Bruce spits out each word as if it's laced with poison.

Drive him home. Let Shelly deal with him.

"I'm going to set fire to the office." Bruce pats the backpack.

"Yeah, well . . . not a great idea with all the water coming down, is it?"

Suddenly he feels nauseous.

"Take me there now." Bruce sounds determined, and worse, he's wearing that mind-blanking expression that hears no reason.

"It won't be raining tomorrow night. If you still want to do this, I'll help you. It's always easier with two, remember?"

"They lifted him out of his life like a stuffed animal."

"Who?"

"They took my boy."

"Michael's in Iraq?"

"Just a baby. Sent him to be killed." He's seen broken and it looks like Bruce.

"Michael's in Iraq?" he asks again.

Bruce doesn't answer. So he puts the car in gear, begins driving him home.

❖-❖-❖

He nearly walks past the hospital. A small gray brick building with three floors that could be anyone's house, except for the barred windows. He drove here straight off his shift. A few hours' sleep might've helped. His head feels spacey; he's not too thrilled with his balance either. Damn pills. Ava offered to drive him to Manhattan—he was touched. But he can think of better places to take her. The front door is the first of several leading to reception, the architect offering a change of mind at any turn. A baby-faced receptionist who has to be in her fifties gives him a paranoid stare before releasing information. Then she tells him outer doors remain unlocked only during visiting hours. In short, he'd better watch the time.

Shelly's in one of the dayroom's orange plastic chairs, a handsome woman with enough energy to run a country. Now she's thinner than ever; dark pouches beneath her usually curious eyes. It seems as if she's crying without tears. She offers up a ragged face and he pecks a quick kiss.

"I got your message. What happened?" he asks. A man sidles along the wall. Three women stretch their necks to watch a mounted TV. He can't figure if they're in or out. Again, he spots the barred window. The tic on his eyelid is back.

"After you dropped him off, wetter than a seal, right, I got him to bed. Wouldn't get out next morning. Kept saying, I don't care . . . isn't worth it . . . what's the difference . . . things like that. Had to get my oldest to help bring him here. The psychiatrist will evaluate him for seventy-two hours. They mentioned shock treatments. I said, wait. Bruce said it wouldn't make a difference. It's as if he made a conscious decision to stop caring—about anyone. Michael, our baby, is in Iraq, you know, but the way Bruce talks, it's not our son but himself he's seeing, young soldier that he was. The memories of then filling him now, god knows what it is he fears."

"They'll feed Bruce antidepressants. They work." He wonders if he should just lie down like Bruce.

"Yeah, hope so. Do you think Murray will keep Bruce's shift open till he's back on his feet?"

He doubts it, but nods because the desperation in her voice alarms him.

"I've brought up three children. A kitchen holds no surprises. I could work two days of his shift till he returns. Would you put in a word?"

"Sure." Murray won't allow her in his overmanaged kitchen, though he'd welcome Shelly's help.

"He's down the hall, last room on the right. I came out here for a break. Wanted my first cigarette in years, but you can't smoke anywhere. Damn."

※-※-※

The hallway is too long, too narrow. He passes a man in a robe talking to something invisible in his hand. The guy reminds him of the time Glory asked him to serve Thanksgiving dinner at a shelter. She found the experience uplifting. The scene depressed him for days. Now, too, the wish to turn around and depart is strong.

No bigger than a walk-in closet with one small barred window and a twin-size bed, which is way too small for Bruce, who's curled up facing the wall.

"Bruce, hey. It's Nick." The pajama-clad backside and bare feet scare him.

"Hey," the voice barely audible.

"So . . . how do you feel?"

Nothing.

"We all go through these dark patches . . . a couple days, you're up, better than new."

Bruce shifts around slowly to give him a who-are-you-kidding look. His face is pale, waxy, lips in permanent frown. "I'm not in the mood for chat."

"I thought you'd have a couple of words for me." He glances out the window at a small square of gray sky. Could they make these places any more discouraging?

"Nick, go home."

"Yeah, in a minute."

Bruce closes his eyes, which is a relief.

He pulls a chair from the wall to the bedside. A few more words, then he's out of here. "I know you're worried about Michael. His tour will end and—"

"He could be dead right now." The sharp words stab his gut. He takes a deep breath.

"You and me, we made it out. So will he."

"You don't know that. Horrible things happen there every day."

"You have two other kids waiting for you to pull yourself together."

"Their lives are their own," his voice barely audible.

"You mean if they're not in danger you don't care about them?" His own voice louder than necessary.

"Something like that."

He flashes on three-year-old Glory riding his shoulders. Each time they reached a doorway, she'd yell, "duck." And he'd quack. She thought that was hilarious.

"My daughter's in the Middle East."

Nothing.

"She's a witness…for peace." Sounds ridiculous, like some religious calling. Even with Ava he doesn't talk about what Glory's actually doing there. Does he know? He wants to believe in her bravery, her expectations, but how can something good hurt him so much?

"She wants to make a difference," he continues, but this too sounds stupid. It doesn't matter. Bruce isn't listening, his eyes still closed, his face expressionless. He could be dead, but he's alive. No mistaking the stone finality of dead: it's the first thing that hits, even before the smells.

"I'll see you soon. Try and get it together." But even as he says this he wonders if Bruce is finished trying. He wants to give his arm a brotherly pat but is afraid to touch him, a man stalked by doom. He heads out but doesn't stop to speak to Shelly, because what can he say?

The receptionist eyes him suspiciously. "Forget it," he calls over his shoulder. "I'm not moving in."

⸙ ⸙ ⸙

It's a few streets to reach his car. He walks quickly, Bruce heavy in his head, the hospital's sour smell with him as well. Not a hint of sun, the air thick, punishing. Heat and traffic noise follow him. He could do with a cold beer. The whole world sucks is what.

Triborough Bridge or Midtown Tunnel, which one to take? He's already having trouble breathing, being underwater won't help. Before he can stick the key in the ignition, Bruce's open-eyed face appears in the windshield. Not a good sign. He switches on the radio. Bruce's face refuses to disappear. He fiddles with the dial to get conversation. Bruce stares at him.

He shuts his eyes. It's a visitation, a warning, the kind Scrooge received. Only it isn't about time past, it's about now, maybe the future. "Anything can happen to anyone anywhere, we know that, man." He's talking out loud. To Bruce. That's crazy. But he can't stop himself. "Our kids want to live. They'll take care same as we did. You and me, Bruce, we share the doom, but that's it, man. Things are changing for me. I'm beginning to get a life here."

He opens his eyes: the grimy windshield holds only a vision of a narrow street of small shops, garbage cans along the curb. Taxis whiz through changing lights. People rush by. Destination is all. He has one, too. He's taking Ava to a late afternoon movie. When was the last time he'd done that? The film could make Ava late for her shift. Rosalyn will stay an extra hour, friend that she is.

The voice on the radio sounds serious. He ratchets up the volume. The man's selling prepaid funerals. He laughs.

6

Butter and Ketchup

Getting out of the shower, she hears the phone, grabs the towel robe, and hurries to the living room.

"Yes? Hello?" A little breathless.

"Dina? It's Rosalyn. You sound funny."

"It's unusual to get a call this early." Actually, phone calls alarm her whatever the time.

"I knew you'd be leaving for Ava's and—"

"Yes, well, what is it?"

"You do sound strange."

"An incident in the shower. It's nothing."

"Did you fall?"

"I didn't." A woman enters her sixties and it's the first question.

"I have to get a pair of shoes for a wedding. I hate going to the mall alone. Do you need anything?"

Since leaving her job she buys only essentials. "No, but I'll keep you company."

"Meet me in front of Baker's shoe store at ten-thirty."

"Okay." An ER nurse, an ICU supervisor, a world within which she functioned for years at high speed, now she is a woman with time on her hands.

Returning to the steamy bathroom—her mug of coffee cooling

on the rim of the sink—she stands for a moment remembering. It was nothing. But there's a tug at her insides, not a stomach problem. No, it's a tug of panic, the second one this morning. The first was brought on by seeing the new rubber mat in her tub, which she placed there last night. It's a surprising state, getting older, the limitations, bodily insults, odd sense of both urgency and mortality. But no one can stop the process. The fading beauty thing bothers her least. When she peers in the mirror, the face of yesteryear still meets her eyes. What she can't hold onto is that step-lightly kind of go. The way Ava wills her limber body to comply without complaint, Mila's seemingly never-ending energy, Rosalyn's jaunty step with no thought of tripping.

The clock on the shelf tells her she has thirty minutes to wake Bobby. Her black slacks and pink blouse hang outside the closet door. Pancakes, Bobby loves them. Now that she has time, he's growing up and soon won't need her. Caring for Bobby—so different than her son—is never a chore. Tim insisted on attention. As soon as she stepped through the door he was all chatter and need. Maybe if her husband had lived . . . her son was so young . . . but who knows? She saw Tim during the last snowstorm. He arrived wearing sneakers. She offered to buy him boots and he wanted cash. She gave him what she could. He stayed less than an hour. She was relieved to see him go, something she can barely admit to herself.

Taking a sweater, though it's a strangely hot spring, she checks for her car and house keys, confirms the toaster and coffeemaker are unplugged.

❖·❖·❖

Driving to the mall from Ava's house, Bobby's on her mind. He was quiet during breakfast, unusual for him. Moodiness is a given at his age. Maybe he's upset about the kitchen guy his mother is dating, not that he'd say so. He's double-digits now, things are happening to his body. Would he talk to her about it? She passes a row of renovated houses with new roofs, landscaped lawns. Beginnings.

Pulling into a parking space, she notices the indoor mall is bustling. Shops, restaurants, and offices occupy two tiers that circle up and around. People dressed for work hurry by, reminding her she's a lady of leisure. Not quite. Still, her recent scheduled-by-the-minute life is done with. The alarm clock is no longer set, but she wakes early anyway. She bought lots of plants, a tomato box she tends daily. There must be more to retirement. Maybe she'll buy a book about it, though she doesn't believe in experts.

Rosalyn waves, a gremlin all wire and vigor, jeans and a short-sleeved shirt like it's already summer. Rosalyn's thick, dark hair frames a face that will always contain beauty. Some faces are like that but she'd never noticed before.

The shoe store is surprisingly crowded for a weekday. Balancing boxes, salesmen scurry back and forth, making her seasick. She finds a seat while Rosalyn studies the display shelves.

"I want to dance, so the heels can't be too high. On the other hand, I need fancy." Rosalyn holds up a black suede pump for her to see.

"Nice, try them." The salesmen interest her more. She searches for one who'd be around thirty, Tim's age. It wouldn't be a job he'd consider. He isn't a server.

Rosalyn, wearing two shoes with different-sized heels, limps across the carpeted floor to sit beside her. "Which one?"

"The left." Even if Tim took a job selling, she doubts he'd hold on to it past the first paycheck. And she remembers all those years ago when he first disappeared, she and the principal searching the empty classrooms. Bobby would never disappear that way.

"How well do you know Nick?" she asks.

"He's not much of a talker. Why?" Rosalyn slips on another pair of shoes, raising one leg to admire the fit.

"Ava's dating him."

"She's a big girl."

"A kitchen guy's not exactly a model for her son." Again she flashes on Tim, wonders if he's working anywhere.

"Model?" Rosalyn laughs a harsh sound. "A cushy job makes a noteworthy man, is that it?"

"A man Nick's age should have a more relevant position."

"What's relevant? Cop? Pencil pusher? Stockbroker? Like that guy Mark, the big business owner from Colorado?"

"Oh don't play that game. You know what I mean. I guess Ava's tired of being alone," she hears herself concede, though she isn't sure she believes it.

"Poor lonely Ava. Comes home from the diner and doesn't have to deal with a man's moods, criticisms, demands. Peace."

"A relationship is more than a list of problems."

"Companion, lover, hand-holding in the dark? How much of that is real, Dina?"

"How cynical," she says.

"It's experience."

"You've closed down, is what."

"With all due love and respect, my past isn't written on my face."

"There are truths in life," she insists.

"The trouble is they keep changing." Rosalyn slips off the shoes.

"You always have a quip."

"Sorry, but I can't sympathize with looking to a man to change life for the better. It's never that simple."

Rosalyn's words resonate, but something in her won't give in. "Of course not. One has to work at it, together." Is that what she did? Filling the few short hectic years of her marriage with all she wanted to accomplish: a new house, furniture, child. Then Howie dies, just like that, and she, too stunned to grieve.

"Dina. You've been a widow how long? Aren't *you* lonely? Why didn't you join Parents Without Partners like so many people around here? Have you slept with anyone since?"

She did have a brief affair with a kind man who sold medical supplies, but it was complicated. Having to build a relationship, meet Tim's needs, work a high-powered job. It was too much. She ended up wanting simplicity more than companionship. "My true love died," is all she says.

"I see." Rosalyn lines up four pairs of shoes.

"You don't see a thing."

"Are we arguing?"

"Of course not. We're just two women talking."

"I'm sharing, you're talking." Rosalyn gazes at the shoes.

"You're goading me."

"If you say so. Listen, Nick's a sweet, respectable guy who's done well as a single dad in these last years, even if he is too quiet."

"Ava talks to you about the relationship? She hasn't said a word to me." Last year she would've been too busy to notice.

"Well, you know. We share different things with different friends."

"How very kind of you to explain," she mumbles, with no attempt to hide the sarcasm.

Rosalyn glances at her. "I need your help. Please tell me which of these shoes I should buy."

She points to the suede pumps.

❖-❖-❖

The sun has ducked behind a cloud revealing the grimy glass dome overhead. The first time Tim went missing, she covered every inch of the mall looking for him. The police were sure he'd return once he saw how miserable the streets could be. He did, but not for a month, a month in which she barely slept, traipsing the neighborhood peering into boys' faces. She blamed herself for his absence. But he didn't come home to stay. Money, he needed as much as she could offer. He cajoled, cried, swore he'd go to rehab. Now when he comes he always wants something from her. She began to pray he'd stay away. What kind of mother would do that?

"Dina, it's nearly twelve. Let's have a drink."

"And forfeit my free lunch at the diner?"

"Ava's not there. She's on full night shift now, though Murray feels no shame in shifting her hours whenever he wants. If I were Ava—"

"You're not. But it's weird, no one gives me a check anymore. I've become a fixture of sorts."

"Murray can afford to be generous. Sylvie's gone back to work, you know. Mila told me gleefully that Murray's not happy. Smart move, I say. A woman needs to have her own money. I said as much to Murray. He looked at me like it was my fault. Anyway, he's fond of Ava and knows what you do to help her."

"That's not the reason for the free meal."

"What then?"

"Older woman, invisible or stand-in for Mom. It's revolting."

"No one sees you that way."

"Not yet," she murmurs. "A drink it is. Where?"

Rosalyn turns her dazzling eyes in her direction. "I know a café." They cross the main floor of the mall, a buzz in the air like dying neon lights.

⋅⊰⋅⊰⋅⊰⋅

The café is blessedly quiet. They sit at a small round table near the window. As usual she takes in the ketchup in its easy-squeeze dispenser. Tim added butter and ketchup to everything he ate. It nauseated her. Sometimes he'd make a sandwich of the two ingredients. And she'd have to leave the room to contain her disgust. She wonders now if it indicated some chemical imbalance, perhaps a lack of potassium or sodium? Even as a nurse she'd never thought of it before. It was simply a stupid, even outrageous combination, the way children can pick out clothes that don't match.

The waiter slogs toward them. He seems exhausted, bloodshot eyes, swollen fingers, pasty skin—either a hangover or untreated diabetes. They order two glasses of wine, a grilled cheese sandwich for her, warm apple pie with ice cream for Rosalyn.

"Strange being served . . . I leave huge tips. Ruined by my profession." Rosalyn glances out the window.

"What did you do before being a waitress?"

"You don't want the list."

"I bet it's colorful." She's fond of this woman's spunky refusal to conform; fond, too, of their talks about anything and everything.

The waiter brings their wine, setting each glass down carefully. She notices the slight tremor in his hand, decides his symptoms are alcohol-related.

"To the good life," Rosalyn says, and takes a long drink.

"So?" she persists.

"File clerk for Revlon, very young . . . free makeup, boring, boring. Go-go dancer . . . had its moments, definitely more lucrative. Affiliated escort service and travel agency."

"Who did you escort?"

"Foreign visitors. Men." Rosalyn takes another big swallow, nearly emptying the glass.

"Exotic?"

Rosalyn gives her a half-smile. "Depends how you define the word. And you, always a nurse," but it's not a question.

"Yes, interesting but no spontaneity. The job was about order and control. The right dose, not just of medicine, but of time with patients. Everything doled out with the next task in mind."

"And grateful people? And the god-docs, they were a trip, I bet."

"True." So many years carrying out duties without making any major mistake. She wonders now whether that counts as success.

⁂⁂⁂

Her house sits between two identical small white clapboard structures with black trim, one belongs to Ava, the other to a family newly arrived from India. She sees a light in her upstairs room. Bobby has a key. Why did he lock the door? "Bobby?" She walks past the orderly kitchen to the living room. Why would he be upstairs? "Bobby," she calls again, and climbs the well-worn steps. Before reaching the top, Tim appears.

"I thought I heard you." His voice is deeper than she remembers.

"Oh my." Her hand presses her chest.

"Didn't mean to scare you. I have a key." But the smirk on his face doesn't reassure her. He looks awful, just awful: skinny as a pole, pale, too, shabby clothes, torn sneakers. Has he been sleeping in the streets?

"I put my gear in my room."

"Yes, good," and she turns to go back down because a sudden dizziness threatens her balance.

He follows her to the living room, drops into the club chair, his feet up on the chipped leather ottoman. "I'm in trouble, I need to hang out here. My partner's picking me up tomorrow."

"What kind of trouble?" Her jaw so tense a pain shoots up the side of her cheek.

"You'd be an accomplice if I told you."

"An accomplice? Tim, what have you done?" She's not shouting, but her voice echoes in her head, the way it sometimes does when she's at the beach treading water.

"Don't get wormy. Stay calm."

"Where have you been since I last saw you?" He seems tired, his eyes red-rimmed. But he's not high, which is something.

"Around. You're looking good, Ma. How's the job?" He reaches up, switches on the floor lamp. In the circle of light, his skin pulled tight over delicate bones has a bluish tinge. There's red in his dirty-blonde hair. Has he been in a sunny climate?

"I retired." That's a word she rarely uses. Left, finished, no more nursing, is her usual description.

"What do you do for money?"

"I have a pension. I get along. You needn't worry." His question, though, is self-serving, and a spark of anger ignites inside her.

He gazes at her with opaque eyes.

"What is it, Tim?"

"Remembering living here."

"Not as long as you could have." Does she want to rake up old ashes? Will there be anything new beneath? A difficult child who slept little, wouldn't play by himself, clung to her with such tenacity she froze.

"I was in your way," he says simply.

The boy knew. The boy felt her impatience. Be honest. Own up to it. But she can't. "Don't be ridiculous."

"Yeah, right, ridiculous, that's me."

"Are you hungry? I have chicken. I can order Chinese. Whatever you want."

"Any beer?"

"No."

"Call Ava, ask if she has any?"

"I'd rather not."

"That too much trouble?" A slow grin spreads across his face.

"I'm glad to see you. I'll cook something. I'll wash what you're wearing. What else can I do?"

"Nothing, Ma, nothing at all." But she doesn't believe him.

In the kitchen, taking the defrosted chicken from the fridge, she knows as if it's written on the wall that this time she's not to be spared. Well, okay, what more can happen? He'll want money. She'll go to the bank, take out a few hundred. He's her son, who else can she give it to? And she remembers that winter morning returning from Ava's, rushing him so she wouldn't be late for work. He became recalcitrant, moving ever more slowly. Finally, she told him she was leaving. He could get himself to school. "But I'll be late if I have to walk there." "Not my fault," she said, striding toward the door. "Ma," he called over and over, but she wouldn't turn around. That afternoon he disappeared. "I'd sure like a beer." He pokes his head in the kitchen.

"Go to the market."

"I'm hiding." His sullen words a cold fist in her belly.

She searches his face, the dark blue eyes with their long lashes, the beauty of them wasted like the rest of him. How could he be so stupid? "I'll go. I'll be back in a few minutes."

⁂

Once again she finds herself in the car heading toward the mall. Was it a bank? A robbery gone wrong, a teller wounded, blood on her son's hands, on his soul? Stop it, she tells herself. Until he shares what happened, she can't know. Years ago she made herself quit planning for his future, which hurt more than his demanding visits.

In the brightly lit market she hopes not to bump into Shelly, who works here. Any other time would be fine. Only two days ago they stood beside the colorful produce stands chatting. Shelly's a talker, said her youngest is in Iraq, which gives her nightmares. Poor Shelly.

She strides down the aisle, picks up a six-pack of Beck's and hurries to the cashier, no time to waste. Around her, people fill their carts as if today is just another day. She envies their indifference. Then consoles herself—no one really knows what goes on in another person's life.

❊·❊·❊

The double-locked front door upsets her, makes her feel sneaky in her own house. He's right there waiting for a beer and follows her to the kitchen. She hands him one, puts the remaining bottles in the fridge. "Why not take a shower while I prepare dinner? Some of your clothes are in the dresser."

He twists off the cap, flips it in the sink. "Yeah. Good idea."

His narrow frame lopes easily out of the room. When he was little he'd curl up on her lap. The gentle weight of him against her breast, the grassy smell of his hair, imprints that never disappear. She begins breading the chicken the way he likes it.

Hearing the shower loud and certain, she switches on the small counter TV as she often does while preparing food. She surfs for news of robberies, murders, whatever. Nothing. Tomorrow's papers may enlighten her. Is that what she wants? Isn't it better not to know? A moment of uncertainty stills her: cook dinner, serve it, pretend everything's normal, then retreat to her bedroom. Or she could confront him. She takes a bottle of Beck's from the fridge and twists off the cap, the cold beer bitter in her throat.

❊·❊·❊

He bounces down the stairs in a too-big pair of khakis and a faded black T-shirt she could've sworn she'd thrown away ages ago. His bare feet leave damp prints on the wood-slatted floor. A fringe of wet hair drips past his forehead.

101

"I bet the shower felt good." Some neutral ground has to be found.

"I forgot to close the curtain for a minute and got a little bit of water on the tiles. I threw down a towel." His voice matter-of-fact, but a challenge in his eyes, as if daring her to run up and fix the damage. The spilt juice, loose jar tops, left-out food, unlocked doors, half-open drawers. She tried to teach him, believed she could, but his habits never changed, and neither did her frustration.

"The floor will dry," she says crisply, and returns to the kitchen. Through the window she sees Bobby walking up the front steps carrying some boxes. Damn. She strides to the door to head him off.

"Hey sweetie, what's that you've got?"

He walks past her.

Tim salutes him. "Bobby, my man. You're a big guy now."

"Oh wow, I had no idea you were home."

Bobby deposits two boxes on the table. "One is a Scrabble game. My mom has two. The other is blueberry pie she brought home from the diner. Did your mother tell you she gave me your baseball mitt?"

"That's cool," Tim says.

"Want to play catch?"

"Not tonight. How's your mom?"

"She's out with Nick, her boyfriend."

"You like him?" Tim's voice deadpan.

"He's okay. His daughter's hilarious. She has a million funny stories. She won at Scrabble the other night and no one beats Mom. We have a marathon planned. The winner gets twenty dollars. I thought I'd practice with Dina."

"We can all play." Tim goes in the kitchen and returns with a beer. "Still too young for one of these, I guess."

"When is your mother expected home?" she asks.

He shrugs.

"Eat with us," Tim offers.

"I'm sure his mother has dinner for him."

"She can save it." Again Tim's voice gives nothing away. Why does he need Bobby here? She doesn't like the feel of it.

"She can save it," Bobby echoes Tim.

"Does she know you're here?"

"Where else would I be?" Bobby looks at her as if trying to figure out something.

She returns to the kitchen, dumps frozen broccoli in a saucepan of water, and waits for it to boil. A watched pot, Howie would've quipped. A man who liked his homilies, kitchen towels that read *home sweet home*, welcome mats, his-and-hers towels. She thought it a waste. They rarely had guests, not with her hospital shifts, but she saw no reason to squabble. Tim, however, wanted her to struggle, tried to engage her on a daily basis. She refused, had neither time nor energy. Sick people awaited her attention. Now she wonders if Tim needed her to fight. Children want to know they're important enough to stir up a ruckus. The water begins boiling. Early dinner, she thinks, then send Bobby home. An evening alone with her son, that's what she'll aim for, what she'll tell them both. She puts the ketchup bottle on the table.

⋯⋯⋯

As soon as they finish the game of Scrabble she suggests Bobby go home.

"Stay over. Why not? We're having fun, right, kiddo?" Tim speaks directly to Bobby.

"I'll call Mom."

"Where will he sleep?" she mumbles, confusion muddying her thinking.

"He'll share my room," Tim says.

Bobby looks at her, waiting for approval. The boy's not stupid.

"Sweetie, do me a favor, take the Scrabble up to Tim's room." She watches him run up the steps, then whispers, "What do you want with him?"

"Insurance policy. Don't worry, nothing will happen to him."

"I am worried." She stares at the hollows and planes of Tim's face, a replica of hers. "Why involve anybody else?"

"Bobby's a member of the family. He's the good boy." And Tim looks at her, mockingly.

"Tim, I'll have none of it. He's a neighbor's boy and should be sent home."

"In case of trouble?" An edge to his voice.

"Will there be any?"

"Depends." Is he toying with her?

"Let him go home, Tim. We can work out things without him."

"What things, Ma?"

"I don't know yet, but if you need to take someone, take me."

"That's a joke, right? You wouldn't know how to leave this place." She flashes on the times he begged her to take him somewhere, away, and always she had a reason—a good one, she believed—not to do so.

"Whatever happens, I'll help you. It'll be easier if it's just us."

"You may regret what you're saying." His eyes steady on her.

"I won't." The room seems darker though the lights are on.

"Okay. Listen . . . if my ride doesn't show, it could mean one of two things: He took the money and ran. Or he was picked up and gave me away. There'll be no way to know which." Tim speaks quickly and quietly.

If his ride doesn't show she'll have a felon under her roof. Still, he can't hang out here forever. It's the first place the police will look. She can't say so, can't have him believe she wants him to go even if she does. "We'll have to wait and see," her tone reasonable, even reassuring, though his face has gone a little blurry.

"Done," Bobby calls, bouncing down. Tim meets him at the foot of the stairs and in a low voice delivers some cockamamy story to send the boy home. Tim's good at that.

❖❖❖

She wakes with a start. Squints to decipher the red digits on the new radio clock, nearly three. Dim voices reach her from downstairs. Did his partner arrive in the middle of the night? Her ears pick up the faint creak of the downstairs closet door. What does he want in there? A coat? Now Tim is climbing the stairs, maybe coming to say goodbye. No, he goes to his room. A minute later footsteps pad down again. Would he leave and not say a word? Let him. Yet she's out of bed peering through the slatted blinds at nothing more than velvet darkness. Slipping on a robe, she carefully takes the steps down.

He's on the couch, the TV volume low, the closet door ajar.

"Do you want a cup of hot chocolate?"

"I just finished the last beer. Go to sleep."

She sees the photo album he's tossed aside.

"I heard voices. I thought your partner showed up."

"I doubt he's coming. I shouldn't have left everything with him, too tempting," his face a screen of regret.

"What will you do?" Every visit ends with the same question.

"Maybe Canada . . . anywhere far from here." He gives a short laugh, almost a bark.

"You don't have a car."

"I'll switch buses till I get there. Can you dye my hair and cut it, too? Buy me a blazer, pants that fit, shoes, socks, and a pair of sunglasses. Can you do that?" The last words a childish plea.

She remembers a stormy night. Crashing thunder, lightning, wind rattling windows. It sounded like the roof would fly off. Tim toddled down, his eyes wide with terror. She picked him up, dragged an old sleeping bag into the living room along with a flashlight. She zipped them in, hunkered there till he fell asleep. There's nowhere to hide him now.

"Yes. I can do that. I'll take out cash too," she says. With whatever maternal influence she still has, she orders him to go to his room and get some sleep. He takes the stairs two at a time.

Switching off the TV, she replaces the photo album, shuts the closet door. She wonders if aiding his escape makes her a felon, too. It's against her nature to thwart authority. He's done something illegal; she's clothing him, giving him money. He's her son for heaven's sake. She'll shop and go to the bank early. If his partner shows up, the clothing and hair dye will be useful. Stretching out on the couch, she can't help feeling she's doing the right thing for the wrong reason.

If his father were alive, he'd pressure Tim to turn himself in and get him the best lawyer possible. She hoists herself off the couch, climbs upstairs.

"Tim, if I hire a lawyer, would you give yourself up?" The suggestion offered through his door. He doesn't respond.

"Are you asleep?"

Nothing.

"Tim?"

"Ma, that'd be easier for you than me, okay. So forget it." Again the childish voice, the boy who hated discomfort, feared difficulty. If Tim were caught red-handed on some video camera, jail would be inevitable. There's no way he'd survive in jail. With faint relief, she descends the steps.

⬥-⬥-⬥

The morning sun wakes her. Problems sometimes dissipate overnight, but the weight of Tim's needs is immediate. Tiptoeing upstairs, her back aching from the narrow couch, she listens at his door, hears nothing. In her room, she dresses quickly. She phones Bobby to say Tim isn't well and can he manage breakfast without her.

❖❖❖

In the ATM vestibule of the still-shuttered bank, she averts her face from the video camera in the corner. Maybe his partner will show up. But maybe not. Tim should've taken his share of the money. What strange thoughts. She isn't used to all this intrigue. It's unreal, scary. Some people take risks for the fun of it—bungee jumping, mountain climbing, sky-diving—none of it anything she ever wanted to do.

The department store opens for business and she goes directly to menswear, no other customers in sight. That, too, feels eerie. Guessing at sizes, she chooses two pairs of pants, two shirts, a blazer, loafers, and socks. She piles the clothing on the counter. "My son won't let me shop for him anymore. They grow up and that's it," the cashier quips.

Taking the escalator to the basement pharmacy, she picks out a pair of wraparound sunglasses. Then she locates the hair dye, two bottles of brown-black color.

❖❖❖

The blinds are drawn and the door double-locked no doubt. She hurries in as if she's the one they're after. Tim waits on the couch, his narrow body on guard.

"Want something to eat?"

"Do my hair first," his voice as tense as his face.

She follows him to the bathroom, drags in a stool, wraps a large towel around his shoulders. She cuts his hair, the back of his neck no longer boyish. A man shouldn't need his mother anymore. Maybe if he'd joined the army like other boys around here . . . There are too many ways to lose a son.

She mixes the dye with the solution, shakes it a few times, and applies it to his hair.

"I had an incident in the shower yesterday," she's surprised to hear herself say.

"Yeah?"

"I squirted a glob of shampoo in the palm of my hand, then rubbed it on my hair, but my hair was dry. I forgot to wet my hair. That's never happened before. It's frightening to forget the usual things."

"I once put salt in my coffee. It's not senility, Ma. It's preoccupation." His words are weirdly reassuring.

Waiting for the dye to take, she sweeps hair off the floor and wipes the steamy mirror, an eerie silence in the house. No radio. No TV. Outside noises are muffled, it's as if they've been sealed in.

"Ma, it's ready to wash off."

She'd leave it on another ten minutes, but he's too restless, fidgeting, in and out of the bathroom too many times to count.

She shampoos his hair and her hands are gentle on his scalp. The dye turns the sink black. Drying his head with a towel, she offers him a comb. The dark color pales his skin, but it suits him. "You do look different."

"Don't recognize me, huh?"

"You think I wouldn't know you?"

"Many ways to know me." He looks past her to the mirror.

She begins scrubbing the sink.

"If my partner does arrive it'll be by three this afternoon. That was the plan. If he's not here by three-thirty, drive me to a bus station near Montauk and stay with me until I pick up something going north. Did you get the money?"

❖ ❖ ❖

She waits on the couch in her blue pantsuit and white turtleneck jersey. Montauk is two hours away. They could be stuck waiting in the car for god knows how long before a bus arrives. They should check a schedule. She's packed a small bag with a toothbrush and nightgown in case a motel becomes necessary. Tim once accused her of never venturing past anything familiar and now she's aiding and abetting a criminal. What's usual about that?

He walks slowly down the stairs, stopping to pose for her approval. He does look handsome in the new clothing. He could easily pass for a lawyer or a doctor, someone respected.

"Tell me one thing." She hands him three hundred dollars in twenties.

"One thing?"

"Was anyone hurt? Or shot? Or dead? Anything like that, I should know."

"Why? Will you love me less?"

"You're my boy, Tim."

"It was about money, that's it."

"I should open the blinds. They aren't usually shuttered at this time."

"Go ahead."

The afternoon sun no longer enters the room. A row of houses, outdoor chairs, closed garage doors, people at work, in school—nothing strange, except she's about to drive a fugitive to safety. He sits beside her on the couch. His loafers without a scuff, the crease in his pants sharp. It could be the last time she sees him.

But it won't be. He'll return again, and again. Of this she's suddenly certain.

"I filled the gas tank," she says to say something.

"Good." But he's not listening, his mind elsewhere, planning lord knows what.

A black Honda pulls up in front of the house. Tim sprints upstairs and returns a moment later with a suitcase he found in the downstairs closet.

"Be careful," she mutters.

Words she ought to say slip away like time.

"You take care." He sounds excited he hasn't been left behind after all.

At the window she watches him slide into the passenger seat. Then he's gone. Just like that. A stab of disappointment takes her by surprise. She stares at the space where the car was. The afterimage contains more than the moment, but she blinks it away. She flashes on another memory: her husband's funeral, Tim slipping onto her lap, offering her his only candy bar.

We give each other what we can, she thinks, climbing the stairs to his room. The window is shut, the lights on, the bedding mussed, the closet door ajar, the chest drawers open. His dirty clothes are piled on a chair and a damp towel is on the floor next to an open magazine. Three empty beer bottles line the sill. Grease marks on the wall. A half-full chip bag sits near the bed. She'll air out the room, then tomorrow she'll sweep, vacuum, and change the sheets.

7

How We Know
Before We Know

Wedding indeed. Rosalyn lifts one shoe from its box. What else could she tell Dina? At least she placed the escorting in the past where everything can be forgiven. More and more, she feels it's where it belongs. The long black skirt and blue silk tunic draped over a chair are waiting for her—whoever he is, he'll like it. It's such a chore dressing up when she'd rather order takeout and watch TV. Still, working for Annie has gone well for her, leaving her with a chunk of savings she'd never have accumulated from diner income. It's the money that bought her little villa . . . well, actually, a condo with terracotta floors and huge windows facing a terraced lawn.

Her eyes linger on the throw rugs bright as turquoise gems, the opalescent vase filled with daffodils, then slide to the sunburst clock on the wall. Jesus. Her father's waiting. He hates flowers, thinks they're a waste of money, promises to toss them when they're given to him.

❖-❖-❖

The winter snows have damaged the road even more than last year. She drives cautiously past old houses, a few with tarps over their leaky roofs, others with cracked windows. This is where she grew up. The area depressed her then and still does now. Holidays were the worst, yet she'd look forward to Christmas every year as if it would be different. Her father would drink less. Her mother would find a gift that pleased Rosalyn. She and her cousins were always shooed in front of the TV, but her ear was on the adult-talk. Josie lost another baby; Marie Rose pregnant by god knows who; Artie can't get it up; Ron's temper is out of control; Tony's got no work again. After each tidbit, someone would sigh, "That's life, what can you do?" She hated their acceptance. Not that they'd listen to her, a mere girl, at least not until she was married with children, if then. They'd hear her out now, though. With wide eyes and slack jaws, yes they would.

She hoists the bag of food from the rear seat, feels a strain in her back. Yesterday . . . lugging boxes from the storeroom. She warned Murray, no more. If it's over two pounds, he carries it.

"Dad," she calls, shouldering open the door. Since the emphysema diagnosis he's remained dormant. His body will disintegrate. She's been over this with him. At least walk to the corner and back, she insisted. He won't hear it. When she phones her brother to complain, he's sympathetic, but rarely comes east. Neither of them is filled with affection for the man. How could they be? For too long after their mother died they had put up with him themselves. If she had the excuse of distance, she'd take it as well.

"Make sure to shut the door," his brusque voice a little wheezy.

"How about hello?"

He's broad-shouldered, with powerful, deeply veined hands, sheltered in his BarcaLounger the small, bomb-shaped oxygen container beside him. Not a trace of gray in his dark mane.

"We don't stand on formalities, you and me." As usual he shouts over the TV, which is on all the time. Does the man ever sleep?

"I brought frozen lunches and dinners. In and out, it's easy."

"You want me to pay you?"

Yes, why not? damn it. The man owns his house. He has a fireman's pension, doesn't spend a penny. "That's okay." How about thank you, she won't say, avoiding a lecture about duty or why have children.

"Can you stay?" He wants her to prepare and serve dinner.

But she's already in the narrow kitchen stuffing food in the freezer. The soiled towels heaped on the chair makes her wonder if the monthly cleaning service she hired is enough. When her mom was alive every room sparkled. After the cancer spread, her mother couldn't leave the bed, so Rosalyn had to mop, dust, whatever.

Peeling off the see-through covering on a turkey dinner, she places it in the microwave, an appliance her mother never owned. It's weird, so many years, yet, recently, thoughts of her mother spring to mind not just when she's here but also in the shower, supermarket, the oddest times. She recalls a story her mom told about living in the Bronx a few streets away from a Gypsy store. One winter evening, when her mother was seven, a Gypsy man scooped her up. Her mother screamed. He put her down and fled. The story was told as a warning to Rosalyn who often wandered away from the house. Her father, listening, muttered good riddance. To this day, she doesn't know if he meant his wife or Rosalyn.

She spoons hot food on a plate and places the meal on the TV tray in front of him.

"Do you think about Mom?"

"What's the point?"

"Memories, I don't know."

"Can't do a blessed thing to change the past. Today is what I have. You too. Make something of it. Where's your husband? Where's my grandchild?"

"Let's not, Dad."

"She's in her twenties now. She'd be a friend to me."

"You sure as hell didn't feel that way at the time," her voice rising above his.

"I was looking after your mother. It was never right. A child belongs with its parents. Period."

She watches him shovel food in his mouth. Damn him. What would he do if she died before him?

"I'll pick you up tomorrow for your doctor's appointment."

She hurries to the car, slides in, slams the door. How dare he mention the baby? The memory is hers, not his. He has no right to it, none at all. She remembers Carl Reese. Another lifetime. Someone told her . . . probably her father . . . Carl's in Iraq. Isn't he too old?

⟡⟡⟡

The hotel caters to conventions. Men wearing name tags wander in and out of the lounge but the bar isn't crowded. Burgundy-flocked paper darkens the walls. Several green-shaded lamps hang over the whiskey bottles and the indirect lighting casts a pinkish glow. She sits at a small square table nursing a glass of sparkling water. Dina should see her now, perfumed, coiffed, new shoes. Annie's message said his name is Jack Temple, a Londoner, carrying a newspaper. Arriving early gives her a chance to catch sight of her date before he sees her. If she gets a bad vibe she's out of there. It's happened once or twice. Annie, who runs the escort service, chooses carefully for her girls, and loves to hear next-day stories. Their phone calls mimic the confessional, with Annie as priest placing details in some universal order that undermines any thought of sin. Still, she can't help but wonder about the wives and girlfriends back home. When she says so, Annie swears it's genetic, that she's never met a man, gay or straight, who hasn't cheated on someone somewhere. Carl didn't cheat on her. Once the baby came, though, it was finished between them. Waiting for a strange man with Carl in her head. Too weird. It's her father's fault dredging him up.

⁂

A tall middle-aged man with a long, bony face and graying hair, carrying a newspaper stops at her table. He's dressed in an expensive-looking dark blazer over pale gray pants, gray shirt open at the neck. She pegs him as very English indeed.

"Rosalyn, I expect? Jack Temple." His bright green eyes carry the younger man he once was.

"Hi. Have a seat."

He seems pleased with what he sees. Why would someone like him need an escort?

"Here on business?" It's her job to help him relax, but he doesn't seem nervous.

"Yes, for a while."

"Let me guess . . . something to do with banks?"

"Not quite. I'm doing research at a lab on Long Island. I work for a pharmaceutical company."

"Impressive." Some men prattle on, which can be boring, but less wearing. It's hard to know with this one. Either way, she'd rather be home relaxing on her couch. Such thoughts aren't permitted. It's her job to be 100 percent present. She's learned the art of it, how to keep her distance and leave an impression of closeness.

The blue-white tablecloth, heavy linen napkins, crystal stemware, and elegant silverware are nothing at all like the diner, and nothing like what she grew up knowing. On the rare occasion her father took them out to dinner, but usually to some less than appetizing place. Here she is in for a sumptuous hotel meal, and not her first.

The waiter appears before she can settle in. He and Jack discuss the merits of Beaujolais or Sauvignon Blanc and Jack orders a bottle. Nodding his white-haired head, the waiter hurries off. She scans the other couples in the room, their intimacy, wondering as she always does if her status as an escort is apparent.

"May I say something about myself . . ."

"Of course." Her dates often attempt to define their goodness in the face of immorality.

"My wife has MS. There are limited hours we can spend together. We don't talk about my needs but she'd understand. A nurse cares for her. My son comes often, but he has his own life."

"That's a lot of information to tell someone you've just met."

"I want the woman who touches me to know something about me. It's less impersonal."

"And are you asking me to do the same?" Usually her dates couldn't care less.

"If you wish."

"I can't rattle off a bio." He's a stranger. It feels intrusive.

"Are you an actress, writer, a painter?"

"Why would you think so?"

"Creative women need to support themselves. And . . . well . . . you're very beautiful, radiant, really."

"This isn't the only work I do. I care for my sick dad, so I appreciate your situation. Shall we order?" She picks up the menu.

❊·❊·❊

Except for an occasional headlight sweeping past, the road home is dark. Her mind replays the last hours. He was attentive, talkative. He told her about places he's visited, blue skies the color of her blouse, sunsets as tawny as Spanish wine. And middle age, how odd it feels to be there. He was an "up-by-the-bootstraps lad," worked his way through college. She found herself sharing snippets of her life—unusual—relating diner stories that had him laughing out loud. He was curious about her and easy to be with. The hours passed unnoticed, also unusual. Still, the faint embarrassment of exposure dogs her. He wants to see her again.

❖·❖·❖

The breakfast rush is in full swing and the cacophony of sounds is jarring. Mila pours coffee with one hand, wipes surfaces with the other while trading words with customers. But that's Mila, her ability to juggle three things at once keeps Murray at a comfortable distance. Nick flips eggs, catches popping slices of toast, pulls plates out from the warmer. The distinct, watery slosh of the dishwasher surprises her. Murray asked Nick not to run it during busy hours, insisting the noise disturbed customers. Murray makes up things like that all the time, but isn't about to criticize Nick who's been pulling double shifts. They've all been covering for Bruce. Even if Bruce were ready to return, Murray's looking to hire someone "reliable." Changing into her work shoes, Rosalyn fights the urge to return home, to catch up on sleep.

Willy beckons her, his ancient arm in the air. A small man in a booth for four, Willy won't sit at a table because he doesn't want to reveal his skinny legs. They are two sticks. When does vanity end? She jots down his order, though Willy orders the same breakfast special every day. If she walks away without promising to return, he calls out, "Rosalyn, I need you." She fills his water glass and pats his arm. "I'll be right back."

Murray's standing at the counter. "Why the long face?" she quips, not expecting an answer.

117

"The whole thing . . . I don't get it . . . Sylvie leaves early, arrives home late. I have dinner alone when there's no reason for her to work. I don't like it. It's eating at me. What's the point of being married?"

"Talk to her. Tell her you're lonely." He won't. He'll never admit need. That feels familiar.

She places Willy's poached egg, wheat toast, small cereal box, and milk in front of him.

"Stay," he orders.

"For a minute." No doubt Murray's watching her. How he got Sylvie to marry him is the real question.

"You look lovely," Willy says.

"You say that every day."

"Sometimes I lie." He winks. "Did I mention . . . my sons are coming to visit? They're wonderful children, but it would kill me to move in with either one of them. At ninety, eating and sleeping are my last best functions. I need to do them on my own." His voice is thin, high, the testosterone long gone.

"I understand," she says sympathetically.

"I knew you would."

Why do people want to hang on so long? Are memories enough? Not that she'll ever see ninety. "How are you today?" she asks.

"My dear, the question is, will I make it here tomorrow?" He adds the third packet of sugar to his cereal, which he never finishes.

"And, will you?"

"Seems so, but my five senses are no longer intact. Tell me, does springtime still smell fresh? If so, it insists on love." They often have this conversation, which leads to his advice about her finding a companion. Usually it amuses her but today it's irritating and she doesn't respond, though Jack comes to mind. After sex, her dates want to sleep, happy to have her leave. Jack was different. He insisted on a post-midnight stroll along the dark flower-scented garden paths behind the hotel. Even if Jack were a free man . . . he's not.

"Did I say something to upset you?" Willy asks.

"Of course not." She gazes at his wizened face, the yellowish skin. His eyes, though, as black and shiny as patent leather. He's alone and as happy as his body allows. Something takes hold inside her, what, she can't exactly say, but it feels like a clutch, a squeeze against the future, a warning to do something now.

"I'll bring coffee in a minute," she calls over her shoulder, hurrying to the parking lot. Wedged between two cars, she takes the cell phone from her pocket, dials Annie. "It's Rosalyn," her voice low.

"How was last—"

"Fine, it was fine. It's not why I'm calling. How should I put this . . . I'm quitting," the words heavy in her mouth. "I'm getting too old for the routine. Or . . . maybe my day shift takes it out of me. I hate having to dress up when I feel like shit."

"Then . . . rest a few weeks." Annie's tone hesitant as if she's talking to someone ill. Her head does feel as if it's about to explode.

"No," she nearly shouts, shocking herself. Lowering her voice again, says, "It all feels . . . suddenly . . . beside the point."

"What point?" Annie sounds truly confused.

"I'm tired of meeting the needs of strangers." It's the best she can do.

"What about the money?"

"I have enough of everything but time." Where are these words coming from? She's not impulsive. "I've got customers waiting."

⁂

Switching on the car radio to interrupt the static in her brain, she pulls into the driveway. Her father walks slowly toward the car, portable oxygen canister in hand.

"I phoned you last night to pick up a six-pack today," he says, getting in.

"We'll do it on the way back from the doctor."

"Where were you?" his tone faintly accusatory.

"Out . . . on a date."

"Who's the boy?"

"Dad. I'm forty now."

For a moment he takes her in as if he might actually see her. Her hands tighten on the steering wheel, her head tense enough to crack.

"The food you brought yesterday was tainted."

"It was frozen."

"Kept me in the bathroom."

"Tell the doc, then."

"You don't care, do you?"

"Dad!"

"Be better for you if I was gone."

"You watch too many soap operas."

"Well, what else can I do?"

"I don't know. Invite more of your old pals to visit."

"They come when they can," his tone testy.

He's more protective of their feelings than hers. She says nothing more.

Accompanying him up the path to the doctor's office, she holds open the door. "I'll pick you up in an hour."

"What's the matter, got ants in your . . ." Hurrying back to the car, she drives to the beach.

With the windows rolled down, a balmy breeze, a hint of spring in it, the kind Willy can't smell anymore. Are there reasons for quitting other than the ones she told Annie, whose surprise and confusion mirrors her own. Forty's not old. Did something spook her? It's all so odd. She stares hard at the sand, water, the last shock of afternoon sun streaking purple and orange across the sky. Then she takes out her cell phone, calls the number Jack gave her.

❖❖❖

Her hands are cold. She eyes a bottle of red wine on the side table, deciding whether to open it. A bottle of white wine chills in the fridge. She paces the living room like an anxious teen, then stops to look out the window. Jack's never been here in the weeks they've dated. She doesn't allow "dates" to come home with her. Hotel bar, restaurant, his room, then home, alone, that's been the routine with Jack, too. Now he's on his way here.

She watches his long legs precede his torso out of a town car. Watches him come up the drive, watches, too, as he takes in the landscape. Too late to change her mind, she opens the door. "Welcome to the villa."

His lips brush hers and he hands her flowers.

"Roses of all things . . . beautiful."

"Yes, they are."

She tosses out the brooding tulips, arranges the roses.

"Lovely villa," he says, looking around.

"I like it. A drink? Some music?"

"Let me." He riffles through her collection, stacks a few CDs, pours two glasses of wine, then sits beside her on the couch. He makes himself at home with ease.

"I'm quite glad you asked me over. I wondered, is the lady hiding a man in her closet." He grins. "By the way, my lab gets theater tickets. Let's take in a play. Also I want to explore the beaches here. People say they're more beautiful than the Riviera. Hard to believe."

"Sure, a play sounds great. I'm not sure about the Riviera, but late afternoons, the shore is wonderful."

"Perhaps this weekend then . . ."

"There's something I haven't told you." Ella's velvety tones float by. "It's the strangest thing . . . I quit the job."

"The diner?"

"No, the escort service."

"How come?"

"I don't know."

"When?"

"A while ago." She won't say the day after they met.

"Well, I hope I was responsible."

"No, at least I don't think so."

"I'm glad you did."

"Why?"

"You'll spend time only with me. It will be absolutely delightful." He folds her hand in his. "I couldn't be more fortunate." He pecks her cheek. "More wine?" He's up refilling their glasses.

⁂

In the shower, his large, firm hands slowly massage her soapy body. Two glasses of wine wait on the sink edge.

"You see," he shouts over the sound of the water. "It has nothing to do with getting clean. We should've done this before."

She laughs. A surprising lightness fills her.

"And also, I don't do all that many things well. This, however, I claim credit for success. Yes?"

"Yes," she shouts.

"The other bit I should share . . . well, my dear, it has to do with your outstanding body."

"Jack, I rarely believe the sentiments of excited men."

"Yes, indeed, you made it clear these last weeks. What can I say to make you trust my . . ." He stops his massage abruptly. "Let's get into bed. I'll warm it up for us."

He rinses off the soap and leaves first. She drapes herself in a large bath towel, follows his wet footsteps across the floor. The waning evening sunlight trickles through the shuttered blinds. She registers the stillness; the music has ended. She slides in beside him.

His arms go around her, his belly pressing her still-damp back, his mouth close to her ear.

"Rosalyn, dear. Something there in your breast."

"What?"

❖·❖·❖

Locked in the diner bathroom, Mila drones on about the number of women who survive, customers who years later enjoy their burgers, women who . . . But she's only half listening. How we know before we know is the competing lyric in her head. It's why her mother's been visiting her thoughts. Why, too, the eerie sense of time. Even more crazy is the strange relief of no longer waiting. The doom she's carried since her mother's death has been born, the truth of it stark, almost energizing in its clarity.

Murray pounds on the door. "Hey! What's going on?"

"Be right out," Mila calls. "Hurry, tell me what the doctor said."

"It doesn't look promising, though the biopsy was inconclusive, which, he says, they often are. Tomorrow I visit the surgeon, the day after I go for a bone scan. Then . . . I don't know, a bunch of tests I guess."

"Ava and I will go with you. She, tomorrow, me the next day, Dina the day—"

"No . . ."

"Rosalyn, you'd certainly go with me." Mila cuffs her wrist. "So just let us do it."

"I do need help with my father. Could your daughter visit him two hours every afternoon for a while? She can put up his supper.

See if he needs something at the store, whatever. I'll pay her eight an hour. I'll tell him I'm away on vacation. I don't want Murray to know either. Look at the way he's treating Bruce."

"Darla always needs money. It's a good time of day for her, after school, before gallivanting."

"Hey!" Murray bangs on the door.

"Coming." Mila's hand reaches for the knob.

"Go ahead, I need a minute."

In the silvering mirror a pale face greets her. She applies lipstick. There's distance between her and that person. Overwhelmed, is what it is . . . all the things to get done. Everything seems set out, no time for rumination, as if her body has sprung a leak. She glances at her watch and sees it's dinnertime. Not her usual shift, but Mila's in the kitchen helping Nick.

The restaurant's more crowded than usual, buzzing with impatient, hungry customers, arms beckoning, voices loud. Murray is greeting regulars as he fills water glasses and he eyes her as she steps through the door. Behind the counter, Ava serves one customer after another. About to wait on a table of four noisy people, the door chimes and Jack enters.

"God," she says low in her throat, on her way to stop him from taking another step inside. No one knows about that part of her life. "What are you doing?" she whispers harshly.

"You didn't call me last night. I won't have that." They stare at each other.

"We had no plan that I can remember," her tone far from welcoming.

"We don't need a plan. We've spent enough time together. You owed me a call," his tone controlled.

"That's a little proprietary."

"Look, it took me hours to find this damn place. I was worried. What happened at the doctor's?"

"I don't want to talk about it with you."

"Why not?"

"You're a married man with a life in London. You'll go back to that life."

"Well, that gets to the core . . . because Rosalyn, I'm here, with you, now. If you don't like me, if you find me a bore, if you would rather be with somebody else . . . say so." He's talking fast, nervously. "Otherwise, let's get out of here."

His eyes on her are wide, his mouth unsure, prepared for a verbal blow. He's vulnerable, like her. "I'll meet you as soon as I finish my shift."

"No. I'll find a table. I'm staying."

❖ ❖ ❖

After the exam, the surgeon sits on the edge of an elegant leather-topped desk. His degrees descend the wall. He's tall, thin, with a head of curly blond hair, a smile to light the way. Is his demeanor part of the healing process? Does he offer it to each patient? No matter, he's too young, his life still beginning. She needs a doctor in his seventies who's seen it all.

He tells her about the statistics, studies, new treatments. How many of his patients have died of breast cancer? she wants to know. Not one of his statistics. He says, do this and the survival rate could be . . . Do that and . . . He says nothing will be known for sure until they stage the tumor. She's having trouble absorbing words—the door in her head is locked. It's too much information, she tells him. Mila, though, scribbles his words on index cards.

The afternoon sun does little to warm her body chilled by the A/C. Mila hands her the index cards, which she stuffs in her bag. The car isn't far, but they walk slowly, Mila's arm linking hers.

"What're you going to do? Breast off, chemo first, or . . . ?" Mila asks hesitantly.

"I don't know."

"It's an awful decision. Are you terrified?"

"I can't talk about it yet," she admits.

"Did you and Darla work out a deal?" Mila doesn't miss a beat.

"We did. She looks more like you every day except for the dark hair. Was her father dark?"

"He was dark all right. Who was the fine-looking man at the diner waiting for you?"

"I dated him for a few weeks. He's married."

"Now isn't the time to break up. You need as many with you as will stay. Sickness, divorce, birth, they take it out of you. Someone has to be there to empty the bucket. Should I drop you off or come in for a while?"

❖·❖·❖

She kicks off her shoes, drops on the couch. The still-blank journal Jack bought her is on the table. Her feelings are muddled, alien, racing, her thoughts filled with the minutiae of things to do, stupid, unimportant bits and pieces taking up space in her head.

Every day, Jack asks how she's doing. Every day she says fine, her tone refusing talk about the possibility of malignant cells spreading like melting butter. He suggested a support group. She told him about Doris, one of her regulars, who attended a group to help grieve her son killed in Iraq. Doris quit after one meeting. She didn't want to hear how she'd feel a year from then. She wanted to make her own discoveries. To each her own journey, it's what she believes as well, and said as much to Jack.

Whatever her mother's journey, she didn't share it with Rosalyn, didn't talk about the disease, didn't reveal what was happening to her body. She never mentioned pain, disfigurement, or death. Then again, at seventeen, Rosalyn didn't want to hear, didn't want to take in the flat chest while her own breasts were flourishing. Her hands cup their fullness. She remembers Carl's head burrowing contentedly in the cleavage, his delight in their milk-laden heaviness. He was with her when the nun brought in the infant. She closed her eyes, lest the baby's face remain to haunt her. Now she wishes she had seen her, someone to hold on to.

The phone rings.

"It's me," Mila announces.

"You're home already?"

"Darla said your dad's cute and funny."

"You're kidding!"

"Swear to whatever. Ava and I hatched a plot to take you to dinner a few nights from now."

"I've had enough diner food."

"Funny, funny. The real stuff. Romano's, remember their salads? Even better, the wine they never tell you the name of . . . heaven. So warn your guy, he can't come. It's just us."

"Sounds great." She clicks off.

Cute and funny? Darla's gone to the wrong house.

❖❖❖

It's a different exam room, small, cold, without windows. Lying on a narrow, padded table, a thin pillow beneath her head, wires attached to chest and legs, an EKG clicks faintly, recording her heartbeats. Yesterday, a whirring plate of light took three-dimensional pictures of her bones. Heart, bones, breasts, her body dissected for study; the tests, their definitions, the possible outcomes, layers of information have all taken their toll on her brain as well. Her voice has begun to echo in her head like a bad telephone connection; she senses herself watching herself, even when applying makeup. It's as if she's two people, one just a hair ahead or behind the other. Is this a heightened state or terror?

The technician removes the wires, wipes the gel off her body. The surgeon scrolls down the long sheet of paper, studying the EKG.

"Rosalyn, your heart is beautiful," he tells her, stuffing the graph in her file. "I'm sending the bloods to the lab. The bone scan hasn't come back yet. But let's look at the mammogram together. Get dressed, come to my office." He helps her off the table. The desire to hang on his arm, to stay in his sight at all times, is strong.

❖-❖-❖

"I left work an hour ago to get here, but the traffic . . . listen, sorry I'm late, couldn't be helped," Jack bustles in, anticipating a scolding. But she hardly noticed the time. As usual he makes himself at home, uncorks wine, pours some in glasses, hands her one.

"I haven't done a thing about dinner," she mumbles more to herself.

"Low on the problem scale." He tugs her to sit beside him on the couch.

"Are you a problem solver as a scientist?" she asks, though concentrating is difficult.

"It's what they pay me for."

"Are you worth the money?"

"Absolutely."

"Tell me one of your great finds." She's trying.

"It'll sound like tooting my horn, is that how you say it?"

"Toot away," she orders.

"I discovered blending two types of old drugs produced a third that raised the number of white cells in the blood."

She stares at him. "Are you doing cancer research? Because that's too eerie."

"I never saw any reason to mention it before. It's where a great deal of the drug investigation is today." He slides an arm around her shoulders.

"You don't have to press me one place or another every time you mention cancer. I'm not that fragile." Actually, though, she's chilled.

"No you're not. In fact, your self-sufficiency is sometimes off-putting."

"Off-putting. That's very British. Aren't your countrywomen very self-sufficient?"

"In their public selves."

"I see." She wonders if his wife is clingy.

"I offended you when it wasn't my intent."

"Men want women to need them so they can feel strong and noble. But here's the thing . . . when women do lean on them, men feel suffocated."

"Wow. That's telling me."

"That wasn't my intent."

He laughs. "Touché. Nevertheless, you've seen the doctor again. What happened?"

"He showed me the mammogram. It's there, a white splat, not small, easy enough to see on the film. Also the staging came back. The surgery is being scheduled." She moves to the window. It's too dark to make out anything that isn't already familiar. He comes up behind her, nuzzles her neck.

"Your touches kind of scare me."

"That's simply terrible. What can I do?"

She wants to say, be cautious, because she's taking in the dimension of things, registering their very essence. She once read soldiers on the front lines create an impenetrable bubble to keep the world at a distance.

The phone rings.

She picks up the cordless. "Hello?"

"You said you were away."

"Dad?"

"Can't stand the sight of me anymore?" his voice explosive.

"Dad!"

"Lie to your father? Great! I actually thought Darla was my granddaughter, but she's only going on eighteen."

"Dad—"

"You've resented—"

"For craps sake, I have breast cancer." She hangs up. "Bastard," she mutters. "And you, too. Just go home."

"My sweet girl. I'm not about to honor your self-pity."

"Self-pity!"

He hands her the wine. "Drink up."

"I don't want it. And I don't want you here."

"Take a deep breath, my dear."

"I want you to leave."

He wraps his arms around her; his hard body a wall. "So you can be alone with your fears."

"So I can muster my strength."

"It's already there, in your eyes, determined jaw, set lips. Believe me, it would take an earthquake to undercut that."

"Why do you think you know me?"

"I don't. You won't let me. You won't share your dreams or your nightmares. Why didn't you tell your dad in the first place? Why must you carry the load by yourself?"

"And you'd like to take me to bed to prove your ability to comfort me, right?"

"I would, but not for that reason."

She gazes at him. Nothing in his expression mocks her. The accent makes him sound flip. "And the reason is . . . ?"

"I'm terribly smitten with you. I didn't want to be. It's why I

130

hired someone instead of meeting a woman on my own. I thought hiring would alleviate better feelings." His voice so earnest it's almost comical.

"You talk funny."

He chuckles. "I'm going to cook dinner. Can I search your pantries?"

"Excuse me?"

⋯⋯⋯

She sets the table, her mind somewhere else. What if she fled? Stuffed the bad news in a corner of her brain the way the doctor stuffed the EKG in her file. What if she took off for California to walk the beaches? Or farther, Rome, Venice. Or maybe Turkey? She has the money. Spend it now. She looks out the window where things are as they were. That's the problem with fantasies. They change nothing.

He places a puffy salami omelet on the table, the garlic and onion smells palpable.

"Looks wonderful," she says, a bit sorry for her cutting words before.

"Now aren't you glad I stayed?" He holds out a chair for her.

"I won't be bribed." She sits across from him.

"Apparently. Yet it's exactly what I want to do. Cheer you."

"You're sweet."

"Not really." His expression clouds and she wonders if he's feeling guilty.

"Are you thinking about your wife?"

"Not thinking so much as worrying a bit. I spoke to the nurse this morning. My wife's been sleeping more. A bad sign."

"Do you like being surrounded by sick women?"

"What a thing to ask." He looks uneasy.

She shrugs. "Well, you are."

"I don't see you that way."

"What way?" She's no longer sure what they're talking about. Like those customers who insist on chatting. She provides trivial questions, and the answers don't matter.

"Like Lillian, incapacitated."

She wishes he hadn't said her name.

"Simply believe this. I'm here for you."

"But then you won't be."

"You're vulnerable. I'll continue to reassure you."

"Jack, that's condescending."

"Good! Sounds more like you."

"I'm in a very strange place," she admits.

"And I'm still drawn to you."

"Who knows what's going to happen to me."

"That's true about any of us," he says.

"You mean, today's what we have? Sounds like my dad."

He cuts the omelet, places some on her plate. She's not the least bit hungry but forks up a tiny piece because he's watching her. Ridiculously, Willy comes to mind. He still worries about what people will think.

"Things still matter," she muses.

He looks up. "What do you mean?"

"I'm surprised, is all."

"Crises propel us to odd places. A bit of an adventure . . ."

"That's inspiring, thank you."

"Adventures have no history, that's all."

"It's more complicated than an adventure," she says.

"Come now. You've heard about the best-laid plans . . ."

She nods, pushes away the barely touched food. "I'm really not hungry."

She drives to her dad's house. She hasn't spoken to him in a week. She considers leaving the bags of food in the driveway and taking off, but then finds herself with a shopping bag in each hand, walking up the scarred path. Fogged windows block anything inside. The house needs painting. Only the maple tree thrives, though no one ever cut back its branches.

"Dad?" She shuts the door behind her.

To her surprise he's in the kitchen.

"What're you doing?"

"Want coffee?" he asks.

"No." She wants out of here. Will resent any discussion about her body. And begins to stuff packets of frozen food in the freezer. He leans against the sink watching her. There's hardly room for the two of them.

"I hired Darla for the summer," he says gruffly.

"You what?"

"Going deaf?"

"You'll have to pay her."

"No kidding," he says.

"Did she agree?"

"She accepted." His eyes steady on her.

She wants to say you finally got off the chair. She wants to say it took the threat of death. She wants to say it's really too late. "Good, Dad. That'll be a help."

⟡⟡⟡

They've taken her street clothes, earrings, purse—anything that could identify her—and stowed them in some room she'll allegedly be wheeled to after recovery. Draped in a hospital robe, covered by a sheet, she's one of several bodies lined up between drawn curtains awaiting surgery. It's still possible, she isn't anesthetized yet. She could chance fate, shout, I changed my mind! Let me out of here! She makes no move, no sound, resignation heavier than the future.

Fingering the cold edges of the narrow gurney, A/C very high, no germs allowed, if she stays calm her teeth won't chatter. Breathing in deeply, she counts slowly on each exhale the way Dina taught her. It's no use. Her thoughts race, collide, refuse to remain long enough to read, as if there's something she must resolve. Dina has the keys to her condo and will take care of everything. Darla will deal with her dad. Ava and Mila drove her here. Ava didn't say much, though Mila went on about her daughter, how amazing it is that's she's grown, how worrisome, too, how she spends money like . . . Mila's chatter was more comforting than Ava's silence. They insisted on staying with her through admission, walked her down the long blue-carpeted corridor toward the heavy double doors leading to the area where a nurse took over. It surprised and scared her then when Ava suddenly hugged her so tight the breath was squished out of her.

Jack, too, on his last night here wrapped her so tightly she feared for her bones. Said over and over she was his godsend. How strange. He wanted to remain with her through surgery and then some, though his job at the lab was done. She wouldn't let him, didn't want him to see her in duress, wanted his image of her to be whole and beautiful. And, yes, she understood none of that mattered to him, but still, it's what she wanted. He wrote down a thousand phone numbers where he could be reached. He promised to stay in constant touch, made her promise to meet him in Europe when she recovered. Said if she didn't, he'd return to fetch her. She believes him.

Her doctor parts the curtains. He's in surgical garb, though his mouth remains uncovered. He smiles warmly; his warm hand squeezes hers. He alone understands what she's about to go through. He promised her a shot to relax her and leans over to inject her arm. He whispers two words she'd never say to herself, "think positive," though they both know truth will have its way.

8

About Time

"Mom, sit down."

"I'm making dinner." The don't-bother-me tone reserved for fussy customers, she's brought it home with her. Okay, she's overworked, working the diner kitchen . . . it's not her thing. Damn Murray. Rosalyn's illness, too . . . it frightens her—fear for those she loves.

"I can't talk to your ass, Mom."

"Darla!" She spins around. Without a bit of makeup, her daughter's a stunner, the contrast, dark hair, light skin. "Okay, what?"

"You're not going to be thrilled."

"Try me." The shag cut frames Darla's small face perfectly.

"I graduate in June."

"I know that." Adolescent nonsense. She reaches for an onion on top of the ancient fridge, notices the scratch marks on the door from a thousand magnets.

"In July, I'll be eighteen. I won't need your signature. It's May," her daughter recites.

She fishes for the missing knife buried under a pile of dishes in the cracked porcelain sink. Christ, the place could use some rehab. "Work the summer for Rosalyn's dad. Save money for the car's down payment. I can't—"

"Mom . . . Forget the car. I'm going to sign up."

She stares through the window at an identical clapboard house. A breeze flutters the short white curtains that need washing. "No you're not," she says softly, her gut cramping.

"It's the best way."

"To what? Die?" She sits across from her daughter.

"Don't be dramatic."

"It's out of the question, Darla." If she raises her voice, they'll fight. She'll lose. She takes a deep breath, tries not to sigh.

"If I sign up now, I get an extra thousand dollars."

"Money?" It's her fault, all her worrying out loud about it. She'll send Darla to her cousin in Arizona.

"You don't have any. I need a lot."

"They're not paying you to attend the opera."

"Mom, I'll be fine."

"You're only saying that because you're young and stupid."

"Thanks."

"It's a horrible choice. There are only downsides." Is this what women's liberation has brought? She needs a drink.

"On top of the thousand, there's a shitload of cash up front, so I could start a savings account. What am I going to do here? Work a few hours for Rosalyn's dad, a few hours more in some supermarket till I save enough to go to a third-rate community college? It's not how I see my future."

"Spend the summer with your cousin in Arizona. I'll scrape up the down payment for that jalopy you've been eyeing." Maybe Murray will let her work Rosalyn's shift as well.

"If you say no now, I'm going to sign up in July. So mull it over." Her daughter strides out of the kitchen.

She kills the stove flame and grabs a bottle of Johnnie Red from below the sink, a glass from the drain. She pours a few inches neat, sits on the couch, and drinks it down. The door slams. Out for the evening. The sigh that's been clogging her throat escapes. The girl's right about one thing—there's nothing special about living here. Darla could meet a guy and get pregnant. Her daughter's too smart for that. How smart is signing up, though?

It annoys the crap out of her that in a few weeks Darla won't need her approval to put her life on the line. Maybe it's true . . . what goes around . . . She devastated her parents when she eloped with Jimmy. But this is different. Darla could be maimed or killed. Christ, she has to do something to stop her. Times like these, a father would be helpful. Good god, it's been years since she had a thought like that.

She pours more scotch, looks around, but there's nothing worth selling. The room has darkened. She doesn't bother with the lamp. Her reflection's on the TV screen, a woman edging middle age with a daughter as old as she was then. The marks of time can't be hidden the way she's hidden Jimmy from Darla.

Sitting here will solve nothing and make her late for work. The overheated diner kitchen, that's what's waiting for her. One more day, Murray said, before a temp arrives and then back to her regular shifts, not that she loves them either. With glass in hand, she searches for a piece of paper, finds an index card on Darla's desk. Writes: *Monday, my day off, we're going out to dinner. The pub you like. Don't make other plans. Off to work.*

⁕⁕⁕

Darla walks the long route to Michelle's house. She needs to think. Her mother reacted as expected. The woman's scared of change. Why else would someone with her looks still be unmarried? She never gets a good answer to that question. It doesn't matter. She has no plan to follow in her mother's footsteps. College, law school, a job on Wall Street . . . she'll make a fortune and buy an apartment in Manhattan. Her mother will see she made the right decisions. The guys who've been in Iraq tell her the girls there do housework. Clean machinery, set up office stuff. They're not running around banging open doors with M16s or whatever they're called.

※-※-※

She rings the doorbell. Waits. "Damn," she mutters, just when you need someone. Not that she's crazy about being here, Michelle's dirty-mouthed brothers always in her face.

The upstairs window finally opens.

"Hi, let me in."

They traipse up the few steps to Michelle's room. "Where are your brothers?"

"Out with my dad."

An intact family she'd rather die than join. Michelle's father, a cop, never stops smiling. She can't trust someone who pretends everything's okay when his wife's messing around with whoever will have her.

Michelle, tall and broad-shouldered, stands in front of the window, her dark, wavy hair backlit by the evening sun. "What did your mother say?" Michelle has no patience for the finer feelings. She wants details. When Darla returns from a date, Michelle phones with clinical questions: What did his tongue taste like?

"Over her dead body. It's a first response."

"Did you tell her I'm signing up, too?"

"She'd accuse me of not making up my own mind."

"We need to go together."

She eyes the posters on the wall, no one she likes. "You're eighteen in June. I won't be able to sign up till late July."

"Work on your mother." Michelle rolls the squeaky desk chair back and forth.

"Like how?"

"The breakdown: you're depressed, no motivation, want to die. Refuse to get up for school."

"My mom thinks I'll get killed."

"Do you agree with her?" Michelle asks suspiciously.

"Of course not. I know she's negative. Have you spoken to any more of the guys who came back?"

"Ian said I was crazy, but he's been high since he came back." She laughs. "Let's smoke at the beach. My mother's car is outside. She won't be home till middle of the night."

⸙⸙⸙

They park in the empty lot. The beach won't be officially open until Memorial Day. Her bare feet tramp the damp sand. The sun has disappeared. They walk to the shore and sit, knees up, listening to the crash of waves. In the gray distance a ship cruises the horizon. Gritty wind blows in her face, her skin clammy. It's fine. She's open to the elements, but worries about how tough army training will be. She's not an athlete. Michelle can carry weight on her back. The thing to do is begin building muscle now. If she puts her mind to it she can do it.

"There's no guarantee we'll be sent to the same place for training," she says.

"Then we'll tell them the deal's off. They need us. They'll agree."

"You don't know that," her tone sullen.

"Did your mother say something you haven't told me?"

"That's not the point."

"Darla, we've been over points."

"What did your father say?" she asks.

"Women soldiers fuck up and complicate situations, then he laughed."

"And your mother?"

"Either she'd just had sex or was flying on chemicals. She looked at me like who was I, then said don't get raped. I told her I'd do my best."

"My mom's stubborn. It'll be hard to change her thinking. If worse comes to worst I'll wait till after my birthday. She can't stop me then." She doesn't say it'd be easier if there were two parents. Even if they both didn't want her to go, they'd have each other to bitch and moan to.

"The sooner we get out of this Long Island swamp the better," Michelle declares.

"I wonder what the desert will be like?"

"Check out *National Geographic.*"

"I bet it has its own silence."

"There's a war going on."

"We'll get time off, sneak behind some dune, look at stars, smoke dope. I thought you brought some?"

"Coming right to you." Michelle digs a small plastic bag out of her purse, removes a joint, lights it, takes a drag, then passes it.

Inhaling deeply, she stares into the hazy nothingness. After the second hit, she sees a distant cloud drop behind the horizon.

❖·❖·❖

Breakfast customers have cleared out, thank god. The lunch crowd will soon descend. Nick stacks salads in the big aluminum fridge; he's filled the bread bins. He's been here all night and must be exhausted. After an hour in the kitchen teaching a temp guy this and that, it became clear he's not a keeper. Damn. She slides onto a counter stool beside Ava, who's nursing a cup of coffee and thumbing through *Newsweek*. Murray hates his employees sitting even on break. His car keys dangle on the hook near the register. Why's he even here on a Sunday? The adjacent mirror reflects a swath of diner along with her sorrowful face.

She sighs loudly and Ava looks up.

"Darla wants to join . . . the army, the Marines, I don't know. Our conversation didn't get that far. Ever see the parents of dead soldiers on TV? It's beyond me how they continue to support the disaster. I'd never be that forgiving." She pulls napkins from the holder, then squeezes them back in.

"That's bad news." Ava folds away the paper. "Why?"

"The military can't get enough fools to volunteer so they're offering pots of gold. I can't compete with that." Would Ava lend her money? Christ, she's on the road to desperate.

"Are you two getting along?"

"Teenage girls and their moms, what's new? We're okay together. Our fights are like summer storms, they're over quickly." Long fingers of sun reach across the countertop, reminding her she'd rather be elsewhere.

"You have to stop her." Ava sounds alarmed, no doubt thinking of Bobby.

"How? Tie her up? Lock her in the bedroom?" She's read about parents who do such things. There's that woman who drove her kids into the water.

"Hell, my husband was killed in Iraq," Ava mutters, as if Mila didn't know.

For a moment they both stare into the mirror, silent. In the near distance trucks rumble on the highway.

"Should Nick speak to her, you know, a man, a vet," Ava offers.

"She'd ride my tail for telling you. The things you hope for . . . the girl's getting older . . . the two of us will talk . . . reason together. Think again." Not totally true. Darla is reasonable. In fact she's damned logical, which is why it's so difficult to win an argument. Her daughter will do well in life. But she has to be alive.

Nick, with gear in hand, ready to go home, comes around and whispers something to Ava, who nods. His hand brushes her cheek.

They watch him leave.

"It's good between you two," she says.

"I think so."

"Don't hurry it."

"What does that mean?"

"Enjoy each moment, I guess. Sounds corny, doesn't it?" But, actually, she means anything can happen and then what.

Murray comes up from the storeroom. So that's where he's been. "Ava? Write down toilet paper, cleaner, dozen rolls of towels, and, also, we're breaking glasses. That has to stop . . . another box water-size . . . they're damn expensive. Mila, nothing to do?"

If Rosalyn were here she'd remind Murray Ava's finished her shift.

Murray stacks some stray plates, dumps them in a bin under the counter with a crash, then takes a fistful of bills from the register, counts them, and slams the register shut. "Temp could use hands-on, Mila. He's alone in there. But maybe you're otherwise engaged."

"Sylvie better sleep with the guy . . ." she whispers to Ava, sliding off the stool to wipe wet silverware that would air-dry in a minute. Murray stuffs the wad of bills in the burlap bank bag. The thought of filling her pockets comes and goes.

❖·❖·❖

The morning sun highlights the faded lime-color walls, water-stained ceiling, sagging beanbag chair. Darla sleeps tight. She perches on the edge of the too-thin mattress, thinks to stroke her daughter's hair, but touchy-feely is no longer a habit between them. There was a time Darla clung to her like an extra limb, her little arm circling Mila's leg as if she feared her mother would disappear.

"Time to get up, sweetie."

"Umm." Darla hugs the pillow, her painted-pink toenails bright against the graying sheet.

"You'll be late for school. Come on." Was she on the phone all night? No point asking, she needs calm between them.

"What time is it?" Darla mumbles.

"Seven-thirty."

Darla lets go of the pillow, swings her legs off the bed. "Why did you wait?"

"Relax. It's only seven."

"Damn! I always fall for your stupid trick."

"Because you're a great student. You'll get some kind of scholarship."

"Mom, I go to a less than mediocre high school. They don't even have a music department. They don't have any AP courses either. I'm not getting any scholarships without that kind of stuff. You just don't understand. I'll get financial aid, but it won't be from Yale or Harvard."

"Is that where you want to go?" It never crossed her mind.

"Eventually. To law school."

"So that's why you want to lose a limb in war."

"Jesus! You're so negative. It's a wonder I have any aspirations listening to you all my life."

"Darla, reconsider it. It's not a smart move. We'll find money somehow, somewhere."

"No we won't. I have no rich relatives or living grandparents. We manage, that's what we've always done. Big deal! Not only will the army bonus help, I'll have veteran's benefits. It'll make all the difference."

"I can't stop you after July, but waiting gives you a chance to change your mind. You sign up today, it's over." She wants to kick the wall.

"Let me get ready."

Reluctantly, she gets off the bed, shoves her hands in the back pockets of her jeans. "Did you see my note about dinner tonight?" But Darla has shut the bathroom door.

She listens for her daughter's tuneless voice to belt out a song in the shower. The staccato beat of water on plastic sends another message. Darla's pissed at her mother's refusal. Someday she'll understand. Maybe. She smells gas. The pilot light is out again. It could be the wind, so she shuts the window above the sink. Instantly, it's too hot. She's beginning to hate this kitchen. All kitchens. Opening the oven door, she strikes a match; it catches. She'll insist Darla apply to a good college. Then she'll find money somehow, at least for the first year. She remembers the costume jewelry, the silver watch, the wedding band her mother left her, the whole package worth a few hundred at most. That should pay for a day or two of college. Christ! Borrow from Rosalyn? She can't ask her now. There's Murray. She'd rather rob a gas station. Then Darla would have two parents in prison. Great!

She grabs a bowl, breaks two eggs and beats them so hard the table trembles.

❖❖❖

"This pub . . . you never have to wait," she says, dropping the car keys in her bag.

"They have good Bloody Marys," Darla offers.

"When did you . . . ?"

"Oh, Mom, you're so predictable. I plan to have one tonight. Is that a problem?" Darla sashays ahead in a calf-length peasant skirt that swirls as she walks. She's built like her father, the long narrow body. Her deep, dusky voice is his as well.

"I'm refusing to argue with you."

"Okay then. Is there a particular occasion for this dinner?" Darla tosses back. "Someone new in your life? Changing jobs?"

"All of the above," she offers, enjoying a momentary lightness.

Beer and fish smells mingle. Netting hangs from the ceiling, a cardboard mermaid caught in one. Blue haze floats under fluorescent lights. Background music adds to the appreciable noise. In a high-backed booth with wooden benches, they open their menus. A woman and four antsy kids sit nearby.

The waiter, not much older than Darla, eyes her daughter appreciatively while scooping away two extra settings. He pours water and whips out his pad, stuff she's used to doing herself. They order drinks. She chooses fish and chips; Darla wants the clam and corn dinner.

"So, Mom?" Her daughter smirks.

"What?"

"You're not dropping fifty dollars here for nothing."

"Then what am I doing?"

"Buying my compliance?"

"Let's eat and enjoy, okay?"

"That'd be good."

The waiter returns quickly, the drinks festooned with celery and slices of lime. Again, he eyes Darla. "I hope she's old enough?"

"I'm her mother, you think I don't know her age? Christ!"

"Okay." He leaves. Darla grins.

"Good, Mom, that was believable. Anyway, I'm only weeks from legit."

"Wrong, sweetie. Legit here is twenty-one."

"That's as retrograde as everything in the burbs." Darla scans the room looking for proof.

"It's that bad living here?"

"Suffocating. People talk about anyone who's not like them."

"You find that everywhere."

"At least in the city there's shame."

She decides not to ask how she knows. "Is Michelle's family that way?"

"Her father is."

"Do you ever think about your father?" Her heart speeds up.

Darla stares at her. "What?"

She shrugs. "Just wondering."

"Mom, you don't wonder. What about my father?"

"Nope."

"You never mention him. He left you with a baby." Darla's eyes are steady on her. "How come you never remarried or even considered it?"

"You don't know what I considered." She tosses out the straw and drinks straight from the glass. The spiciness nearly chokes her. More likely it's the conversation. There are truths she's still afraid to tell this girl. That's the horror of a lie. You have to keep lying.

"Mom? Where are you?"

"Right here. The drink is dynamite."

"Answer my question."

"I never married because I was never divorced." She speaks low, as if the woman in the next booth were interested.

"There's a statute of limitations. All these years of abandonment . . . you don't know where he is . . . it's automatic . . ."

"You'll be a good lawyer."

"This isn't about me."

Yes it is, she thinks. And ponders ordering something stronger, a double scotch neat, but that'd be a giveaway.

"How come you don't date?"

"I went out with that Luke guy, remember? You didn't like him."

"Mom, that was ages ago. Don't tell me you stopped seeing him for my sake." Her daughter glares at her.

"Of course not. He turned out to be mean. Drank too much, too. I don't know. He didn't appeal to me. I'm having a hard time discussing boyfriends with my daughter."

"We're not discussing your habits in bed."

"Darla!" She finishes the drink and immediately wants another.

The waiter sets down their plates. Her food looks greasy, heavy, impossible to digest.

"Mom?"

"What now?"

"Are you a lesbian? I don't care, I'm just curious."

She stares at Darla, whose sudden childlike expression breaks her. "I don't know how to stop you from signing up. If there was a father around, he might change your mind."

"How would that work?" Darla sounds angry, but anything's better than that scrunched face. "My father would say, don't go, and I'd be scared to disobey him?"

The sudden clamor in the next booth is a relief. Water's wiped up, new napkins brought, children reseated.

"You still didn't answer my lesbian question." Darla's eyes on her again.

"I'm not a lesbian."

"Do you hate men because of how he treated you?"

"He treated me well."

"Oh what a consolation. A sweet guy who left you hanging."

"You're getting drunk."

"On one Bloody Mary? I doubt it, Mom. But it's good for us to chat like this. Not that I learn anything. You have a way of telling me zip, you know that?"

The girl's right. Mila, the queen of doublespeak, but it's no longer enough, not by a long shot. "Do you worry about what you don't know?"

"That's an interesting question. At times."

149

"I'm going to order another drink, then I'll tell you something." Maybe *she's* drunk.

"Uh-oh." Darla teases, though her eyes widen some.

She hails the waiter and orders a scotch neat. Then she chews on a piece of bread to put something in her stomach. "How's the food?"

"Fine."

Two of the kids climb noisily on and off the next bench. She can feel the vibrations. Someone should stop them.

"I bet those kids are a handful."

"Mom!" But she won't look at her daughter.

"You were like that, couldn't sit still. I can remember, I think you were five—"

"Mom!"

Her gorgeous girl will leave and maybe never return. What then? What now?

The waiter places the scotch in front of her. She takes a sip, the medicinal taste a reminder of the unpleasantness to come. And why is she doing this? Her cheeks are hot, her face flushed, a slight buzzing in her ears. She remembers like it was yesterday the two policemen at her door, the baby she didn't know how to comfort fidgeting in her arms.

"Mom, I'm waiting."

"Your father's in prison. He's been there sixteen years. We agreed you shouldn't know. That you should grow up without feeling stigmatized by his mistake." Each word a piece of flint cutting her throat.

Her daughter stares at her.

"My father's a criminal!" Darla's voice rises.

She nods. Her heart pounding now, she chokes down the scotch, which isn't helping, it's hard to breathe.

"You think lying about it makes me less the daughter of a criminal?" Darla pushes away her plate. "Did he murder someone?"

"There was a robbery. A person was shot. The law said anyone involved was guilty." Her robotic tone isn't helping. If she stops to take a breath she won't be able to go on.

"Did the man you call my father pull the trigger?"

"No. He was there, that's all."

"That's all! Jesus frigging god!"

"Darla!"

"You visit him on the sly?"

"I've never visited."

"Beautiful. You don't know where he's locked up, or it's just inconvenient?" her voice scary sweet.

"That's not important."

"What's important is how manipulative you are, lying to me all these years, laying it on me now to paralyze me. Think again, Mila, and think hard. Because you've given me even more reason to get the hell out of here."

Mila? She's been banished. "Your father—"

"Stop saying my father like I know him."

She takes a deep breath. "Jimmy was in the first Iraq war. It ruined him. He came back more restless than ever. He could hardly sit still, never mind keep a job." She can taste the bitterness. Even in bed he slept in fits and starts, except when he made love, the only time he could get out of his head. "He wanted money quick, just the way you do."

"Must be in the genes," Darla shouts, and bolts from the table. The woman in the next booth looks up.

⬧⬧⬧

Driving slowly, she rolls down the windows and scans each side of the road for Darla. Christ! What did she accomplish? Alienated her daughter . . . broke a promise. God knows what Darla thinks about any of it. And what did she expect from her daughter, a smile, a freaking hug? She opened the damned box, didn't she?

The heat in the car is suffocating; there isn't a breeze. It's hot like it was the last time she saw Jimmy when the A/C in the motel room was broken. He was afraid to open a window. They made a bed out of an empty dresser drawer and sat hunched over the baby talking softly. Jimmy's earnest expression, his hands pressing hers, his positive tone so certain. He knew the way for her to follow. He'd get to Florida, set up and send for them. If he was caught, ended up in jail, Darla must never know. He left money and took off. The baby woke up crying. She rocked her till morning and never did crack a window.

Her daughter's nowhere she can see, probably doubled back and called Michelle to pick her up. One thing is certain: Darla isn't on her way home. She doesn't want to go there, either. She heads for Sully's bar.

❖·❖·❖

It's dark inside. A few regulars stare at the muted TV screen or maybe at their own ravaged faces in the mirror. She finds a small table in the rear. Fraying high school pennants decorate the wall, a faint yellowish light from the jukebox playing oldies. She hears the front door open and close but doesn't look up. She's tempted to cry but it won't do any good. The lying is over but not the anxiety, which fills her with cold, hard fear. She calls her home number. Useless. She leaves a message on her daughter's cell phone to contact her immediately. She scrolls down to Michelle's number, calls her. No answer. Leaves a message there, too. Where would Darla go this time of night?

The bartender, a tall, slim man in his fifties, waits impassively for her to decide. She glances at the soiled page that stands in for a menu, the smudgy print hard to decipher. Nothing she wants. She orders a double scotch neat, water on the side. Jimmy drank bourbon. She did, too, all those years ago. She liked so much of what he liked.

Her finger traces the table's gouged surface. Jimmy carved their initials in whatever tree trunk caught his fancy. It pleased her, the same as their long walks did, her hand in his the whole time, chatting about anything and everything. Old memories flickering again in her brain, it's her fault, saying his name aloud like he's part of her life.

The bartender places a sizable glass of scotch in front of her. Jimmy wrote her one letter from prison insisting she go on without him. That it was the only gift he could offer. She took it. Things happen to people every day; she knows that. Still, after his arrest, the separation was unbearable. He lived in her head, walked at her side, appeared wherever she went, at work, bars, laundromat, the supermarket. Holidays were hell. The pain was so intense something inside her finally switched off, released her. What exactly that was she never figured out. Explain that to her daughter.

How is it possible for someone who never knew her father to follow in his footsteps? It's eerie. She tries Darla's cell again. Damned gadgets go to voice mail after a few rings. How many times can she say call your mother? Darla often mentions clubs where they hang out, but did she listen to the names? Hopeless. Oh lord. When did he come in?

Murray, carrying a drink, strides toward her in dark slacks, white shirt. "Look who's here? Can I sit?" He doesn't wait for permission.

She nods anyway, helpless.

"How come you're here?" He's drinking neat like her.

"I could ask the same question."

"No one home yet." He sounds mellow, unusual for him.

"I fought with Darla, don't know where she ran to."

"These kids," he offers. "What about?"

"Wants to join the army." God, is she really sharing with Murray? He doesn't have a clue about her daughter. When Darla occasionally comes in for a meal, he doesn't chat with her, just notices the food she eats.

"That's crazy."

"I thought you liked the war."

"It's no place for women. Better stop her," his tone more dismissive than interested.

"After July she won't need my signature." The powerlessness of it all threatens to drown her.

"Tough, tough. Kids test us."

"You don't have children."

"Doesn't mean I'm stupid." He scowls at her.

Man's still her boss. "Of course not." She finishes the drink, which isn't doing a thing to calm her.

"The truth about kids is . . . they grow up."

"Murray, she'll be sent to a war zone. Growing older may not happen. Get it?" She can't help herself.

His hand covers hers.

She stares at him. "What's going on?" She removes her hand.

"I'm a little drunk, a lot lonely. Let me buy us a round." He holds up two fingers for the bartender to see. Then gazes at her as if she's the answer to a question he's been pondering. It doesn't take a shrink to know he wants her to probe his misery, help him unburden. Men like him expect that from a woman. An instant fantasy, bed down with him, then ask him to pay for Darla's education. The only thing more ludicrous would be doing it.

"One more and I'm off," she says. No doubt the man looked old when he was thirty. Some men are like that, wheelers and dealers, anxious about next steps while peering over their shoulder to see who's stalking them. It wears out the face. Jimmy was open, boyish, probably doesn't look much older now.

The bartender serves the drinks, places their empty glasses on a tray, then wipes the table with a rag and leaves.

After a quick sip, she reminds him, "Really . . . I have to go find Darla."

"Sure. Sure. But stay a few minutes. If something bad happens to me, Sylvie will be sorry."

"Why's that?" she mumbles. Because who cares. An unhappy man with a lot of money doesn't rouse her sympathy. One quarter of what he paid for the house would cover four years of college.

"The woman isn't being attentive the way it's supposed to be. She works late, sometimes even on weekends, but doesn't need to work at all. She cooks when she can, then freezes the damn food for me. I sit there alone with the dogs. The house is so big it echoes. Why did I even set it up? I don't know, Mila, I don't understand her. Women tend to be devious."

"Thanks, but I refuse the insult." He looks at her bewildered. She chooses to conserve her energy, which is dissipating with each drink.

"Maybe Sylvie's having an affair, but I don't think so. A man can smell that kind of thing. You know what I think? I think Sylvie doesn't know how to be married. No one taught her. Maybe we both need a few lessons," his tone gloomy.

"Well, amen to that," she says. "Murray, go home. Sylvie will be there by now. She'll worry."

"That's what I want," his tone defiant. "See—"

She'll trawl a few bars, find one of Darla's friends who can give her some place to search for her. Oh Jesus and Mary, the beach . . . she and Michelle always go there. At this time of night? Maniacs lurking in the shadows? Two beautiful young women walking alone in the dark?

155

"What I believe is—"

Christ! Panic has her by the throat. She grabs her purse.

"—sooner or later, everything has a solution," he says.

❖-❖-❖

"Darla, I can't drive around all night. My father will have the force out. Stay at my house. We won't answer the phone."

"No." Not with Michelle's brothers parading around, she doesn't like sleeping with them in the next room, either, probably jerking off. "Drive me to Rosalyn's dad, the guy I work for. It's right down the road."

"This time of night?"

"He naps on and off all day and watches TV forever. I'll knock . . . just try it." She stares out the window seeing nothing. So what if this Jimmy guy fought in Iraq. That was a million years ago.

"Well, sorry for thinking you're nuts."

"It's around the corner, second house."

Michelle looks at her. "You can still change—"

"Wait to see if I get inside."

She runs up the old driveway, the blue and white TV screen flickers through the foggy window. She knocks hard at the door. Hears the slow plod of feet.

"Who's there?"

"It's me, Mr. Joseph, Darla." She waves at Michelle to leave.

He opens the door. "What are you doing here? Something happen? A guy chasing you?"

She smiles. Because what could the sick old man do about it. "I had a fight with my mom, and don't want to go home. I could sleep on the couch, do some work for you in the morning. You don't have to pay me. Sort of a trade-off." She hears the quickness of her words and wonders if he's gotten it all.

"Come in. Shut off the TV. Make some coffee."

She turns off the TV, goes in the kitchen. The coffee's already made. Old man probably forgot. This Jimmy guy could be old, too . . . more likely Mila's age. Who cares? It's all so stupid, the lies, the whatever. It probably made her mother feel powerful. Secrets can do that.

She's hyper enough but pours two cups, brings them in. The old man sits in his BarcaLounger but doesn't touch the coffee. She eyes the oxygen canister, the long tubes extending into his nose, the slow hiss of air, hypnotic. Dropping on the couch, she feels the springs. There's an unused bedroom. Later.

He removes the oxygen lines and hangs them over the chair arm. "What did you fight about?" His wheeze is more pronounced than usual. God, don't let him get worse while she's here.

"My mother revealed a long-held secret to stop me from joining the army. She figures if I'm going to die, I might as well know the truth."

"What secret?" He looks concerned. Sweet old man.

"My father's been in prison sixteen years. He didn't want me to see myself as the daughter of a criminal." Her mom's setting her up, that's what. Her mom wants her to talk to this Jimmy guy who went nuts in Iraq. Isn't going to happen.

"Well, maybe you're not."

"Mr. Joseph, they don't put people away all those years for no reason."

"Circumstances make people do stupid things, then they have to pay. Doesn't mean he's a horrible person. He could be. Doesn't mean he is."

"You're only saying that to make me feel better."

"I knew good people who did a lot of dumb things. Some ended up in jail, some in rehab, some in the ground. I've seen my share . . ." He gazes past her, his mouth slightly open.

"My mom's determined to keep me from signing up, but soon I'll be able to go without her permission. Thing is, the next few weeks with her will be hell. I wish I could leave tomorrow."

"I know a woman who had a baby when she was around your age. She gave it away, couldn't care for it properly, so she said. Your mother didn't do that." He takes a sip of coffee. "It's cold," he hands her the cup. For a moment she stares at it, then returns to the kitchen to make a fresh pot.

While it drips into the pot she checks the fridge. Stuff there for breakfast. The old man likes his food. She'll remind Mr. Joseph to replace the oxygen lines. The last thing she needs is for him to have a breathing attack. What if this Jimmy guy is sick like the old man, some disease or cancer? Shouldn't she know about this for her future? Everyone says she looks like her mom, still . . . how come this Jimmy guy wasn't curious about her? Prisoners always want contact with spouses and children. He sounds like a selfish prick. How could her mother love a guy like that? No wonder she doesn't go out much, scared of repeating the mess she made.

She carries in a steaming cup of coffee. His eyes are closed. She leaves the cup on his TV tray, tiptoes into the spare bedroom. She switches on one of the dim lamps. It must've been his daughter's room, though there's no sign of life anywhere. The bed's made, nothing on walls or dresser top except an old, grimy mirror. She could check the closets but she doesn't want to. Okay, she's surprised. Okay, shocked. Her mother gabs about every little thing. What else hasn't her mom told her? Who cares? Sooner than later she's out of here. Her mother will adjust. She'll have to. She checks her cell phone: five missed calls from her mother. Anyway, no one asked her mom to be a martyr. If *she* got pregnant, she'd have an abortion. There's also a message from Michelle. She listens. Her mother called the house and woke her father, who yelled up to ask where Darla was. "Obviously, I was fast asleep."

Tiptoeing out, she sees the old man is still napping. Should she reattach the oxygen? That's another thing. Stay home with her mom and then what? Become a nurse. Take care of sick old men. She's fond of Mr. Joseph. But he's not her future. And the hellhole he lives in isn't either. Maybe old people don't care where they live. That would never be her. Her house, too, is disgusting. It's clean, her mother keeps telling her. But what the hell does that mean? Clean? You can't call something so run-down clean. Jesus. These people fool themselves because they're either too lazy or too scared to change. Or worse, they don't know any better. It's depressing. Her cell phone vibrates and she takes it into the spare room, stares at it till it stops. Her mother's having a heart attack. She picks up the last message; Mila's walking the beach looking for her. She calls her mom's number.

"Darla?" her mother's breathless voice.

Who else, she wants to say. "I'm signing up day after my birthday. Period. Otherwise I'll live at Michelle's until its time to leave."

"I hear you."

"I want an agreement."

"I won't nag you. Come home. Where are you?"

"Rosalyn's dad's."

"Christ. You woke the old man?"

"He wasn't asleep. Mom, something else."

"Yes?"

"Why did you listen to this Jimmy guy?"

"I was young and scared and he sounded so sure."

"Are you sorry?"

"I don't let myself go there."

"All these years you didn't think about—"

"I did a lot at first."

"Were you heartbroken?"

"Let's talk more about it when we see each other. It's easier that way."

"Mom, easy isn't the way life is. Never mind. Just pick me up."

Mr. Joseph wheels the canister to the doorway. He's reattached the oxygen. Suddenly she feels like an intruder. He didn't offer this room. "My mom's coming to . . . I'm sorry if I . . ."

"Get me a six-pack on your way over tomorrow." He shuffles out.

She waits on the lawn, her back against the rough bark of a tree; light opening in the sky, the heat of the day beginning. Does her mother know where Mr. Joseph lives? Even if this Jimmy guy suddenly wants to see her, she'll refuse. What kind of father waits sixteen years to offer a hand? No kind she wants to know, though she'd probably get a lot of pointers from him about the desert.

❖·❖·❖

Mila glances out the car window. Leaves hang precariously from tree limbs. In another week they'll fill the gutters. It's been a summer hot enough to wilt anyone's spirit. But now, a cool breeze ruffles her hair. The map's open on the seat beside her. She's terrible with directions, giving, taking, or following them. On long trips, her daughter was the guide. She's avoiding the highway, going through small towns different from her own. Huge houses that don't resemble each other remind her of the one Murray built. Her foot on the gas pedal is bare, though high-heeled shoes lie on the mat. Darla would get a chuckle seeing her in the sexy green dress she hasn't worn in years.

Darla's last e-mail said she might get a leave after basic, but "Mom, don't count on it." God knows she counts on nothing, trying to adjust is all. Less shopping, less cooking, no checking the clock to wonder where her daughter is, but none of it gives her an ounce of comfort. Dread dogs her even at the diner where she hoped to be too busy to notice. Morning, noon, night, she tells herself, what's done is done. No use. She can't accept the danger.

Iraq? Afghanistan? It's where Darla's headed. Friends try to help. Ava offers words of support, Shelly, who should know, assures her that all will be fine, that time passes quickly. Even Sylvie sent a message. But, really, it's a crapshoot. The truth is no one has a clue what will happen, she least of all.

And truth is what's she's after. It's about time. He doesn't know she's coming. He'll recognize her, though. She's the best prize he ever won. He said so too many times to forget, his face lighting up whenever she came in view. She, too, always excited to see him, now as well. She's nervous, yes, but not scared. Years get used up; she can't fill them in for him, even if Jimmy does ask. Maybe he'll bow his head, reveal graying hair, or offer her that grin so close to sadness. Maybe he'll search for the girl in her that's no longer there.

9

Happiness Exists Somewhere

The news stuns her. Still seated on the exam table, legs dangling, she stares at the dove-gray suit hanging on the closed door as if it belonged to someone else, the person who walked in an hour ago. She can't go back to the office. A dental appointment, she lied. Her purse is beside a tray of instruments and she takes out the cell phone. The receptionist's voicemail picks up. "Hi, it's Sylvie, I'll be back a little later than expected. That is, if anyone asks. Thanks."

If she hadn't called in sick a few days ago she'd take the rest of the afternoon off. That, too, was a lie. She went to Liam's funeral. The entire service at the East Hampton church was bleak: a scattering of old people, the urn buried in an unmarked hole behind his house. Gone, all signs of him. Murray would've accompanied her, but she didn't want him to see her cry, didn't want to deal with the insistent questions that would follow.

He's already badgering her. In bed last night he wanted to know why she had to work? Why does she stay so late? Why can't she be home for dinner? Reasonable questions. She feigned sleep. He won't stop asking. She knows that. He's not an easy man to live

with. He dotes on her but that's the problem. There's nothing con-
crete to hang her discontent on, except who he is.

Sliding off the table, she tears off the paper robe, stuffs it in the
receptacle marked *waste*, and dresses. She needs to walk.

⁂

Fifth Avenue sometimes distracts her, even lifts her spirits. She
allows herself to study the well-dressed people, stylish storefronts,
soaring architecture, St. Patrick's Cathedral. She peers into the
FAO Schwarz window of toys, decorated for Christmas, though
it's weeks away. Grieving takes time, she reminds herself. Holidays
don't help. But it's more than Liam. The sad eyes of a stuffed giraffe
nearly as tall as the real thing stare at her. She turns away, surprised
to see Shelly across the avenue, and finds herself striding toward
her. Shelly's a woman of endurance, what she needs right now.

"Hi. What are you doing in the city?" Shelly's black coat does no
justice to the lovely combination of her dark hair and light eyes.
The woman should wear greens and purples.

"Hi to you. Bruce attends two days as an outpatient. I drive him
in, walk around, then pick him up. I don't mind."

"How's he doing?"

"Up and about. They found medicine he can tolerate. Until now,
the stuff they fed him made him a maniac. What are you doing
here?"

"My office is nearby. A cup of coffee?"

"I wouldn't mind a glass of wine."

She leads them up a side street to an easy-to-miss Irish pub stuck
between two restaurants. Inside there's no hint of afternoon light.
The coziness suits her. No one would look for her here. People
stand two deep at the bar, office workers, unemployed, lunchtime
trysts, who knows?

They find a small table and a waitress appears dressed in slacks and a sweater. Maybe she's just helping out. Shelly orders a glass of house red. She asks for club soda.

"How's your youngest son doing?" What she wants to ask is how to go on when things are beyond control.

"In that horrible place." Shelly sighs. "The kids face death at every turn, not that I would say so to Mila. I can't pick up a newspaper or listen to the radio, forget TV. If Michael came home Bruce would recover faster. The doctor thinks Bruce has confused his own soldier past with Michael's war, which I could've told him weeks ago if he ever asked. I worry because so many reservists are being made to stay longer than their terms. Two months ago, my middle guy wrote to the National Guard that Michael has to come home for a family emergency. No dice."

"It is frightening. I'm so sorry." Shelly looks worn, her heart-shaped face thinner. "Have you eaten lunch?"

"Food isn't friendly lately. My oldest brings me takeout. First-borns are worrywarts."

"You must've been a baby yourself when you had him."

"I swore I'd never go through the pain of it again, but the memory evaporates. It's the way of the world. Are you thinking of . . . ?"

Heat flames her cheeks. "Well . . . Murray's in his fifties."

"Unless they've given up their favorite pastime, age isn't a factor."

The waitress sets down their drinks. She's glad for the interruption. "Your children sound devoted. It must be comforting."

"I don't know. They have their own lives and a life takes time. If Bruce got sick like this with a bunch of youngsters in tow . . ." Shelly shakes her head.

"I'm sure now that Bruce is on the right medication he'll be on the mend shortly."

"He'd like to put in a few hours at the diner but full-time is still iffy." Shelly looks past her, clearly embarrassed to be asking.

Murray doesn't want Bruce coming back but she'll appeal to his sympathy bone. Bruce is a vet, son in Iraq. Murray likes feeling noble. He's always announcing how much food he sends to the shelter. "I'll talk to Murray about it. Nick's overwhelmed, I'm sure."

"That would be great. I hear you did a fine renovation job in the house. It must be lovely."

"Seems so." Is there nothing in her life greater than that damned house?

Shelly searches her face. "Is everything all right?"

"A dear friend died recently. It still grieves me." It was Liam who encouraged her to return to work, who said her unused energy was festering. The photo of Liam's dead son, what happened to it?

"You need to find something uplifting to get it off your mind. While Bruce was in the hospital I bought a print of women dancing in a circle. I hung it in my kitchen. I look at it and think happiness exists somewhere. Sounds silly, I know."

"God, no, Shelly. It's a wonderful thought. But . . ." she shrugs.

"What? You can tell me."

She gazes at Shelly, whose features blur slightly in the ashy darkness. How can she say she's pregnant with no idea what to do? Shelly will think her foolish for throwing away everything for a bit of pleasure. Is that what she did? Is that what she wanted to do? "My house feels too big," she says inanely.

"I can't say I know what that would be like."

Of course she wouldn't. They probably live in one of those tiny . . .

"I envy you," she admits. "You have a family who cares about you."

"Sylvie, everyone at the diner can see Murray's crazy about you. He'd do anything for you."

"Yes, he would," she agrees, letting the truth of it sink in to no avail.

⊰-⊰-⊰

At her desk, the computer open on the columns of numbers and names on the sales screen, but her mind refuses to focus, is everywhere but here. Another woman would be excited, perhaps even relieved. Not her; she's amazed, yes, but mostly scared and confused.

When her cell phone rings, her eyes flit to his corner office, *vice president* stenciled large. "Dinner tonight?" Harry's voice certain.

"Well . . ." she hesitates. "Can I get back to you?"

"Why?" he insists.

"I had tentative plans."

"Cancel them."

She doesn't answer.

"Buzz me." He clicks off.

There's nothing spontaneous about Harry. Most likely his wife called to say she'll be busy this evening. Across the wide expanse of desks separated by see-through walls of Plexiglas, salespeople talk into headphones while watching computer screens. Most here are starting careers. In the cafeteria and hallways they gab about ad agency profits and losses as if it were personal. The top echelon doesn't care a whit about any of them, the indifference palpable in Harry's anecdotes, which she counters. A spunky woman, he calls her.

It's no use, she can't concentrate, presses a few buttons and the document disappears. Endless white flakes drift across the snow-filled screensaver. Why choose a winter scene? She didn't; it was simply here, like Harry.

⊰-⊰-⊰

Harry waits at the cloakroom to check their coats. His elegant cocoa-brown suit fits smoothly across his broad shoulders. His

stylishness first attracted her. They chatted a few times at the pro-
verbial watercooler. He asked her to accompany him to account
focus groups; wanted her input. She was flattered. In the chauf-
feured car maneuvering through crowded midtown, Harry didn't
talk about work. He discussed foreign cinema, Italian films were
his favorite, art shows in unexpected places. A man interested in
museum exhibits, who'd been to the theater too many times to
remember. Her acting background enthralled him. After their second "work" day, Harry asked her to dinner. She accepted easily,
which surprises her still.

They're ushered to a table near a window of mullioned glass.
Except for the warm coral blush of streetlamps, it's too dark to
see much outside. Logs crackle in a nearby fireplace, the ambience seductive. People dine here late, usually after a cocktail party.
They bustle in full of the cold outdoors, reluctant to give up their
coats, impatient for whiskey to warm them. Most other nights, she
frames the scene as if in a play, but she doesn't know what her role
is now.

The menu is in his unblemished hands, manicured nails. She
glances at his wedding band and hers.

"Shall I choose for us?" he asks as he does most evenings they're
together.

"Why not?" she replies as usual, though not a bit hungry.

"I do like knowing you," he says softly, studying her face, which
isn't as concentrated on his as he expects.

"Why's that?" she responds, also softly, while another scene plays
in her head. I'm pregnant with your baby. Why didn't you use con-
traception? Because I had unprotected sex with my husband for a
year, and nothing happened. I thought my fertility was gone. Likely
story, he'll say. She glances at him. A man with four grown sons he'd
never disappoint. He made that clear from date one.

"Your attitude makes me think. It's a challenge." He's trying to engage her. Who wants to bed down with a distant icy woman? Is that who she is tonight?

"My repertoire is endless," she offers through the fog of worry that threatens to dull her mind.

He smiles. Lovely teeth, strong chin, dark eyes that glitter. In the theater, he'd be the matinee idol but never Sir Laurence, whose talent reined over appearance.

"In my position, people tell me what I want to hear. You don't. That's what makes you refreshing."

"I try to be entertaining," she says lightly. Conversing about nothing feels almost beyond her.

"See, like that."

He can't see and he isn't curious either, not really. He's killing time till they're ready to leave for the corporate apartment, his to do with as he pleases. She suspects their encounters there are unlike anything he experiences at home.

The waiter pours a finger of wine in each glass, waits for Harry's nod of approval, then leaves. Harry is about to top hers but she places her hand over the rim. He glances at her but says nothing. She rarely has more than two drinks at any time, her mother's vacant alcoholic eyes never far away.

"There's something I can't figure out about you," he says.

"What could that be?" she asks, hoping miraculously he'll force the truth out of her.

"Are you ambitious?"

"Meaning am I after your job?" she teases, though disappointed.

"No, that would be stupid." He laughs. It's a nice sound, deep, warm.

"Which I'm not." She takes a sip of water. "Tell me," she probes gently, "why are we here, together?"

"Don't you think it's a little late in the day to be asking that?" His careful tone reminds her she's not delivering the correct lines.

"No, it's never too late." She shrugs, then fakes another smile.

"The brutal truth is I'm bored at home. And I find you appealing. I have from the beginning." He reaches across to stroke her hand. Two people married to others acting as if they're engaged in some dramatic first experience when passion's at its highest. Her interest in any of it tonight is less than nil.

"That doesn't sound so brutal," she says.

"Why the sudden curiosity?" He places the napkin on his lap. The man doesn't want to know.

"I'm interested in marriages. Why some go sour and some don't." No, Harry, I'm interested in how you'd react to my having a baby. I'm interested in knowing how disastrous your response would be. Interested, yes, but unable to put it to the test.

"My wife and I have been together twenty-eight years. Relationships plateau. Some get past that, other's teeter." He's reciting probably the same litany he gives all his women. Once she lied at an audition, said she was sixteen, and had to pretend for the duration of the play. But how long can she pretend not to be pregnant?

"An amount of time not to be sniffed at," she quips.

"You don't say much about your marriage . . ." He refills his wineglass.

"A bit stultifying," she offers. How to describe what she doesn't understand. Even if she did, it would feel disloyal to discuss it.

"You haven't been married that long," he reminds her.

"You can pepper me with questions in the boardroom, not here," she quips.

"In the boardroom I'd already know the answers."

She laughs. "So I hear." Rumor has it Harry's a hard man, that he fires people for first offenses. If she hints at her predicament he'll insist she deal with it immediately. She isn't ready, has no clue what ready would feel like.

Harry raises his hand and the waiter hurries over. He gives their order, pronouncing the French dishes with ease. He's comfortable in his skin, doesn't want to be anyone else. Onstage, she's been a mother, a wife, a lover. It's easy to play other people.

❖❖❖

Her car, a dark shape beneath a sputtering lamp, is one of a few still at the station. She beeps open the door and slides in. On the road, an occasional light shimmers in the distance, the sense of the ocean near. She ratchets up the heat. Dead winter's on the way. Her refusal to go to the corporate apartment surprised him. She said dinner lasted longer than she expected. Harry didn't press her. He walked her to Penn Station, chatting easily. He kissed her cheek, his aloofness apparent. She didn't perform well tonight, didn't provide the pleasure the world owes him. He doesn't need her—she's a whim, a toy like the ones in the store window. Yes, the first weeks with him were exciting. Even now it's easy to imagine them in Bali, something they talked about. She sees them lying hand in hand on a sparkling white beach and she tells him she's pregnant, her voice languid, reassuring.

❖❖❖

The dogs bark as she nears the door. Inside, they wrap themselves around her legs. Stroking their sleek bodies, she murmurs, "Hush," refusing to say their hateful names. Murray, in a thick terry cloth robe, watches like a pleased proprietor. He offers her a sip of his wine, which she declines. "Tired, I'm off to bed."

"I've been waiting up. I have something to say about us," he declares.

Is this the moment where everything changes? Has he had enough, wants out from this woman who fills so few of his needs.

Oh she sleeps with him, but is she affectionate? Does she make him feel important? Or has someone told him about Harry? Is he about to send her away? She wants to say can't this wait till the weekend, that she doesn't like being blind sided, but Murray's withheld fury can be frightening. She follows him to the living room.

He sits too close on the ridiculously long sofa. She glances at the refurbished room, new chairs, lamps, and tables, paintings hung; the dogs are asleep in the corner; the silence broken by the sound of the surf, which pulses like an angry heart. Is now the time for truth? When he takes her hand, she feels only trepidation.

"I want to make you happy. But you're not behaving the way a wife should."

"Behaving? I'm not a child."

"Cut me a break, okay? I don't want to fight over words." He drops her hand. "I've decided we should go away for a week. I can't leave the diner longer than that. Lie on a beach, relax together." Oh god, he's climbed into her Harry fantasy. Is he toying with her too? Does he know more than he's letting on? Except it isn't like him to be subtle.

"And I don't like your job . . . it takes all your time . . . the hours . . . the nights . . ." The familiar lament goes on but she tunes out.

She sighs loudly. He stops talking and gazes at her.

"Having a beautiful house doesn't fulfill me the way it fulfills you. It's why I went back to work." The truth in pieces. It's the only path that seems possible.

"Why do you have to come home so late?" his voice plaintive, his expression sorrowful, deepening creases track the sides of his mouth. He can't fathom being the cause of her distress.

"A day or two . . . then I promise we'll have this talk. Now, though, I need to get some rest."

"We can't put it off longer than that." He strokes her hair. "Okay, go to bed."

She walks away quickly, praying he won't call her back. Coward! He turns off the lights, follows her, then slides in bed spooning her. He kisses the back of her neck, presses her shoulder to turn around. She does, easier than explaining why not.

⁂

She prepares the morning coffee, then leaves quickly to take her shower. When, finally, she hears his car backing out of the garage, dogs in the backseat, the relief floods her. She phones the office, leaves a message that she won't be in without saying why. Indecision churns her insides. Pulling on a pair of sweats and heavy socks, she finds her sneakers, and wraps a scarf around her neck. She grabs her old peacoat from the hall closet and stuffs gloves in her pocket.

⁂

Walking along the muddy shore, hair whipping her cheeks, spray dampening her face, she misses Liam again. He knew about Harry. She told him the affair was opening her mind to possibilities she'd forgotten existed. That Harry's hand might lead her out of her marriage. Liam thought she was searching for her feelings the way a painter seeks light.

She makes her way to where Liam had his lean-to. All traces of it are gone except for a vague shadow where the coal fire used to be. Up here the sand is drier. She sits and stares at the dusky horizon, the black water. A few gulls sweep over her still-discernible house. There's no hint of sun. The fast-moving clouds are dizzying. She never saw Liam work. He painted in the early morning but often he'd leave out a canvas for her to see. She'd marvel at his ability to see so many different scenes in the same place. He explained it's what made creating exciting.

Almost overnight, it seemed, he stopped painting and retreated to a chair on his patch of lawn. She brought whatever creature comforts she thought he needed, though he never asked for a thing. He wouldn't discuss what was ailing him. He hardly ate, barely talked. He took to his bed and stayed there. His last weeks remain painful to contemplate. He'd look around the room with faint wonder or study his hands as if they held some final secret.

Two of his sea paintings hang in her living room. Murray likes them because they prove where he lives. No doubt Harry would appreciate them as well.

Murray and Harry, each with his version of her. If she has an abortion, neither man would have to know. So what's stopping her? Nothing but a clump of cells moving toward recognition, that's all it is now, the doctor said. Soon, though, it'll resemble Casper the ghost in those ultrasound pictures women bring to the office. Except it'll be *her* ghost taking shape.

Dolls never attracted her, fake babies with silly big knees. A real baby will have needs she can't even fathom. She used to imagine being a mother different from her own. A ridiculous memory, as ridiculous as thinking she could care for a child by herself. Food, clothes, rent, sitters . . . her theater-days are over. And so too any chunks of money they used to bring in. Besides she's too old for anything but character roles and would have to wait eons between them.

The screams of wheeling gulls split the air. Wind bites her cheeks, sand lands on her lap. A coin of sun peeks through the clouds, then disappears, the entire scene bleak. If Liam were here he'd remind her that place reflects feelings. If she shared her ambivalence, he'd no doubt say there's such a fine line between delay and denial.

Hoisting herself off the sand, brushing herself off, she wraps the scarf around her head and trudges back to the house. If she dresses quickly, she'll make the afternoon train to Wantagh.

❖-❖-❖

She pays the driver and watches the taxi head to the mall to pick up a fare. In the graying late afternoon light the neon sign flashes *Murray's Diner*. A silver-striped bus with polished aluminum siding. The long, wide windows clean as new morning. Murray's as fastidious about the diner's appearance as she is about her own. Dressed now in forest-green slacks, lime color sweater, makeup, she's ready for an audience.

Pushing open the door to the tinny sound of chimes, the sizzling smells of burgers and fries greet her along with the faint scent of barbecue sauce. Ava waves, eyebrows raised with questions. Why isn't Sylvie at work? Is something wrong? Did she quit? Questions only slightly offtrack. Once the affair ends, so will her job. Mila, wrapped in her puffy jacket, is ready to leave. The shift changes at four but everyone's putting in extra hours to cover for Rosalyn. The wall clock reads ten past five. She hangs her coat on one of the hooks.

"How are you?" Mila asks on her way out.

"Fine. And how's Darla?"

Mila shrugs, frowns. "Haven't heard bad news yet. Murray's in the storeroom, want me to get him?"

"No. I'll find him, thanks."

"I'm out of here, " Mila swings past, allowing in a burst of cold air.

"Coffee?" Ava calls.

"Tea, thanks." She sits on a stool, elbows on the counter. "You look wonderful." Ava's newly styled hair frames her slim face with soft curls.

"You think so?" Ava half turns to catch herself in the mirror, then leaves to set up two customers. It's not quite dinnertime, but half the tables are filled and there's a low buzz of voices.

Nick carries out a heavy tub of clean coffee mugs and places it under the counter. He looks a bit sleepy but handsome as ever; perhaps he just came in. He nods to her; she smiles, wonders if he opens up with Ava. Their romance upsets Murray, who fears that Nick will walk if he complains. Murray brings home each employee's transgression and wants her sympathy. It pisses him off when she defends the staff. He *is* holding open Rosalyn's job for another month, though he's sure she's not coming back. Even more surprising, he visited Rosalyn twice, once in the hospital, once at home. He said Dina was there helping out. She would've asked for particulars, but Murray's more about what's right or wrong than descriptions.

The leather booths, small, square tables, inlaid floor, low ceiling, Formica counter, familiar reflections in the gold-flecked mirror. At this very counter, she and Murray spoke for the first time ahead of a short courtship full of activity: bars, restaurants, sightseeing, Saturday nights at B&Bs in the Hamptons. Weekday evenings he'd show up outside her office full of enthusiasm about a new dinner place he'd discovered. He seemed indefatigable and it charmed her. He admired her, it was clear. He listed all the things about her that pleased him, and not just once. He was open about why he never married, how most women bored him. He told her what he wanted, what he was waiting for, drawing her into the simplicity of his confessions more than any chemical attraction.

What of that matters now? she wonders. Her face in the mirror offers no clues; her resolve dissipates by the second. She must get this scene over with. How else to go on? Leaving the comfort of other people's presence, she descends the storeroom steps slowly. The urge to turn back remains strong. Halfway down, the dogs leap up to greet her, nearly toppling her. "Easy, easy," she cautions. There are boxes piled against walls, supplies fill metal shelves that reach the low ceiling where a dim overhead bulb casts an eerie light.

Murray in rolled up shirtsleeves and an old cobbler's apron from who knows when stares at her as if she's a ghost.

"Didn't mean to shock you. I just wanted to—"

"Why aren't you at work?" he scolds. He fears surprises even more than she does.

"I took the day." She scans the room, which has no chairs and only two tiny windows. It's a cellar. A faint whiff of pesticide threatens to nauseate her.

"Why are you here?"

"Can we go somewhere else to talk?"

"Why?" his tone suspicious.

"I can't talk here." Either the room has contracted or claustrophobia has her by the throat.

"What do you want?" He's not going to make this easy.

"Murray . . . please," she begs. "Meet me somewhere."

He stands there as if his feet are nailed to the floor, wearing an angry anxious expression that asks why is she doing this to him?

"Murray? Where? Please?"

"Sully's," he says reluctantly. His eyes are steady on her.

"I'll be there." She turns away quickly lest he find a way to keep her in this dungeon.

The dogs follow her up the steps. "No. Stay."

"Rummy. Cheney. Down, now!" Murray shouts. His voice goes through her. The dogs obey.

Upstairs, a temp is wiping tables. Ava watches the woman with a mournful look, maybe thinking of Rosalyn.

Sylvie grabs her coat. "See you soon," she calls without turning. The door chimes shut behind her.

Snowflakes drift and whirl in the sudden wind, a purple tinge ahead of the darkening sky. Sounds of highway traffic fill her ears. The distant small houses with doors shut tight remind her there's no one available to help her. Why not simply disappear . . . woman last seen at diner . . . Pulling her coat close, she hurries toward the glittering shop lights of the mall.

❖-❖-❖

The smell of spilled beer and old cigarette smoke lingers in the air, but it's warm inside. If Sully's were well lit all would be revealed, the warped floor, aging walls. Like an old theater, it's weathered many tales. She finds a table in the rear where early on she and Murray had drinks and spoke of past events. He described how badly he'd wanted to be a boxer, the hours he put in at the gym. But his hands were too small; no one would take him on; how awful the rejection. She told him about her mother's drinking problem, her father's suicide. He said simply, she'd turned out fine. What didn't she see then?

Her eyes travel the dark corridor leading to the door and his arrival. He'll explode, of course he will. He'll be enraged, incoherent, ask—no, demand—over and over why she took up with Harry as if any of her answers will register. He'll accuse her of being wanton, loose, a betrayer of everything good. Or is that what she thinks? He'll be devastated as well. Lord knows what it will do to him. Any other scene she'd know her cues, but not here, not now.

Her thoughts whirl dizzily, her throat tight, perhaps a shot of bourbon to warm the cold fear, or a martini for courage? The bartender is on his cell phone with his back to her. She's the only customer. The table holds a smudgy one-page menu she can't imagine consulting, and remembers Harry fingering last night's menu.

It's finished with Harry, has to be, of that she's certain. What's weird is how little she cares.

The door bangs open and Murray rushes in, unzipped ski jacket flapping, woolen hat in hand; snow glancing his hair. His face scrunched tight, his eyes find her.

"I didn't order drinks," she says before he can sit. "I'll have club soda." He looks at her with alarm, then strides to the bar. Knocks hard on the counter to get the bartender's attention, then his eyes remain steady on her. She turns away, nothing on the wall but frayed pennants, old photos.

Murray slams down her soda, the spray wetting the table. He takes a long pull of scotch, then drops into a chair without taking off his jacket. His jaw is locked, his hands balled in fists, his shoulders hunched defensively. He's breathing hard. It's unnerving.

"Talk." His imperial tone, the one he uses with the dogs. Her stomach clenches. She takes a sip of soda. Truth in pieces, she reminds herself, first the pregnancy, then Harry, then she'll flee.

He leans his face close to hers, the smell of scotch on his breath mingling with aftershave. "Talk," he demands again.

"Murray, I'm pregnant, but it's not . . ."

He leaps up. "What the fuck . . . I thought you couldn't . . ." He's shouting.

"I thought so too."

He peers at her, eyes narrowing, face reddening.

"Murray, it's not—"

He grabs the back of her chair, slides it right and left, emitting little squeals or maybe he's choking. He's creating a scene; the bartender's watching. "Murray, stop, please."

"Okay, okay," his raw voice nearly breathless. "Oh baby, that's so marvelous. I'm happier even than when you said you'd marry me. I'm not happy, I'm thrilled. God, Sylvie. When did you find out?"

"Yesterday . . . but Murray, it's not . . ."

He clasps both her hands, kisses them. "How are you?"

"Good," she says, somewhat confused.

"Anything you want, baby, anything, just name it, it's yours for this great news." He's talking so fast, his certainty is overwhelming. Harry's response would look nothing like this.

"You really are happy," she murmurs.

"There's that empty room at the end of the foyer."

She knows where it is, knows where's he's going, and something snags in her throat, a pill too big to swallow.

"We'll make it into a nursery." He's still talking very loud.

She says nothing.

"We'll buy funny wallpaper, we'll hang those little musical toys. The dogs could be a problem. But they took to you real soon. I bet they'll protect the baby."

She says nothing.

He drains his glass. "Of course there's things I can't do. Diapering stuff. I don't know . . . maybe I can learn." He sounds faintly embarrassed. "I need a refill."

He hurries away. A deafening silence fills her head, the kind that occurs after an explosion. For a moment she can't remember where she is. Her eyes flick to the bright screen of the mute TV. Heavily equipped soldiers traipse through strange terrain, reminding her of Shelly who bought a painting of merry women, who refuses to be laid low by Bruce's condition, who makes the most of her situation. A customer enters and sits at the bar. He, too, leaves his coat on, wet with snow. Maybe he's staying for only one drink. She's not wearing boots, how will she manage the slippery outdoors? Her heart is pumping, her mind gone numb.

Murray's loud gleeful voice is offering to buy the man and bartender drinks. Her mother often offered her presents, old scarves or sweaters that stank of whiskey and cigarettes. She hated them. Once she wouldn't take the item. Her mother, angry, grabbed her arm, pushed her face close, and said in no uncertain terms, it was rude and unkind to refuse anyone's gift.

Is she giving Murray a gift or is he giving her one?

Whatever he's saying to the customer, she can't make out, but is sure he's boasting . . . a father . . . first time . . . never thought . . . His face is hidden but she imagines him grinning with flushed cheeks, the way he does before they make love. The customer lifts his glass in a toast. Did he turn to her?

The sad march of whiskey bottles across the back mirror leads to the door. It isn't far. She could run past Murray into the cold night. But what would she find there that isn't already here? Her eyes slide to the flickering yellow light of the jukebox. Maybe, somewhere, there's music.

10

The Things in Between

She's going crazy. Each morning, now, she talks to her image in the mirror, says, Rosalyn, life isn't half bad yet. Then she intones Sister Judi's words from long ago, everything can be gotten through—how did Sister know? Crazy, indeed, but so what? Spying a parking space, she pulls in, flips down the mirrored visor and checks her head scarf.

Dina's car pulls up beside hers.

They walk across the crowded mall, the heat of the day apparent in everyone's slow trudge.

"It's good not to have lunch at the diner. Murray's drone...should he sell, shouldn't he... who cares?" Dina asks no one in particular.

"He does sound serious," she murmurs.

"See what love can do?" Dina reminds her.

"All for Sylvie, right?"

"And the coming baby, don't forget."

"The baby . . . of course," she says quietly.

❖-❖-❖

The café has A/C, thank heavens. It's crowded. Voices are loud; people seem indifferent to anyone hearing what they say. Jack, too, doesn't care. She has no idea where he is when he phones her—at work, a pub, in the street—only that he tries to probe her deepest thoughts, wants her to unburden.

The young, attractive hostess in a T-shirt, long skirt, and flip-flops leads them to a table, drops two menus, fills their water glasses. Beautiful is dangerous, her father would mutter when she was that age.

"Did you see her earrings . . . four hoops in one ear," Dina says, her lobes free of adornment.

"I'm having a glass of merlot with my sandwich."

"Okay, me too. Why not?" Dina agrees.

"Anything from your son?"

"If they caught him I'd know. Anyway, it hasn't been that long." Dina's dismissive tone surprises her.

"Are you worrying?" she asks.

"Thankful not to hear and ashamed to admit it. I can't bury my feelings anymore," Dina asserts.

"That's wisdom."

"Yes . . . compensation for the insults of aging and . . ." Dina stops. "Sorry."

"Don't be. You've nursed me through the whole rotten treatment. What would I have done without you?" Dina still shows up at ten every morning. Maybe she anticipates a time when Rosalyn won't be able to get out of bed. If so, she hasn't let on.

"I'm glad I had the skills to help," Dina says simply.

"Oh shit. Let's not talk about me. Your remarks about Tim . . . I understand. He's a problem that can't be solved easily."

"The guilt, the love . . . mixed together . . . that's hard too." Dina picks up the menu.

"Is there anything I can do?"

"Like what?" Again, Dina's faintly challenging tone surprises her. The truth is she's no longer curious about lives she needs to let go of.

"I don't know. It's what friends say," she offers.

"I suppose. I'm having a tuna melt." Dina closes the menu.

The waiter steps up to the table, wipes his hands on a stained towel tucked in his waist. Messy hair, sullen expression, clearly he'd rather be elsewhere. "We'll make your life easy. We'll both have the tuna melt with a glass of merlot."

"Did you return this morning's call from Jack?" Dina asks.

"I spoke to him three times this week, four last week."

"Are you avoiding him?" Dina searches her face.

"He's after me to go abroad."

"So?" Dina's chin lifts combatively.

"It's too far to travel." She doesn't say time has edges now. That there are things here she must do first.

"You're done with chemo for a while."

"I'm done with treatment, period. Anyway, Jack . . . it's complex."

"You mean he cares about you but since you're sick it's a waste of time?" Dina's serious eyes fasten on her.

"Don't be crude."

"Well, then, explain it better," Dina says matter-of-factly.

The waiter serves their drinks. "Food's still being prepared," he mumbles.

"Do you know how I met Jack?"

"At a bar, I thought."

"Well, that's true . . . I worked for an escort service. He paid for an arranged date with me."

"Oh." Her friend attempts to sound casual.

"I quit the service months ago," she assures her.

"Aren't those one-night stands," Dina's voice low.

"Jack was the guest who stayed. Why am I even telling you?"

"You wanted me to know," Dina says, her composure restored.

"Probably." Except it wasn't her intention. Lately, it's as if another person inside her decides what to say without her permission. It's what she fears, isn't it? Jack will hear what she isn't ready to share.

"Rosalyn, how you two met doesn't explain why you won't join him in Europe. Obviously he wants to show you around."

"You're one persistent lady. Let's say, I'm not in a vacation mood."

"What kind of mood is that?"

"Drop it. Please."

"For now." Dina takes a sip of merlot.

⁌⁌⁌

Glad to wave goodbye, she drives off. Dina's chatter about Jack felt intrusive. She doesn't want to think about him. He senses that but won't accept it. He can be endearing yet exasperating. She stuffs a pillow behind her lower back to ease the muscle spasm. She passes a row of refurbished houses with freshly painted porches and non-leaking roofs, a hard sun ignites the front lawns. Her father could move into one of the houses. She offered to arrange it months ago but he refused. It's been a few days since she saw him. It feels even more difficult to be with him. He stares at her like she might die in front of him, or else won't look at her at all. The man doesn't know how to be supportive. Simply doesn't. At least he approves of the high school student she hired to help him. She finds the boy aggressive.

She pulls into his driveway. Good, the student's car isn't there. She beeps to let her father know she's arrived. To her surprise, he walks out carrying the new oxygen container, which has a handle and resembles a thermos. "Let's go to the beach," he says, sliding in slowly.

"What?"

"Forgot where it is?"

She starts the car. "Why?"

"I want to be outdoors while it's warm."

The truth of that doesn't sit right, but she never could figure out how he thinks. She glances at his strong, craggy profile; he'll out-live her. She said as much to her brother, who reassured her that wasn't so in words that held no weight. The rest of the relatives are equally Pollyanna. No doubt family members need to believe what they will for their own comfort.

❖-❖-❖

They sit on a boardwalk bench facing the water. A few clouds play hide-and-seek with the sun. Blankets, towels, umbrellas arrayed on the sand; lifeguards in high white chairs, whistles at the ready. Parents watch their children cavorting in the water, the noise of it all distant. She and her brother played here winter and summer, though her mom wouldn't allow them in the ocean even on the hottest days.

Lotion and salt air, she smells both, but feels outside, a witness. Yesterday, too, in the supermarket, she felt at the far end of a tunnel. Snippets of conversations reverberated in her head. It's as if what's said matters less than the things in between she must still uncover.

"Dad, do you know how to swim?"

He nods.

"Mom didn't. She was afraid of drowning."

"She was afraid of a lot of things."

"Parents pass on their quirks. I can't swim."

"Worse things have happened."

"When Mom took us here, she sat in a tiny canvas chair, her feet buried in the sand if it was warm. In the cold, we were all bundled up. She wore boots. You were never with us."

"The fire station didn't believe in time off for the beach."

"Or weekends?"

"What is this?"

"Just mulling stuff over, remembering . . . Mom made us wash our feet with the hose because you hated sand in the house. In winter, we had to leave our boots outside. It was a rule. She always wanted to please you."

"What do you want, Rosalyn?" She hears him breathing.

"Was Mom a happy person?"

"Who's happy?"

"It's a question I regret not asking her."

"That was a long time ago. Stop torturing yourself. And me."

He must've known what her mother felt; they lived together for god's sake. "Did you love Mom?"

"I was nineteen when we married." He lifts the oxygen container from the ground to the bench.

"Did you love us?" He spent more hours with his fire team than with them. The guys were his buddies, drinking mates, the ones he confided in if he confided at all.

"I supported my family, took care of all of you. What else can I say? What else do you expect?"

Is she stirring him up? Or will he switch on the TV as soon as he gets home to blot out the past hour? In third grade, she begged him to come talk to her class in his fireman's uniform. He refused, said, what for? She cried bitterly. Her mother whispered he was too shy; he wouldn't be comfortable. Comfort's what he always craved.

"I just want to understand you better," she says.

"Why?"

"Dad, you're exasperating."

He glances at her, then looks away. "Something I want to say . . ." his voice a hoarse whisper. "I have a bit of money. If there's a treatment out there your insurance won't cover, I'll pay for it."

"I have enough money."

"You never let me give you anything."

Is that true? She looks at him but he continues to face the water.

"Okay. Thanks, Dad. If I come up against that, I'll ask you for help." It's the best she can do.

"I meant what I said a while back about meeting my grandchild."

"Don't go there," her voice rising in desperation.

He inhales shakily. Then silence.

She could ask about the student helper or if his pals have visited, the ball games he loves, anything to break the silence. But, suddenly, she's weary of the ancient dance between parent and child. And she wonders, is it too soon to take him home? She mentioned a doctor's appointment at three, which is a lie, but the truth would be impossible to share.

He's hunched over on the bench, still staring ahead. Whatever he sees out there has captured his attention or is simply easier to look at.

❖-❖-❖

From the driver's seat she watches him take small steps up the path. The maple tree in full leaf casts filigreed shadows, its thickly gnarled roots heaving the old lawn. She used to pray those roots would lift the house off its foundation so they'd have to move out. The prayer came back to her during the weeks of chemo. The intravenous bag was slowly deflating, her body exhausted, her mind, though, was wild with memories and fantasies. Faraway countries she'd visit, Zanzibar and Saint Kitts, names she heard somewhere but knew nothing about. Where's Zanzibar? She composed letters in her head to lots of people, but sent only one.

Her father reaches the door but doesn't turn or wave goodbye. She beeps to let him know she's leaving, glances at her watch. Nearly two. Arriving first is out of the question. If he's a no-show . . . but his terse phone message was explicit. Three p.m.,

Friendly Fishermen's Pub, Bridgton. He was never one for long phone conversations. What will be will be, she reminds herself, and refuses to give the next few hours form or content.

She knows the pub, which is dark in the afternoon and well lit in the evening. She ate there several times with Mila. Poor woman can barely talk about Darla's going to Afghanistan. Mila who will only step in a church to get out of the cold said she made a pact with God, promised not to complain if He brings her daughter back intact. On the other hand Mila talks nonstop about Jimmy, his gray hair, beard, handsome as ever, so recognizable, how each visit with him pleases her, his compliments about her youthful looks, how he loves seeing her and doesn't take his eyes off her. She even jabbers to Murray about him.

❖-❖-❖

At a minute to three, she slides out of the car, walks up the back ramp, pushes open the heavy door, and enters near the bar. She scans two customers' faces, a muted TV screen, the bartender fiddling with a cranky A/C. Then she follows a long narrow corridor to the rear booths. She sees him in one, looking out the window. Is that buzz-cut marine, or army? Is he balding? His big shoulders the same as years ago, the chest broader, though. Wearing a white T-shirt, his muscular arms tanned, the short, flat fingers unchanged. She slips into the booth across from him. "Hey Carl."

"Rosalyn. Rosalyn. How the hell are you?" He grins; his wide black eyes no longer merry, his sun-weathered face creased. Years ago, his smooth skin was soft, no five-o'clock shadow either. Now the beginnings of a beard sprout under his chin.

"Not sure how to answer."

"Yeah, your letter said . . . sorry about . . ."

"Me too."

"Have a drink." His shot glass empty, his beer stein nearly drained, he hails the waiter, who looks no older than they were when they met. "Beer or bourbon?" the waiter asks, indifferent to her presence. Carl orders both and wine for her. "A very long time," he muses, taking her in.

She nods. He used to tease that she had two words for each one of his. Now she's strangely shy. "I heard you were in Iraq."

"Three stints. Reserves. I'm getting too old but I'd go again if they ask me."

"You don't look old."

"Yeah, friends never do."

"Are you working?"

"Helping my brother fix up a basement. I've only been back a few months. It feels forever. Can't fit in . . . it's like trying on an old jacket that won't button. Everything's too tight."

The waiter brings their drinks. Carl drains the last drops of beer and hands off the glass. "Last I heard you were at that diner."

"Who told you?"

"I can't remember. My memory's shot and so is my hearing, so talk loud."

"Was it awful?"

"Nothing good."

"Thank heavens you weren't injured."

"Not where you can see." He chuckles.

"But you want to go back?" Easiness creeping in between them.

"Funny, huh? The weird crap happens here. Bad sleep, jumping at sounds, drink like you know . . . but over there I know the sounds, sleep like a seal in the sun. Still drink like a . . . Hey, why talk about it? It comes out like a long whine." He downs the bourbon, takes a sip of the beer. Some of his color is from the booze. "How'd you find me?"

"I called some old friends . . . heard you were married." All this banter with someone she hasn't seen in too many years to count. Still, it's what one does, she supposes, except these questions are not what she's here for.

He gazes at her a moment. "Katie left me after the last tour, took a job in Atlanta. Couldn't get far enough away, I guess." He finishes the beer and looks around for the waiter. "Hey," he calls too loudly. "Another round."

The waiter frowns and the diner floats into her head. Murray barking at someone, customers impatient for service, Ava whirling from the counter to the tables. And Willy? She holds him there in his booth.

"Sorry about you and Katie. It's none of my business anyway."

His fingers drum the table, eager for his drinks. "You still have that terrific face. I'd know you anywhere."

Terrific face, unforgettable eyes . . . His husky voice comes back to her; so, too, the gentleness, how he cared for her. How could she forget? "That's sweet."

"And you, babe? Married a few times or still with the same lucky guy?"

"I never married. My aunts, my cousins, my father all point this out whenever they can. Not that any of their marriages are very inspiring either."

"Yeah, family. Best stay away from the bunch of them . . . or so I've learned. Anyway, if you never married I must've left an impression." He tries for boyishness, but sounds sarcastic. Jack's gentle, comforting, though persistent voice comes to mind. But Jack's older, hasn't been to war, his tragedy endured slowly over time, water on a rock.

"An impression . . . absolutely," she agrees. An impression she made sure to erase the way she managed to turn away from whatever needed tending. She won't let that happen again. She can't.

As soon as the waiter serves the drinks, Carl downs the shot of bourbon.

192

"You do that often?" She points to the empty glass.

"As often as I can. Don't worry. It takes a whole lot to knock me out. I'll be right back, going to visit a man about a—"

She watches him saunter to the restroom in his camouflage pants, a few bulging pockets with unbuttoned flaps. She remembers his tight jeans the night they broke up. She couldn't fit into hers. Her stomach was puffy and stretched. The stitches hadn't disappeared yet. Her breasts were still heavy. Her body felt unrecognizable, unlovable. His looked untouched, everything in place, without pain or scars.

It was a summer night and they took a blanket to the beach. Other couples were scattered about. They found a space to themselves. She remembers the water lapping gently at the shore, occasional laughter from somewhere nearby, a sky invaded by stars. He tried to kiss her. She turned away. He began stroking her hair. She told him to stop, said he made her want to vomit. He kept asking what's wrong, promising he could fix it. At first she didn't respond, then a stream of invective she's ashamed to recall burst from somewhere so deep inside and left her trembling. He drove her home without a word, didn't call again. It was what she wanted. She'd just given up her baby.

He slides in the booth and takes a long pull of the beer.

"I was remembering our breakup."

"Oh yeah?" He doesn't sound interested.

"I owe you an apology."

"Yeah . . . right . . . okay, I accept."

"You're not the least bit curious?"

"Hey, I figured out why you didn't want to see me anymore."

"Whew, that's a load off." She wipes her brow.

He chuckles. "Why are we here, babe?"

"I need to know about our daughter." There it is, the pussyfooting finished.

"What exactly?" She detects reluctance.

"I need information. Your sister's best friend took her." She can still taste the weird mixture of emptiness and relief.

"Rosalyn, Rosalyn . . . Why would she want you in her life now?" He finishes the beer and looks for the waiter.

"I made a will. I'm leaving her my savings, my condo. The attorney needs to be able to contact her when the time comes." Heat rushes to her cheeks as if she just spiked a fever. It's all she can do to sit still. But she can't take off, not yet.

He leans forward. The bourbon's worked itself into his face, sweating now. "I can't help you. I have nothing to do with her."

"She doesn't know you're her father?" her voice rising. Why would she? They gave her up. They have no rights. It's there again, the tunnel with him at the far end.

"The girl knows she's adopted. I hear the girl's mother filled her in some about us, how young we were . . . so on." His eyes are on her, but she's not sure what he's seeing. Suddenly his reticence, her powerlessness, the whole encounter pisses her off. And his drinking doesn't thrill her either.

"Think! Remember *something* for god's sake." She stares hard at him.

"Jesus where's the fucking waiter?" His hands open and close, his jaw slack. He used to be laid-back, pliable. Now he's brittle enough to break, and he knows it. Jack comes to mind again, his ability to withstand turmoil, his voice asking her to lean on him.

Two people talk softly in a nearby booth, their words hum past her ears. A few streaks of bright sun invade the room, land on the stained wooden floorboards. She takes a sip of the wine. It tastes old, rancid, vinegary, and she remembers the Chablis in her fridge.

"I'm going up there to get another drink. Fucking waiter." He grabs the table to steady himself. "Her name's Lacy Marino." Then sways toward the bar, his head bent beneath the mess of his life.

❖❖❖

Home at last, the drive back was endless. Phone messages blink on the machine. Her flowers need fresh water. When they begin to wilt, she tosses them. These, though, meaty yellow roses, she bought yesterday. The girl's name repeats in her head as it has since he said it. A name matters. A name gives substance, rhythm, color—allows an image to form. Lacy as a grown woman, a combination of Carl and herself, dark eyes for sure, thick, wavy hair. Maybe she's petite like her or sturdy like Carl.

She finds herself in the bedroom closet pushing aside shoeboxes, scarves, purses on the too-high shelf till her fingers press the soft leather-like surface of an old photo album, which she retrieves. Dropping on the bed, she turns pages, a picture of her mom—who loved her children—reading the newspaper, which she did from back to front, wanting to fill her head with trivia before letting in bad news. Photos of friends she hasn't seen in years. And here's one of her at Lacy's age now. She's wearing jeans and a tank top, leaning against some guy's old jeep, holding back a curtain of hair to reveal what must've been new dangling earrings. She's grinning. When she was Lacy's age she flaunted her appeal yet worked hard, saved money, had lots of friends. Someone Lacy might approve of. Removing the photo carefully, she returns to the living room, slides it in the manila envelope on the coffee table. Then she picks up the cordless and calls Dina.

"It's me. There's something else I never told you."

"Hold on." She can almost hear Dina settling into her chair.

"Yes, Rosalyn, what is it?" her friend careful not to sound eager.

"When I was seventeen I had a baby . . ." she begins. It's a story she no longer wants to keep secret, the names and events unfurling easily. Lacy, Carl, the Manhattan foundling home where she lived for the final trimester, the nuns who cared for her, Carl's sister who took away the baby she never saw, her meeting with Carl today. She doesn't stop there but goes on about the envelope on the table, which contains her will, her father's address, other documents, and now a photo of her. "We'll never meet but Lacy will have something of me, of mine. Don't you see?"

"Rosalyn, you should meet your daughter," Dina declares.

Her eyes flit to the black-and-white print on the wall that resembles a Rorschach blot. "Well I hadn't thought."

"What's to think about?"

"Lacy, her family. I can't just walk into their lives and—" Again, saying her name feels gratifying, proprietary.

"She must be curious about you."

The phone at her ear, she pads across the gleaming terra-cotta floor, the aqua rug catching the last light of day, wondering what it would be like to actually see the girl. In the kitchen, she pours Chablis in a glass and takes a sip.

"Are you there?"

"I'm thinking. And drinking."

"I'll say one thing: do what pleases you, never mind the result."

"You speaking from experience?" She's aiming to tease her, but finds she's listening intently.

"I rarely did what pleased me, only what was necessary. After a while, I didn't know the difference."

It's not entirely true. Dina loved her work. Perhaps she's speaking of Tim, but it's too coded to get into now.

"Dina, I'm sorry."

"That's not the point. It's a lesson to share. Or at least to ponder."

"I hear you."

"It won't be that difficult to find her."

Suddenly the success of learning the girl's name slips away, the closure she sought reopened. "Listen, I can't talk about it right now."

"I didn't mean to—"

"I know. See you tomorrow." She clicks off. Though she's not sorry she told Dina—her secrets less amazing to others than she would have expected—a claw of anxiety tears at her.

The yellow-striped watering can sits on the counter. She fills it and steps out onto her small patio, scanning the darkening lawn, the starless sky. She hopes for a better night. The last two have been fitful. Sleep came late and only for several hours, kaleidoscopic images racing around her head leaving blurry smears.

She waters the spider plants, their tendrils nearly touching the ground, then goes in to look at her messages. There are three. Two from Jack asking her to call him, he misses her, he's worried, please phone him. One from Carl, whose slurry voice recites an address. She replays it twice to be certain.

❖-❖-❖

Her car inches along in the early evening rush-hour traffic. The MapQuest directions Bobby downloaded are on her lap. Reaching Bruckner Boulevard, the lanes fan out like fingers on a hand. It's bewildering till she spies the North Bronx exit sign underscored on the map. Then it's one bleak street after another toward Gun Hill Road. What a strange name. She's never been in the Bronx, though her mother often talked about her childhood there. She tries to recall the stories but her memory has become selective, permits only events involving her. She understands. She's rechewing experience, can taste it. It's made her talkative.

She chattered on and on the other night when Ava and Mila visited. She described her work as an escort, her dates that never mattered, except for Jack. Then Lacy, all about Lacy, how Carl wanted to marry, how her mother dissuaded her. How her father wants to know his granddaughter. How Dina suggested meeting her daughter. How what to do feels beyond her. Ava said little, refilling Rosalyn's wineglass till she was dizzy with words and drink. Mila, though, made comments all along . . . mothers and daughters, great stuff, unbeatable, deep love but not easy, even after a million years together, and warned that the girl might not jump for joy on hearing from Rosalyn.

Also on the phone with Jack, she gave him what he wanted, a dose of her life. Then she added her indecision about Lacy, her confusion about what to do next. To her surprise he didn't recommend a path, instead assured her she'd figure it out. But she hasn't. She thought about sending the girl a note. If no reply came, well, then it would be an answer of sorts. But she doesn't want an answer. What does she want? A reconciliation, a meeting, a sighting . . . she has no idea. If she were a private eye, she'd park the car near where Lacy lived, camera at hand, hat pulled low. She has no hat, no camera, no plan, and no clue what the next hours will bring, only the destination.

❖·❖·❖

Her car scales the lengthy incline of Gun Hill Road. Six-story buildings climb the hill with her, gray brick façades, small-paned windows, some curtained, some not, others protected with bars. Worn stone steps lead to run-down entrance courtyards. Covered garbage cans cluster in front of locked alleys. Do poor people live here? She sees no boarded-up or half-gated shops, broken pavements or skinny kids sitting on stoops. Is it more or less impoverished than other places in the city? It's difficult to say.

Cars are parked on both sides of the street. There's an empty space in front of Lacy's building and she pulls in.

The summer's evening light is waning, the sky a mass of clouds. She turns off the A/C, rolls down the windows. A weak breeze crosses her shoulders, bare in a pale blue T-strap sundress; her head wrapped in a navy scarf. Choosing what to wear was a trip in itself, trying on and discarding one outfit after another. She felt she was preparing for an audition. Exasperated, Dina finally decided for her. How many times did she check her face in the mirror, thinner, longer, her eyes, thank god, no different. Her skin, though, not the least bit rosy.

If Lacy appears—perhaps on her way home from work—will their glances meet in some mystical recognition? More likely the girl will walk past her. How will she know it's her daughter? She's given Lacy a height, a weight, even color and style of dressing, created an image out of a name. What if Lacy doesn't resemble her or Carl? It happens. What image does Lacy have of her? The seventeen-year-old her adoptive mother glimpsed? Or one Lacy cobbled together from bits and pieces of overheard conversation. Whatever it is, it's not a woman without hair, sick, pale, in bad repair.

No doubt Carl told his sister that she plans to leave everything to Lacy. No doubt it's how he got an address from her. But did anyone tell the girl? Her watch reads seven. Could be Lacy won't get home till later. Could also be the girl's in her apartment and won't leave till morning. Does she sit here all night? She stares at the building. It's a sixth-floor apartment. Does she have the strength to climb up? Maybe there's an elevator? Doesn't matter. She'll get there, somehow, find 6J and ring the bell. The door will open. She'll introduce herself. Lacy could freak out. Then what? Answer correctly and win a daughter? Answer incorrectly, and . . . one thing she does know, a mother is more than the woman who birthed her.

And what is it she can add to her daughter's life? Who is this visit for? If she invades that life and then disappears forever—because that's what will happen—would that be fair? If she were going to be around for even a few years none of this would matter. They'd have time to know each other, time to compare likes and dislikes, disappointments as well as revelations. Without time, the girl will be left with sorrow, perhaps regret, what might have been, what isn't. How can she chance that? How can she impose this perverse need on her daughter? Dina's wrong. Consequences matter.

Something else tugs at her, something she didn't want to think about before driving here. Lacy could've found her if she'd wanted to. They were never more than an hour apart.

Once more she stares at the gray building, its prison-like façade, littered courtyard, forbidding back ally. Her clean, pretty condo comes to mind, with its small patio, its array of plants, glass-topped table, pillowed chairs, so comfortable, so inviting. All of it will belong to her daughter who can sit there with a glass of wine, a husband, maybe children. It's this she'll take away from being here. It's this she'll hold on to.

Carefully, she maneuvers the car out of the small space. The sky is darkening. Behind her, the streetlights brighten the pavement with an evening sun.

⁂

A jet flies low and loudly over the car as Dina pulls up in front of the departures building and pops the trunk. "Take your bag. I'll park and meet you back here."

With trepidation, she watches Dina drive away. The crowds make her nervous. People push past her. It's loud. Cars drive up to the curb nonstop. Redcaps hurry by, tugging trolleys of bags. Long lines form in front of outdoor check-in podiums. The every-which-way of it is confusing, how to get by, which direction to go? Figuring out anything here feels beyond her. A strong urge to be at home where it's quiet, predictable, assails her.

It'll be better on the plane, she assures herself. In her own seat, calm, maybe she'll sleep. She steps through the first set of automatic doors. A second set leads to the ticket counters, but she doesn't enter, fearing Dina won't find her. A spasm tightens her back. They occur more often now, but over-the-counter meds still help, though she has stronger stuff if she needs it. She fishes in her purse for the red pills, shakes out two, finds her water bottle and swallows them. Cars continue to pull up, unload, and drive away. Endless. Automatic doors open and close incessantly, hordes of people in and out. Where's Dina?

Jack's call this morning, he wanted to erase any last-minute concerns. Said he was aching to see her, had taken care of every little detail. Repeated some of the many places he'd show her. How gorgeous the weather was, the ocean something else. His tone was gentle, his words meant to reassure. She didn't say leaving home frightened her now.

Leaning against a wall, tempted to close her eyes, she goes over the checklist. House and car keys, her father's phone number and address to Dina. Done. Clearly marked envelope with will, deed, and financial stuff on coffee table should Dina need it in case she . . . Jesus, she's only going for two weeks. Could she be any more dramatic?

"Oh Dina," she exhales, "I thought I lost you." In her summery yellow dress and sandals, her friend looks cheery, youthful.

"Check in and we'll go sit somewhere. It's early."

The line is long and disorderly, baggage everywhere. People study their tickets, eye children, each other, emanating anticipation, annoyance. And what does she feel? The last time she flew was ten years ago, to Florida. Her newly divorced friend was anxious the entire trip about leaving her children. It wasn't much of a vacation, and nothing like what Jack has planned. Still, she's never flown across the ocean. She's never been unable to trust her body.

"Did I give you Jack's cell phone number?"

"And his e-mail address at work. Yes. Relax. I'm exceedingly efficient. I ran the ICU, remember?" Dina glances at her, then away.

From the ticket counter they weave through the crowd toward a small restaurant filled with travelers, tables crammed together, loud voices, scraping chairs. The bar is festooned in outer-space décor, silver stars shoot away from blue and red planets. They find a small table near a Plexiglas wall overlooking the tarmac, and order two cosmopolitans. Huge unmoving planes line up ready to take off, the weight and wingspans challenging the idea that they'll do so. The ground crew in orange jackets as bright as their wands of light that cut through the air in semaphore code. She watches it all, a moving tableau that her plane will soon join. Dusk is beginning to settle, the late sun falling somewhere in the sky.

The waitress sets down their drinks and hurries away. "Serving an airport crowd can't be easy. It makes the diner seem like a breeze. Mila gave me a note from Willy. He wrote, *Miss you, always will.* Then asked when I'm coming back. I'm not, you know. I haven't told Murray."

"I'm sure he figured it out."

"Ava says Murray actually wants to sell. Amazing, Murray no longer there. He's a fixture."

"More like a relic." Dina looks in her bag for a tissue, her expression troubled. "Something I'd like to ask you—it's none of my business and you can say so."

Afraid to hear anything disquieting, she wants only protective custody from those around her, cages of love. How silly is that? "Go ahead," she says, and takes a long pull of the drink. It's strong, tangy, cold. She decides she'll have another.

"Why did you decide against more treatment?"

She gazes at Dina, the small, round face, eyes that penetrate. She recalls the sleepless nights, anxious days weighing another round of chemo against the agony of side effects when no good outcome could be promised. Even now, the turmoil of that decision is easily resurrected.

"Jack's a cancer researcher. My doctors faxed him results after two rounds of chemo. He didn't want to mix doctor with boyfriend but I begged him. My mother had only snippets of information. She had to intuit on a daily basis. I told him that would send me bonkers way before the disease got me.

"He wasn't happy with what he saw. A pernicious cancer, invasive. The stats on treatment weren't promising. He said no one ever really knew how much time, that miracles happen . . . that word clarified things. Why spend the time I've got left throwing up, tasting mouth sores instead of food, becoming so weak I couldn't walk by myself. You know the rest of it."

"Yes. I can't imagine what I'd do," Dina says more to herself. "I think you're brave," her friend's eyes moist.

"Dina, it's okay—"

"Sorry, Rosalyn. It's not like me to be—"

"I know it's not. You're all steel wool, right?"

Dina smiles. "Not exactly, but after years in a hospital you grow some tough skin."

Her glass is nearly empty. "Let's have another."

"You do. I'm driving." Dina's eyes watch her.

Seeing the waitress zip from table to table, she decides to order at the bar, which is three deep with people whose raucousness tells her they're pain-free. Two young men smile, bow, and part to make room for her. She grins. Ordinary consideration feels extraordinarily reassuring these days.

"Damn, I forgot to throw out the flowers." She places her drink on the table. "They'll dry up and flake all over the . . . Christ, why am I still worrying about such unimportant crap? Is that crazy or what?"

Dina says nothing.

"Before you picked me up, I ran around the place, a bundle of indecision. Should I apply makeup at home, on the plane? Who cares . . . makeup for god's sake? I'm dealing with life and . . . Dina I expected to let go of trivia, though what that would feel like is beyond me. It does happen. I've heard it said often enough, but maybe closer to the end." Her throat tightens. She takes another pull of the drink.

Dina's hand slides across the table and squeezes hers. "I've been with lots of patients, and sick isn't dead. Yours is a warm body to touch and a mind to think and feel. You're alive, Rosalyn. Why shouldn't everything matter?"

"But the junk that fills my thoughts . . ." she shakes her head. "This morning . . . never mind."

"Oh go on, rattle away. Lord knows what goodies I'll hear."

"I was in the shower. The shapes on the curtain reminded me of Halloween when I was a kid, maybe eight. My mother cut out the face of my pumpkin. She made one eye round, the other square. God knows why. I wanted them to match. She tried to fix it, but only made it worse. I stamped my feet, crying I wanted another pumpkin. My father grabbed the damn thing, opened the door, and flung it out as far as he could. I was inconsolable, hated him for days. But this morning the memory struck me as funny, my father, in uniform, heavy boots tramping across the living room floor to throw out a little pumpkin. I laughed out loud. It's been that way recently. Events transformed by circumstance."

"Or time. As the years pass, I see things differently, too."

"Like what?"

"My husband's death. I didn't really grieve. I sucked it up as another glitch and soldiered on. Maybe that was necessary, but he deserved more. Thinking about it lately, the sadness is there, untouched. On the other hand, Tim's difficulties growing up . . . they don't seem as enormous now as they felt then."

"What do you do about any of it," she murmurs, watching the planes move silently down the runway. Flares light the way now, the darkness complete. People at the adjacent table noisily push back chairs, assemble their luggage and file out.

"Aren't we the serious ones?" Dina quips.

"You think?"

"You're about to take off for unknown parts. I think that's serious business." Dina glances at her watch.

"A house by the sea in a place called Mumbles. Sounds pretty grave. Have you been to Wales?"

Dina looks at her as if to say when would that have happened.

"Well, neither have I or a zillion other places. It's an adventure, isn't it?" The drinks have produced a comfortable buzz in her. She stands to gather her stuff. The waitress rushes over with the check. She leaves an outrageous tip.

⁂

They amble past food counters, bookstores, newsstands, kiosks selling all manner of things, luggage, watches, even jogging outfits. So many people going somewhere, it's as if two disconnected worlds exist, one here and now, another elsewhere. She is a bit drunk.

"The whole point of this uprooting trip is for you to have a marvelous time. Can you remember to do that?" Dina asks as they reach security.

She takes in her friend's face, the combative jaw sturdy as ever. "I'll try. But I'm a bit shaky," she admits.

"Who isn't?"

They hug for a long moment. Dina gently disengages. "I'll stay here till you get past security."

Several lines snake around awaiting passage through to the gates. Unlike the earlier ticket line, there's an air of expectancy, even gaiety. Women in jeans, shorts, flip-flops, men, too, in casual wear, all leaving, same as her.

Searching the large tote for her boarding pass, her fingers brush the address book. She promised to send postcards from every-where. As the line moves forward, she loses sight of her friend, but knows Dina's there, watching, waiting. Her friends are like that, loyal, constant, strong-willed, and opinionated, like her. When she returns there'll be wine and laughter as they extract every detail of her trip. These women love stories.

She slings her bag onto the conveyor belt, tosses her shoes, purse, and sweater into plastic bins, all of which slide slowly through loose leather flaps into a tunnel to be scanned. It occurs to her she's done with scans. No more machines that click and buzz looking for hidden flaws, no more unwanted reports, no more uncertainty. She can drink as much as she wants, eat whatever pleases her, stay up late or sleep for hours, because why not? She can have or reject anything within reach. Everything out there is open to her, which is exciting yet weird.

Walking barefoot through the metal detector, a strange question pops into her head. Can people die happy even if they're not happy to die?

11

She was Definitely Here

"What is it?" She puts aside the fashion magazine someone left at the diner, the clothing nothing she'd waste her money on.

Nick is pacing with a beer bottle in hand. It's distracting.

He glances at her, his usually expressive eyes opaque, then walks out. She hears him in the kitchen. Is he worrying about his daughter? He said he was relieved Glory decided on the Peace Corps.

She picks up the magazine, flips pages looking for something besides skinny models with big lips. A window fan sends currents of hot air in her direction. A shower might help to cool her. He returns with another bottle of beer, though the one on the floor is half-full, and resumes pacing.

Ignore him, she thinks. If he wants her attention he'll have to say so; she isn't in the mood to read minds. It's too hot. The magazine is open on her lap, but her thoughts tick off chores she plans to accomplish. It's her day off. Her daily visit to Rosalyn, of course. She, Mila, and Dina follow a schedule of care with the help of Hospice. Rosalyn wants to be at home. Who can blame her. After Rosalyn, she'll drive . . .

He plops noisily on a chair and like a sullen adolescent moves the beer bottle back and forth on the dining table, leaving wet rings.

Glory pads in barefoot through the unlocked door in shorts, her

T-strap top revealing glowing tanned skin. "Hi all." She registers her father, who's pacing again.

"How was the beach?" Ava asks.

"Hot and crowded, but fine. The three of us had fun in the water." When Nick's back is turned, Glory mouths, "What?"

She shrugs. "Where's Bobby?"

"Outside with Hamid." Glory told her Hamid's upset about her upcoming departure. They've been seeing each other a few months and plan to stay in touch. The girl's more open with her than Bobby is with Nick, whom he pegs as Glory's father and therefore off-limits.

Nick's at the window now, fingers drumming the wall. "Ask Hamid in for a beer," he says suddenly, eagerly, as if Hamid's presence will undo whatever's troubling him.

"Dad. How many times . . . he does not drink, it's against his—"

"Of course, of course. I can give him a soda."

"He's sandy, doesn't want to. Ava we're going to the antiwar vigil in Sag Harbor. Bobby's coming with us."

"He is?" Glory's invited him many times. He claims it bores him to stand there. It must be that he's taken a shine to Hamid. She remembers Bobby's difficulty letting go of Mark's friendship, which was more like a courtship.

"I hope he doesn't get restless . . ." But their eyes are on Nick, who trades his empty bottle for the one on the floor, then stares out the window again.

"Dad, I've raided the fridge. See . . ." Glory jiggles a bulging canvas tote.

"Sure, why not?" Nick doesn't give a glance, his foot tapping nervously. Whatever's out there has his full attention. She and Glory exchange a quick look.

"Are you feeling okay? You sound strange," Glory says.

"Don't I always? Next time tell Hamid to come in, sand or not."

"I'm not keeping him away, I promise. Dad, I'm leaving." No response.

"We'll see you later," she pats Glory's arm reassuringly because now she's worried, too. He's always responsive to Glory. What the hell's going on?

"Should I stay?" Glory whispers.

"No, it's better for us to be alone," she whispers back, not sure if that's true.

When the door closes, he says out of nowhere, "Glory's reliable."

"And right on the mark about you. You can't find a place for yourself. Are you anxious about something?"

"That's it," he agrees, then strides to the bedroom. She follows. "About what?"

"About telling you," his high-pitched tone a cry.

A rush of adrenaline fires her system. "Me? What?"

"I'm getting a beer. Want one?"

"No. Take it easy with the stuff."

He lopes out in his bathing trunks and undershirt; his shoulders burdened by whatever she's about to hear. Her mind races through recent talks but nothing troublesome surfaces. An illness? He hasn't been to a doctor. Is he about to confess about an affair? Except their relationship is smooth, loving, Nick constant, loyal. He always wants to be with her.

Damn, she wishes they were at her house. The ambience at his less than reassuring. Though used to the warps and creaks of floors and doors here, it's less cared for than her own place. Her eyes sweep the yellowing walls of the bedroom, the tiny windows, paint cracks along the ceiling. Nothing attractive. Still, they've bonded in his saggy bed with its unmatched sheets and pillowcases. Their schedules are so erratic; to be alone with him she steals a few hours and comes here. Sometimes Nick's asleep. Always, though, as soon as she enters the bed his long limbs wrap her. The gentle strength of his hands is a constant surprise, so too the satisfying turbulence of their lovemaking. His almost childlike subsidence afterward follows her home, makes her feel safe, though she can't say why.

What's taking him so long? "Nick," she calls. Outside the window, the small lawn appears as thirsty as the white sky. The sprinkler is on though they're supposed to save water. It's been a week-long heat wave and the humidity has been merciless.

"I couldn't find a beer cold enough so I stuck a few in the freezer." He fiddles with the secondhand A/C in the window. He switches it on high and for a moment the whirring noise is everything.

"Let's talk in bed," he says.

"That's ridiculous."

"That's me, ridiculous," his serious tone is disconcerting.

He props up some pillows. "Get in first."

"I don't have to listen to you, Nick."

"Yes you do, for the next few minutes, then, maybe, never again." His large dark eyes beneath his thick brows stare at her unblinkingly.

"Christ, you're scaring me. You know I hate surprises and I hate being set up. You know that, Nick." She sits on the side of the bed, her feet planted on the floor.

He pulls up a chair. "It's hard to say everything because there's so much." And looks at her imploringly. Her stomach cramps.

"Are you sick?" Rosalyn's decline is never far from her thoughts.

He shakes his head. He holds both her hands as if he's sure she'll pull away at his first words. She won't. She'll listen to everything. It's what she does with Nick because sometimes it takes a while to figure out exactly what he wants.

"I have a plan that'll change our lives. For the better, is how I see it. I've thought through every angle. I don't find any flaws."

"Tell me."

"The diner's up for sale. We have to buy it."

Now it's her turn to stare. Has he gone off his meds? Where would they get that kind of money?

He lets go of her hands, begins pacing. "I know what you're thinking, but we can do it. If we get married, sell your house, move in here together, we'll raise enough cash for the down payment. The diner income will pay the mortgage and then some."

"Wow! And whoa," she says.

"Look at it any way you want, it's good." But he won't look at her.

Move in together? Marry? The diner? Sell her house? His words feel threatening. Words make things happen. They start wars.

"Nick, look at me. Did you expect me to say an immediate yes or no? You know me better than that."

"What scares you most?" His tone so earnest, she nearly relents to put him at ease.

"Well . . . buying the diner," she offers because she can't go near the rest. "That's big, Nick, too big for me to comprehend." The A/C isn't doing its job. The room is hot. They should open the window.

"Murray sells to some asshole, which is likely, we'll have to live with the consequences. The asshole will micromanage. They always do. Then what? Murray's no picnic, but he knows how far he can bug me. And what about you? The new guy will make you work things his way. And think about this." He begins pacing again. "New bosses bring in their own people. They fix up and sell. We might not have jobs. It might not stay a diner. We know the business . . . the customers. We'll change the name, spiff it up, place a few ads on the highway . . . that'll bring in more people, more profit," his arms gesturing, appealing. "Hard work isn't my problem. But here's the thing . . . No way can I look for a new job. No way. All that adjustment shit, can't do it. I don't want to." He's shaking his head.

She's stunned, can't remember the last time—if ever—he said as much at one time.

"Ava...you and me, we're good together. I couldn't...I wouldn't do this without you." He stops pacing, gazes at her with frightening intensity.

"You're generally so iffy about things," she murmurs, his sudden forcefulness unwelcome. He drops back on the chair, his body visibly deflating. But she can't tend to him now. A heavy band has wrapped her chest. She needs out of here, where she doesn't care, but not here. She needs air. "Let's talk later. I have to be at Rosalyn's at four. I'll see you after your shift. Okay? Lay off the beer, it's only three." She leans over to kiss him, breathes in his familiar peppery scent. His fingers circle her arm.

"You can't leave without giving me anything back."

"I need time, Nick. I can't get my mind around any of it. I can't even formulate the questions I know I have. We'll talk. Don't worry. We always do." She's beginning to sound hysterical.

He tugs her toward his lap. She knows where that'll lead, and pulls away.

⁕⁕⁕

On Sunrise Highway, cars whizzing past, A/C blasting, she presses the gas pedal but where she's headed remains a mystery. She lied. She's not due at Rosalyn's till five. She had to get away. Felt knocked over by a wave with nothing to grab onto, the old sensation that ebbed and flowed after her husband was killed. That, too, alarms her now.

Houses pass in a blur. She's seen them a million times before, old, worn, fractured windows, dirty aluminum siding, lawns too small to notice. Her house is better than that though not by much. Yet it's home. Her parents left her the place. Shouldn't that count for something? Rosalyn's gorgeous condo comes to mind, and so what? Okay, upheaval frightens her.

Her eyes land on a familiar exit sign. She heads toward the ramp leading off the highway. A few minutes and she's at the open wrought-iron gate. She drives through, turns onto a dirt path and parks. Her husband's grave is one hill over. During Bobby's first three years, she brought him here to visit on her husband's birthday, then Bobby began having bad dreams. They stopped coming. It was a relief.

Sparrows flit from tree to tree no doubt looking for some moisture. In the distance a few people attend a burial, fortunately their grief too far away to see. She remembers her husband's military funeral, the phony solemnity of uniformed strangers tending to the bereaved. She hated it. When they offered her the flag, she shook her head, wouldn't touch it, as if doing so would jeopardize the baby inside her. They handed the flag to his mother, too bent over in sorrow to see what she was accepting. It was a hot day like today. Everything dry, including her eyes, because she couldn't afford to cry, needed to conserve her strength for Bobby.

It isn't that she didn't love her husband, she did. When he proposed in his father's cluttered Ford, she said yes immediately. But at nineteen what did she know about anything? A lot less than now, and yes, she loves Nick, too, but it's different; she's different.

The thing is, she's been in charge of her life for years, with no one to answer to. She's made ends meet, god knows how, taken care of the house, her son, a job, made decisions on her own, big ones, little ones, daily. Why would she want to change any of it to buy a diner? They'll have to work even harder. They're not going to be much richer, either. Nick's drug bills alone are through the ceiling. He won't step into a VA hospital for free help, says he'd rather put a bullet in his head. Besides she's comfortable, even happy with the present arrangement. Why disturb that?

She flashes on her cop father. He'd analyze a homicide from every angle, yet each time he came up with a solution he'd shoot it down with another theory. It astonished her how many ways he could look at a situation. Nick can't do that; he's too impatient. It's not that he's going to undercut her response, but he won't get what there is to discuss. Either she agrees with his plan or she doesn't.

Sunshine rolls slowly down the hill leaving shadows . . . like a life. What's she doing here anyway? There are no friendly spirits, only sad memories. She drives back to the highway.

❖ ❖ ❖

It's four-thirty when she pulls up in front of Rosalyn's condo, her head more muddled than it was an hour ago. A drink will help. Mila makes sure there's wine in Rosalyn's fridge. There's even left-over vodka, gin, and scotch from the night after Rosalyn returned from abroad. With a table filled with sinful food and drink, they partied hard. She, Dina, Mila, the four of them . . . drunk, wild, high on laughter, Mila snapping one picture after another with her cell phone. Rosalyn was like a kid who's been given everything she wanted for Christmas. She couldn't stop yakking about every unbelievable place Jack took her, banishing illness as only Rosalyn could.

❖ ❖ ❖

The front door isn't locked. She finds Mila in the living room, looking half her age in a sleeveless shirt and shorts, hair in a ponytail. She takes in the surroundings as if for the first time. Teal-colored couch and chairs facing the plant-filled patio outside a large window, colorful rugs, black-and-white prints on the wall. Nick wouldn't care about any of it.

"Hospice hung another morphine drip. She's been mostly sleeping. Damn, it's unfair." Mila sighs deeply. "So energetic, now maybe a nod, a word..."

"I know. I was remembering her at our party. It wasn't that long ago."

"And at the diner, how she challenged Murray, telling him to give Sylvie room to breathe and didn't mean house space, either. Remember?"

"Yes. Always the odd yet correct take on a situation and not afraid to say so."

"Each day I come here it hits me again. There's no getting used to it. I was surprised when she sent Jack back to London. I wanted to say keep him around, who wants to die alone. Thing is, we do anyway, don't we, even if someone's in the room. Anyway, this is morbid. You're early. Is something the matter? Pale, too. Is it the heat?" Mila studies her a few seconds.

"Must be," she mumbles behind an urge to reveal everything and have Mila decide.

"I'll get my stuff." Mila gives her arm a squeeze.

"Wait. I need to talk." She sits on the couch.

"Oh lord, Ava, not bad news. I can't deal—"

"Nick wants to buy the diner."

"Great!" Mila claps. "You guys as bosses. No more Murray...hooray."

"Nick wants me to sell my house, use the money for the down payment, move in with him, marry, and—"

"Huge." Mila can't help grinning.

"It's such a big commitment, everything at once. How can I—"

Mila sits beside her. "Hold on a sec. If it doesn't work for you and Nick, you move out, find another place."

"It's not that easy."

"Nothing is."

"But I've been on my own so long."

"Yeah, change is horrible, but only for a short time." Mila still sounds gleeful.

"I don't want to sell my house."

"Don't. Sell his for hell's sake."

Why didn't that occur to her? He doesn't have a mortgage either.

"And listen to this . . . you don't have to marry him. Last I heard living together isn't against the law."

If only Mila's words could seep through the certainty of her resistance. But memory is in the way and trust comes hard to her.

"Do I want to change anything?" she blurts out.

"Hey, I'm no fan of unnecessary inconvenience, struggle for struggle's sake . . . all that bullshit, not when life's too ready to surprise you on its own. You didn't expect to be a widow. Rosalyn didn't expect to die young. I didn't bring up Darla to send her into danger?" Mila's face tenses, any mention of her daughter upsets her.

"True," she admits.

"The alternative, though, is some crazy attempt to hold it all in place. It can't be done. You know what I think, change isn't about taking chances. Uh-uh. It's about using time differently."

"I know."

"You can't know . . . it's all unknown. Did I believe I'd see my Jimmy again?"

"My Jimmy—" she repeats. My Nick, she wonders . . .

"The last great hurrah, Ava. We need it, even if—"

Mila's cell phone rings. She fishes it from her pocket. "Hello? Hello? Darla! Wow! Baby! Where are you, I mean right now? I'm with Ava at Ros . . . Hellohellohello . . . shit." She stares at the phone as if it will tell her something, then throws it on the couch. "Disconnected. Happens nine out of ten. I get to speak to the girl never, hardly. I can't stand it. It's like coitus interruptus. Not quite, but hearing her voice for two seconds, then gone, it's a frigging tease. Okay, I promised I wouldn't complain. But I can't get used to this crap, Ava. I just can't. Another six months in that terrible place, but who the hell knows, they could send her back again, they're not about to ask my permission. Bastards. I hate them. Hell and more hell. I need a drink."

"Are you on shift tonight?"

"Yeah. So what? Murray says one wrong word I'll let him have it." Mila seems to be channeling words Rosalyn would say. Is that what happens between friends?

She thinks to slip an arm around her friend's shoulders, but Mila's batting her eyes with the back of her hand to conceal tears.

"I'll check on Rosalyn," she says.

❖-❖-❖

Light leaks through half-closed bedroom blinds. On the dresser, a vase with fresh lilies does little to mask medicinal smells. A portable commode, bedpan, oxygen tank crowd the space. Wipes, cotton balls, lotions, scented oils are on the bedside table. Soiled nightgowns are puddled in a corner. A silky robe drapes the chair, slippers beneath. Rosalyn's no longer walking.

Once upon a time Rosalyn spent hours shopping, choosing lamps, rugs, whatever doodads she envisioned would create a beautiful room. Now the lamps are gone, the rugs rolled up, furniture pushed to the wall to make room for the hospital bed, everything topsy-turvy to facilitate treatment. Material things suddenly made trivial, replaceable.

"Hey there." She perches on the side of the bed, strokes Rosalyn's cool, slim hand, the fingers splayed lightly on the coverlet. Rosalyn's wrists are the size of a child's, her body beneath the blanket shrinking back to where it began. Her hair, grown in some, is a dark halo around the thin white face, which becomes smoother each day as lines of definition disappear along with worries. Her eyes, though, remain luminous, feverish. Dina says morphine can do that.

Any other day she'd be applying moisturizer, adjusting pillows, fixing covers, chattering away, the whirlwind everyone says she is. But something unusual in Rosalyn's calm but distant expression warns her movement or noise will be distressing. She thinks to drape an arm around her friend, simply to be there, except that too might be disturbing, even painful.

She remembers the two of them out on the patio. Rosalyn half-reclined in a well-padded chair. It was early evening, the end of spring, not too hot or breezy, chips and dips and wine on the table, though Rosalyn took most of her sustenance through an IV hung on a stand beside her. Still talkative, though her voice weak, gravelly, her speech slowed, she described colorful dreams with real stories played out as if on a movie screen. Said with all the sleeping she does they kept her from being bored, and if they were chemical hallucinations, so be it. When the cell phone on the table rang, she handed it to Rosalyn. It was Jack. Rosalyn murmured a word or two, mostly listened, said "Me too" a few times before clicking off. Then turned to her and whispered love was a learning curve.

Rosalyn could do that, offer a usable truth in a few words. That night, long ago, at Murray's housewarming. Rosalyn traipsing the cold beach in high-heeled boots, so spry, so eager to be on the go, persuading her to leave the safety of the car to look at the stars, hear the waves. Rosalyn could do that too, insist on life.

Gently, she touches Rosalyn's forehead. It too feels cool. Asleep she looks young, vulnerable, far away, unwilling to be called awake. Tawny stripes of early evening sun slide across the blanket. She sits there till they disappear.

After tossing for hours, the sheets are hot, clammy. Her head filled to aching with Mila's words, Rosalyn's translucent face, Nick's earnest expression. She wants to be with him, of course she does. He loves her, relies on her. Pleasing him pleases her, yet her brain can't wrap itself around the future he proposes.

The chores she planned to do today didn't get done, that weighs on her too. Bobby needs another pair of summer pants, even if he won't take off those stupid jeans. And what about new sneakers, which he actually wants? Except none of that is important. Her friend is dying, her relationship with Nick threatened, her sense of order dissolving faster than ice on a grill. It's a test, a challenge to her resilience. All those years ago, everything crumbling, when going on seemed impossible, what did she do? Was it Bobby, his needs, his very being? Maybe. She sighs and switches on the lamp. It's after five.

Tiptoeing past her son's room, she considers two aspirin, anything to get another hour of rest. Instead she stands gazing out the living room window at the empty street of houses still shuttered against the day, wondering if somewhere others, too, are staring into the darkness edged now with pale blue light.

"Mom?"

"Oh honey, did I wake you?" How scrawny he looks in his long T-shirt, one he'll wear even during the day. The summer sun has whitened his hair and darkened his skin, her beautiful boy. After a few weeks indoors, the paleness he shares with her will return.

"Why are you up?" he wants to know.

"Why are you?" she teases.

"Can't you just answer?" one hand on his hip.

"I keep thinking of Rosalyn."

"Oh." He sits cross-legged in his faded TV chair, with it's food stains and god knows what else. He's offering her his company. She tries to read his face. But, really, what can the child know about illness? Nothing she hopes, ever.

"Want breakfast? It's getting light out."

"I'm starving." The boy eats like a logger and never gains weight.

"The whole deal? Pancakes and eggs?" she asks.

"Yup."

Life intrudes and that's encouraging. Children can do that.

Her arm around his shoulder, they traipse to the kitchen, where Bobby disentangles and plops on a chair. A surprising memory of the pristine, modern kitchen in Colorado comes to mind. If she and Mark had worked out together, there'd be no relationship with Nick. How strange.

"How would you feel if Nick moved in here?" Just saying so increases her adrenaline.

"Is he?" her cautious son, not willing to take a stand till she does.

"Honestly, I don't know. It's an ongoing discussion and how you feel about it matters."

"Would Glory come, too?" He studies the table as if the answer's written there.

"She'll be leaving in a month or so." Opening the fridge, she pulls out the eggs and milk, then pancake mix and syrup from the cabinet.

"She'll be here on vacations and holidays. Kids always come home for those," he informs her.

"Well . . . she may be too far away. But yes if she does she'll come here." She eyes the coffee, accepting the end of sleep.

"It's okay if Nick stays, except there have to be a few rules."

"Oh?"

"Nick can't use my computer or my TV chair or my bike or—"

The phone rings and the sound slices through her. She sprints to the living room and grabs it. "Yes?"

"It's over. Ava, she's gone, really gone."

Bobby follows her in.

"Dina, you shouldn't be alone."

"Hospice is here. Mila's on the way."

"Me too."

Her son looks at her.

"Rosalyn . . . it's over," she says. "Can you make some breakfast?"

He nods.

She ought to take a minute, talk about his feelings, reactions, what a mother's supposed to do. Later. She rushes to the bedroom, dresses quickly in shorts, shirt, flip-flops. Then phones Nick at the diner to tell him it's over. She can't bring herself to say Rosalyn's dead.

⸙⸙⸙

She steps outside. Her legs feel heavy as if the aches in Rosalyn's bones have landed in hers. The sky's heavy as well, and white, the sun pulsing somewhere far behind. The adjacent house is there same as yesterday, the dried-up lawn littered with sad little toys. Someone inside opens the blinds, someone alive. Anger surprises her throat.

In the car she rolls down the windows. The hot morning air, she needs it to breathe. She drives through streets too quiet by far. Noise, traffic, daily distractions could help. That's a joke . . . nothing helps. She knows that. The two baby-faced uniformed men who arrived to give her the news, who wanted to come in, sit with her, commune, she shut the door in their faces. Rude, yes, but weird things happen around death. Or maybe nothing that happens is weird. For days after, she of small appetite couldn't stop shoving food in her mouth. Chatted nonstop on the phone, but not about her husband. Friends tried to pry out her feelings but she would have none of it. Weeks after the funeral, leaving the obstetrician's office, she turned her ankle. Strangers had to help her, hugely pregnant, to a nearby bench. Waiting for a promised ice pack she began to cry, no, wail, and couldn't stop, her head screaming he's dead, gone, never again.

His death was a shock, yes, but Rosalyn's death she knew was coming, thought about it each day, tried to prepare herself for a world without her friend. So why does it feel sudden, cold and sharp? Why is it tearing away at something inside her she can't name but needs to hold on to? Why does she want to shout she'll never forget her? Some people pass through, not Rosalyn. She was definitely here.

12

Stop Here

The buzzing alarm wakes her. Reluctantly hoisting herself out of the warm bed, Ava reaches for her robe and slippers. She goes to the window. Snow again. The lawn and the shrubs are blanketed. Nick's car is gone. Her car, though, is shoveled out, rescued, the big shovel left lying in the driveway. She shuffles into the kitchen, rubbing her hands together for warmth. How sweet, he brewed the coffee. She pours a cup, sips at the hot liquid quickly, no time to linger. She scrambles two eggs, sticks the plate in the microwave for Bobby to reheat. She leaves jam, butter, milk, and cold cereal on the table, places two slices of bread on top of the toaster. She'll let him sleep. It's Saturday. The other morning he mumbled some criticism about Nick living here. She zeroed in with a bunch of questions but couldn't pin him down. He offered small grievances . . . Nick's odd sleeping hours, used his towel, TV on too loud . . . what he wanted was assurance that all would go on as before. She couldn't promise that.

She, too, is adjusting. Nick brought no furniture, a few bags of his and Glory's stuff, yet the house seems tighter. Or is it how she feels? What isn't in question is Nick's disdain for routine. Structure and expectations make him suffer, feel hemmed in, managed. He's explained this to her and she tries to understand, but it can be annoying. If the diner makes lots of money, she'll build an extension on the house. Fat chance. Nick would hate too much space, if it takes him too far away from her. He's grateful for her presence. And her? She's here with him, isn't she? That means something.

Pulling the list off the fridge, she grabs a pen from the cracked mug on the shelf, crosses out *electrician, phone company, tires*, adds *baker, toothpaste, bulbs, laundry, Dina's birthday gift*. Nick snickers at her sense of order. Well . . . tough. There's much to be done.

Another sip of coffee and she hurries to the bedroom to dress. Constitutionally unable to leave a mussed bed, she tightens the sheets, then tugs the yellow spread into place and remembers last night's pillow talk. Their voices low, her son a door away. Unexpected things can happen, she said. Would they have enough money? Someone could slip and fall, she warned. And what about the insurance policy, did he change the name? Does he realize that how people see, feel, talk about the diner will reflect not only on business, but on them as well? That whatever happens they're still accountable for paying their employees? He pulled her close to stop her chatter, murmured the diner isn't her house or her sole responsibility. "Yeah, I know, but . . ." the words muffled against him. "All we can do is our best," he declared, sounding more solemn than wise.

⬥⬥⬥

She pulls into the parking lot, relieved to see that the snowplow has come and gone. Slowing to flurries, the snow lands daintily on the windshield. She sits for a moment unwilling to begin the busy day. It's there, waiting, solid and snow-covered, undaunted by weather or change, a long bus with steamy windows, and as Nick likes to remind her, the only diner for miles. The other day Mila asked how it felt to be a proprietor. She had no idea. It's difficult to absorb the idea that the diner is theirs. Things need to be around awhile before she can claim them.

Enough musing, she chides herself, getting out of the car to hurry up the few steps. She pushes open the door and smells paint. Odors will not do. Also that ridiculous chime, they have to get rid of it. One more item for her list. The diner's been closed a few days, something Murray would never allow. How else would they get things done? Workers have installed indirect lighting, repainted inside and laid new floors. The wood tables with captain's chairs arrived yesterday. Nick would've left more of the old stuff intact, but she insisted. The room looks younger, inviting, warmer, which is a plus in this freeze.

Days ago workers removed the neon sign with Murray's name, and a new one needs to replace it. Baptism, christening, a party . . . it was Shelly's idea to have friends participate in renaming the diner. Leaving her boots at the door, she slips into shoes and hangs her coat on the new set of wooden pegs nearby. There are still a few hours before people arrive.

Murray, yakking loudly, hovers around Nick in the kitchen where she heads. He arrived so early. Damn. Rumor has it he's looking for a house in San Diego, maybe another restaurant there. Mila swears the man has more than enough to retire on. Still, what would he do at home except drive Sylvie crazy? Not her problem. Finding time for a hot bath is a problem.

The unusual clatter of dishes tells her Nick's trying to drown out Murray's prattle. She slides an arm around Nick's waist and whispers, "Thanks for shoveling out my car."

He doesn't respond, his face a tight mask, Murray's impinging on his space.

"—and always make sure there's enough toilet paper. It can turn off a customer like that." Murray snaps his fingers. "Also the paint smell. Do something about it."

"What can we do?" she says quickly, ready to wring her hands if needed.

He looks surprised to be asked, and describes some solvent spray that lifts off smells. The man does know the business. Wearing a black turtleneck sweater and black slacks instead of his usual rolled-up shirtsleeves and jeans, he appears faintly sinister.

"Great, that's a big help. Show me how the light panel works?"

He leads her behind the counter, teaches her what she's known for ages.

"How's the baby?" Really there's no time for chitchat.

"A tiger. He grabs my finger. The strength in him . . . a real toughie."

"I bet." She smiles, about to walk away.

"The dogs keep watch in front of the crib. You have to get my permission to—"

"Hello . . . Anyone? I need some help," Mila calls from the doorway, letting in the cold air.

Nick and the electrician hurry out to carry in Darla's wheelchair, too heavy for Mila to push up the snow-covered ramp; they set the chair down near a table.

"Hey, the conquering hero," Murray says.

"Shut up," Mila snaps, her face permanently tense. The woman has lost weight. Her hair's falling out, her eyes red-rimmed from lack of sleep. Dina suggested antidepressants. Mila shrugged her off, said there's no comfort to be had.

Mila's ragged, pain-filled voice calling to tell her of Darla's injury, she can't forget it. Did she receive a wire, a phone call, a man in uniform at her door, she never asked. Instead torn between grief for her friend and relief her son was intact, she drove fast to Mila's house and found her in bed, sobbing. Consoling words felt impossible, inadequate. She climbed in beside her and held her all night.

Embracing her friend now, she whispers, "I'm glad Darla came."

She'd embrace Darla as well, but the girl's closed expression warns off hugs or questions. Darla takes in the new décor but says nothing. Her silky skin and thick dark hair remain, but her lovely full lips are pressed in a fixed line. Dressed in a down jacket, her useless legs in corduroy slacks. After weeks of pleading, threatening, cajoling, a zillion phone calls and VA visits, Mila managed to enroll Darla in a clinical trial for spinal nerve stimulation. If the trial succeeds, fingers crossed, Darla could someday get around with a walker or crutches. Maybe then, Mila hopes, her daughter will soften toward meeting her father.

When Willy opens the door, it gives her a start. It's been months since he was in here. He seems even tinier inside a long coat and fur hat, a scarf wrapped around several times. Last she saw him was Rosalyn's funeral where he kept muttering, "Not right." Lots of people attended, the church cool and cavernous but far from quiet, emotions flowing freely, including her own.

"I told Willy to come today." Mila leads him to a booth, begins to undress the old man.

❖❖❖

Holding aloft a tray of hot finger foods, she carefully backs out of the kitchen, her friends' chatter loud and insistent. People who know each other. They've moved chairs into a tight little circle. Wet coats are piled high in one of the booths, the damp smell raising memories she has no time to decipher. The snow is coming down heavy now, layering tree limbs along the roadway, hushing traffic sounds. Inside, though, it's warm, safe, and promising, the indirect lighting softening people's faces. A red paper tablecloth covers the newly tiled countertop. Red and yellow balloons cling to the ceiling, trailing a broken spiderweb of strings.

"Ta-da," she announces, setting the tray on the counter near several champagne bottles. And remembers to add, "Bruce prepared these last night."

Nick, in new dark jeans and a navy crewneck sweater, pops the first cork to applause. His expression, focused, in charge, different from any she's seen before. She watches him pour generously into plastic cups. Murray would insist on glasses that could be washed and reused. But this is Nick, her Nick.

Bruce lifts his cup in a salute to Darla. "Glad you're home. My son's redeployed." Darla nods but says nothing. What can she say? I'm sure he'll be fine?

Bobby, seated beside Dina, sneaks glances at Darla, someone he knew before she enlisted, before the wheelchair, before he could ever imagine such damage. Well, okay. Forewarned is good.

Shelly weaves around chairs offering a tray of deviled eggs she prepared. "Ava, I told my oldest I'm coming in to help with the Sunday breakfast rush. He looked at me like I'd lost my marbles. You reach a certain age and these kids think you're finished. Think again, I didn't say."

"There's more hot food," Bruce lumbers toward the kitchen.

"I can get it," Murray says, but Bruce walks past him.

"A toast to Rosalyn," Willy's reedy voice insists.

"To our lady of the flowers," Dina chimes in, raising her drink high, dressed for a party in the long black skirt and blue tunic Rosalyn gave her.

"Rosalyn, dear Rosalyn," she murmurs, locking eyes with Mila. Both remembering, she's sure, the night of the funeral. The two of them plus Dina, sharing Rosalyn stories, laughing, crying, drinking at Sully's bar till the wee hours, none of them willing to go home alone with the loss.

At the counter, too near to where she's standing, Murray refills his drink and raises the cup. "To my old diner and now yours." He claps Nick on the shoulder. "To—"

"Hear, hear," Mila interrupts, sitting close to her daughter, whose jacket she's removed revealing Darla's slim torso in a deep purple Nehru shirt that could pass for festive.

"—the place where I met my wife," Murray continues, "where I spent most of my life, where all of—"

"A shrine will be built," Shelly says not too softly.

"When I opened the restaurant it was a nothing. If you could've seen the way—"

She takes a long drink of champagne, the lemony flavor the same as the one they shared after Nick closed on his house. They brought the bottle to bed, passed it back and forth till it was nearly empty. Trying to muffle their giggles, Bobby in the next room, they stared stupidly at TV sitcoms she can't remember a thing about now.

"—on the couch in the ladies room, I used to sleep there." Murray's voice drones on. "That's right. Once in a while I had company, before Sylvie." He turns to Nick, "And one time—"

"Enough," Nick says, his tone leaden. Grabbing a full bottle of champagne, he walks around refilling cups and returns to top hers as well.

Murray, watching, finishes his drink. "There's a lot you don't know—"

"Take a load off," Bruce orders, kicking out a chair, which Murray ignores.

"Look at all this new crap," Murray's arm sweeps the room. "It'll turn off old customers. Ask Willy. They're used to what was here. Too much alteration . . . What's with these lights? Armchairs? Pictures? It looks like a cocktail lounge. People come here for food, not entertainment. Next thing you know, there'll be some guitar player." He shakes his head, slides a hand across the counter, then again refills his cup.

"Murray, new management always makes—"

"What new management," he scolds her. "You guys have been here for years," his voice going up a few decibels.

"I like the way the place looks," Bobby speaks directly to Murray. She flashes her son a grateful but warning smile.

Murray steps around a stool to get closer to Nick. "You can't hide in the kitchen anymore. Customers need to be chatted up, catered to, they—"

"Hey, Murray," Bruce growls, "give the man room."

"It takes more than kitchen savvy to make a restaurant work. You'll need to consult with other owners. I won't always be around."

Damn him. He's no longer the boss. How dare he take center stage? Rosalyn would get rid of him in a hand wave. With blood thrumming in her ears, she grabs a huge wooden spoon and bangs hard on the counter for quiet, which works faster than she expects. A tableau of faces turn to her and, for a dizzying moment, she's bewildered. Nick, too, seems to be waiting, but for what? Murray's eyes on her are challenging, his expression refusing to understand the moment. It's Bobby's expectant look that releases her. She hears herself declare loudly, "Names, everyone, I need names. And nothing more."

Bobby pops up. "Resurrection Diner."

"Great," she replaces the spoon, adrenaline high, and pulls a pad and pencil from her pocket to jot it down.

"Tiptoe In," Dina adds quickly.

"What kind of name is that?" Murray scoffs.

The door chimes. Chairs scrape and people turn to see. Hamid in a suit jacket over a cable-knit sweater, his hair covered in snow, rushes in. "So sorry to be late."

"No problem," Nick says gaily. Clearly, a welcome intrusion. "It's a party, not a meeting. Everyone, this is Hamid, Glory's good friend."

"Ha-mid," Murray draws out the name. Where you from, Iran?"

"Morocco."

"Oh yeah. Here in the US to—"

"Take some food," she interrupts.

"No, thank you." Hamid shrugs off his wet jacket, pulls up a chair beside Bobby, who looks pleased. "Glory e-mailed me two names." He waits.

"Yes?" pencil poised, her voice loud, ready to talk past Murray, who watches her warily.

"First name is Come Back Diner," Hamid pauses, no one says anything.

"Got it. Next?" her voice more normal though everyone's eyes are still on her.

"Welcome In Diner," Hamid offers with some assurance.

"That's as silly as Tip-toe In," Murray heckles.

"Hey—" Nick says evenly. "Everyone here participates equally. You want to give us a name or what?" He stares hard at Murray.

"Nick and Ava's," Murray replies sourly.

Mila rolls her eyes.

She writes it down. "Others?" she asks.

"A-One Diner," Mila raises her thumb.

"New Place," Willy points a bony finger at the additions.

"Fine Dine," Dina tries again.

Murray inches toward the door, god willing he'll slip out.

"Chow Down," Bruce offers.

"Eat Out," Mila declares.

"Food for Thought," the electrician perched on a stool suggests shyly.

"Second Chance," Shelly says loudly.

"Ace Diner." Bobby grins the way he does when he's playing Nintendo, aware this isn't a game but wanting to win.

She's writing now as fast as she can. When she looks up, her son's watching her. His admiration fills her with the kind of love only a child elicits. Her steady gaze embarrasses him. She turns away. Outside, a blanket of white as far as the eye can see. Bad weather curdled Murray's mood. It doesn't bother her.

"Hey, Ava?" Murray calls as if reading her mind. "What's your contribution?" He's leaning hard against the newly painted wall.

She hasn't thought about a name and admitted as much to Bobby yesterday, who took pains to explain that a name was important. A tag, he said, without a tag you're unknown. Lord help her, a lot rides on the diner being known. Her eyes scan her friends' waiting faces.

A name, she thinks. Give them a name, any name, but her mind blanks, wiped clean of names forevermore. She glances hopelessly at Nick, a name, she begs him silently, any name.

"Best Deal," he says softly, but loud enough for others to hear.

"It's Ava's turn," Murray shouts.

Darla's hand shoots up. "How about Stop Here?"

❖❖❖

She sits at the bedroom window, watching the blue edge of dawn emerge. In the weeks since they closed on the diner she wakes at the same time each night. It's eerie. A scattering of illuminated snow-flakes tumbles past the streetlamp, reluctant to hit the ground. The party's on her mind, though it ended hours ago. When Murray finally shut the door, she felt both relief and a chill of fear. The diner was theirs. In the twilight darkness people left in a group, Bobby went home with Dina. She and Nick watched the cars' red lights come on and then snake away. Alone, silent with their own thoughts, they tidied up some till hired cleaners arrived to finish the job.

Tomorrow the diner opens for business, the name, though, still up for grabs. All agreed Nick should make the decision, which delighted him. He's excited to be an owner. It's there in the way he palms the storeroom keys, responds patiently to salespeople who phone nonstop, checks and rechecks condiments, floors, appliances though no customer has yet been served. She's careful not to undercut his pleasure, careful to keep certain worries to herself.

Because, really, it's not the best time to start a new venture. Look at how difficult it was to secure the mortgage, and what if they don't make enough to cover it? What if all the stuff they bought and still have to pay for doesn't result in more customers? What about her friends, now employees? They, too, must wonder, can she and Nick pull this off? If the diner fails, they'll be out of work. What then? These are the thoughts that visit before her day begins.

It's not that Nick's free of worry, he frets all the time, always has, about something happening to her, about Glory in Mali, whatever. Yet he sleeps, one arm up under the pillow. Amazing. Her eyes flick to her dead husband's portrait, a man who didn't fret. She offered to remove it. Nick said, no, he's gotten used to it, feels some affection for the guy.

Slipping out of the flannel robe, she climbs into bed. He curls around her back, warm, reassuring in its way.

"Couldn't sleep again?" she's surprised to hear him whisper.

"Umm."

"Want to say why?"

"Uh-uh."

"Nervous?"

"A bit," she admits.

"Me too. Things tank. We could live in a tent, no expenses, go from park to park."

"What about winter?"

"Problem," he agrees.

"We could go south."

"We could," his words low in his throat.

"There's Bobby—"

"Don't be real," he admonishes softly.

"That's a challenge," she whispers more to herself. The streetlamp flickers off and milky morning light brightens the sky.

ACKNOWLEDGMENTS

My deep gratitude to Jane Lazarre for her talent, time, and unwavering eye on this book; to Jocelyn Lieu and Jan Clausen, whose attention to all on the page continue to impress me; to Tom Engelhardt for getting me started on the long journey here; to Denise C. for her insight and encouragement; and to Judi Brand, Elizabeth Strout, Barbara Schneider, Marsha Taubenhaus, Vickie Breitbart, Prue Glass, and Liz Gewirtzman for constant support and friendship.

Huge thanks to Dan Simon, Publisher extraordinaire, for his ongoing belief in this project; to my editor, Gabe Espinal, whose intelligence and easy ways made the process more than pleasant; to Gail Heimberg for her technical wizardry; to John Samuel Wiggins for his video; to Jesse Lichtenstein, Anne Rumberger, Elizabeth DeLong, and everyone at Seven Stories Press for their thoughtful and tender care in making this into a book. And deep and abiding appreciation to my agent, Melanie Jackson, a national treasure.

As always I remain grateful to my beloved, Charlie Wiggins, for his unfailing devotion, enthusiasm, and faith in what I do. And to the lights of my life, Georgina, Dónal, and Maya, you make it all matter.

ABOUT THE AUTHOR

BEVERLY GOLOGORSKY is the author of the acclaimed novel *The Things We Do to Make it Home*, originally published by Random House in 1999, reissued by Seven Stories in 2009, named a Notable Book by the *New York Times*, Best Fiction by *Los Angeles Times*, and a finalist for the Barnes and Noble Discover Great Writers Award. Her work has appeared in anthologies and magazines, including the *New York Times*, *Newsweek*, *The Nation*, and the *LA Times*. Former editor of two political journals, Viet-Report and Leviathan, she is acknowledged in the publication *Feminists Who Changed America*. She lives in New York and Maine.

ABOUT SEVEN STORIES PRESS

SEVEN STORIES PRESS is an independent book publisher based in New York City. We publish works of the imagination by such writers as Nelson Algren, Russell Banks, Octavia E. Butler, Ani DiFranco, Assia Djebar, Ariel Dorfman, Coco Fusco, Barry Gifford, Martha Long, Luis Negrón, Hwang Sok-yong, Lee Stringer, and Kurt Vonnegut, to name a few, together with political titles by voices of conscience, including Subhankar Banerjee, the Boston Women's Health Collective, Noam Chomsky, Angela Y. Davis, Human Rights Watch, Derrick Jensen, Ralph Nader, Loretta Napoleoni, Gary Null, Greg Palast, Project Censored, Barbara Seaman, Alice Walker, Gary Webb, and Howard Zinn, among many others. Seven Stories Press believes publishers have a special responsibility to defend free speech and human rights, and to celebrate the gifts of the human imagination, wherever we can. In 2012 we launched Triangle Square books for young readers with strong social justice and narrative components, telling personal stories of courage and commitment. For additional information, visit www .sevenstories.com.

A SEVEN STORIES PRESS
READING GROUP GUIDE

Stop Here
by Beverly Gologorsky

The following questions are suggested to enhance individual reading and invite group discussion regarding Beverly Gologorsky's
Stop Here. We hope these questions provide additional topics for
consideration and generate a stimulating dialogue with others.

For a complete listing of Seven Stories Press books featuring Reading Group Guides, please visit our website at www.sevenstories.com.

DISCUSSION QUESTIONS

1. War affects most of the characters, both directly and indi-
    rectly. How does each character react to the effects of war and
    what do their reactions say about their personalities?

2. Most of the characters in *Stop Here* are struggling to make
    ends meet and have limited opportunities because of their
    economic situations. How does each character respond to the
    stress of supporting themselves and their families? How does
    each character feel about their economic situation and how
    does that reflect their view of the world?

3. How does money affect the way the characters view Murray, the owner of the diner? How does it affect the way they view Sylvie, Murray's new wife?

4. What role does romantic love play in each character's life? Why do you think Ava is so hesitant about falling in love, first with Mark and then with Nick? How does Rosalyn use her illness as an excuse not to get close to Jack?

5. A prominent theme in this novel is the betrayals of the body—we see this through Dina and also Rosalyn. How do Dina and Rosalyn's reactions differ as their bodies start to fail them? What do they find comfort in to help them through these experiences?

6. What did the author accomplish by telling the story from multiple points of view? How did you feel when returning to a character after spending a few chapters away from him/her?

7. Many of the characters spend time fantasizing about what they thought their lives would look like or actions they would take if they could disregard the consequences. What role does fantasy play for each character and how does exploring their inner fantasies help you understand their characters?

8. Murray has never fought in a war and his thoughts on war differ greatly from other characters' opinions. How does his attitude compare with Bruce's, Liam's, and Ava's views on war and its place in society?

9. Do you think Sylvie loves Murray? What are her reasons for marrying him and how does her view of their relationship

change when she gets pregnant and lets Murray believe the baby is his?

10. Shelly advises Sylvie to "Take what you can when you can where you can" (page 37). What do you think of this advice and how does this sentiment tie into the novel as a whole?

11. What is Sylvie searching for in her relationship with Liam? Does caring for him at the end of his life change anything for Sylvie?

12. What would you do if you were in Shelly's place, deciding between leaving Bruce and helping him through his debilitating depression?

13. Does Dina blame herself for her son Tim's actions? Do you understand her decision to help him escape and her refusal to ask him what he did? Do you think it is hard for her to admit that she prays that Tim stays away from her?

14. Do you understand Mila's reasons for keeping the truth about where Darla's father is secret? Do think she made the right decision in keeping the information from Darla? How might things have been different for Darla if she had grown up knowing her father was in prison?

15. The employees of Murray's diner feel like a family. What role in the family does each character play?